UNFORGETTABLE

LANDMARK MOUNTAIN
BOOK 1

WILLOW ASTER

To all who have read my books and come back for more,
thank you with all of my heart

CONTENTS

CHAPTER ONE

CHANCE ENCOUNTERS

SCARLETT

I like a plan.

Lists.

Checking things off the list.

Occasionally I write things down after I've done them just so I can cross them off, but mostly, I need the lists to survive.

It's more than a compulsion to be organized, it's an

absolute necessity. Without my lists, I wouldn't have kept the Landmark Mountain Lodge & Ski Resort afloat.

Big things, little things, it's all there.

Months ago, my list looked something like this:

- *Laundry.*
- *Email.*
- *Make a dentist appointment.*
- *Family dinner at Granddad & Grinny's house, 5 p.m.*
- *Find a new supplier for the resort's linens.*
- *Fire James B and Lori S BY TUESDAY, no more putting it off!*
- *Pick up taquitos and clementines from Cecil's.*
- *Pay the electric bill.*

Today's list had three things on it:

- *Drive to Boulder.*
- *Watch my life be signed away forever.*
- *Get back to Landmark and figure out what I'm doing with the rest of my life.*

And as of thirty minutes ago, I'd crossed off the first two things on the list…but for the past twenty, I've driven aimlessly around Boulder.

That was *not* on the list.

I keep passing the boutique hotel where my best friends Holly and April brought me for my twenty-first birthday a couple years ago, and on a whim, I pull into a parking spot in the front when one opens up.

I stare at the exterior for a few minutes and the next

thing I know, I'm getting out of my car. The wind whips around my bare legs as I hurry inside the hotel, barely taking in the grand lobby as I walk toward the check-in counter, but instead, I take a last-minute turn and head to the bar.

I've already detoured so drastically from my plan to drive the two hours back home once the dreaded meeting was over, what's my rush anyway? It's not like I have anything to return to anymore.

Nothing about this is my typical M.O., but right now, I need to hear the buzz of conversation and laughter around me. I just don't think I can face home tonight, not when everything has been forever altered. I slide onto the barstool and the weight of exhaustion hits me hard.

It's been the longest day…the longest eight months, really. I'm tired to my bones.

"What can I get you?" the bartender asks over her shoulder.

"Lemon drop, please." This drink usually cheers me up after a long day, but I have a feeling I'll still feel like sobbing after I drink it tonight.

I watch the activity behind the bar, drinks being prepared before gliding to a stop on the glossy wood in front of customers, one after the other. The distraction eases some of the tension in my shoulders.

Someone sits down next to me and for the first time, I wish it was a little less crowded in here. The guy's either large or he's doing a full-on manspread on his barstool. I look over to see which it is just as his head turns toward me.

Wow. Okay, that jolted a little energy into me. Not the kind of beautiful specimen I'm used to seeing in Landmark, where the only single men are my brothers, tourists, and my exes Danny and Regg.

His full lips part into a grin, faltering only slightly when I don't return it. He doesn't turn away from me as the bartender asks what he's having.

"A Manhattan, please." And then he surprises me by saying, "Why the sad eyes?"

I sigh, and when my drink is placed in front of me, I take a leisurely sip, enjoying the perfect blend of sour and sweet.

"It's been an awful day," I say softly.

His lower lip pokes out slightly as he tilts his head, his eyes thoughtful. "I'm sorry to hear that. Would you like to tell me about it?"

I shake my head, trying to place his accent. He's definitely not from Colorado. When he says *hear*, it's with a very soft *r*.

"No, I really wouldn't…but how about you tell me something good."

He smiles again and it seems to come so easy to him. His eyes light up, crinkling at the edges, and he turns to face me, his knees brushing against mine. I feel slightly winded from the contact.

"Something good, huh?" he asks, his thumb brushing across his lower lip.

I nod, taking another long sip of my drink. His Manhattan is placed in front of him, but he doesn't seem to notice it.

"Well, I'm almost sorry to tell you that I've had one of the best days I've had in a long time…and then I come back to my hotel and end up next to you, so from where I'm sitting, there is *only* good."

"Smooth," I say, smirking. "And how often do you pick up women in hotel bars?"

He lifts his drink to his lips and I'm envious of the curve of the glass against his mouth. He leans in slightly, his eyes leaving mine briefly to glance down at my mouth.

"Never. I prefer to let a woman walk on her own two feet." His voice is low and husky and I find myself squeezing my thighs together as I lean in to hear him better.

My lips pucker to keep from laughing. "Well, that's a shame."

I didn't know I was capable of the sexy voice that just came out of me, but in the past thirty seconds, I've realized this is exactly what I needed to get through this day…an unexpected flirtation with the hottest stranger I've ever seen.

"You *like* to be picked up then," he says, his white teeth shining as his smile grows. His eyes gleam with the candlelight and maybe lust. It's intoxicating. "Do you prefer bridal style or legs wrapped around a waist?"

I gasp, my mouth parting at the visual he's just imparted. I've had a dry spell, okay?

It's been over a year since I had sex with Reggie and that was so lackluster it may as well have not even happened. I've never contemplated a one-night stand before this moment, but I am so tired of doing everything right. Tired of staying in the lines and following the rules and checking things off, working night and day to please everyone all the time…

That hasn't worked out so well for me.

And I've never had a guy carry me, period, so I can't be sure, but…

"Definitely legs wrapped around a waist," I hear myself saying.

His tongue dips out over his lower lip and I watch it like it's porn close-up and personal, for my very own viewing pleasure.

"Noted," he says, his voice hoarse now.

He picks up his drink like it's an afterthought and takes a long swallow as I watch his neck, mesmerized, then follow his hand to the tie that he loosens after he sets his glass down, all while sneaking glances at the expensive suit he fills out perfectly.

"You're not from around here," I say quietly.

He shakes his head.

"I'm not either," I tell him, smirking as I take a long swig of my drink.

Landmark is a picture-perfect world away from here right now, but home is the last place I want to be tonight.

"You're unbelievably beautiful," he says.

He looks at every detail of my face, lingering on my lips before his eyes wander down my body, pausing at my nipples and taking a deep breath at what he sees there. I'm afraid to look—I know it's obscene. I'm wearing a thin long-sleeve silk blouse and my nipples are fighting to be released into the wild. Preferably as close to his chest as possible. He swallows hard and closes his eyes for two seconds before he opens them and looks down, frowning slightly as he puts his hands on my bare knees.

I stop breathing.

"You're cold," he says.

"Not anymore I'm not. Your hands are the size of oven mitts…and warm. Thank you."

A loud laugh erupts out of him and I stare at him, smiling, feeling like the sun has just come out on this chilly March night.

When he sobers, he looks at me for another long moment before saying, "What else can I do to make your awful day better?"

"Well, I don't normally wrap my legs around a stranger's waist…"

He laughs again and damn, is it ever a great laugh.

"No, I don't either," he says. He leans in and when his breath warms my ear, my heart thuds violently against my rib cage. "So please tell me your name and then you won't be a stranger…"

"Scarlett."

"Pretty."

"What's yours?"

"Jamison," he says.

A hot name for the hottest man.

"What else would you like to know?" he asks.

"I think I'm good with Jamison," I say, unable to stop the giggle that slips out. "How about you?"

He looks at me, amused, and his head tilts. "Oh, there's *so much* more I'd like to know," he says. "But first things first—would you like another drink before…I wrap your legs around my waist? Maybe dinner?"

Again with the thudding heart and heat spiking down my face and chest and well, everywhere.

"Nope," I say, letting the *p* pop. "I'm ready."

I wink and his eyes widen slightly, that amused smirk on his face making me even bolder, and he tosses money on the bar.

I don't even know who I am right now, but when I stand up and tug down my pencil skirt and Jamison stands and towers over me, I look into his eyes and don't have an ounce of doubt.

No fear, no hesitation.

He holds out his hand and I take it, feeling lit from the inside out when our fingers weave together. When we reach the lobby, his hand shifts to the small of my back and he guides me onto the elevator, pushing the highest floor.

And then all the air rushes out of me when he turns to face me and tugs my body flush against his. I feel like I'm about to drop from the steepest incline on a roller coaster, and I put my hands in his thick, dark, wavy hair, holding on for dear life as he dips and lifts me like I weigh nothing. My skirt rides high as I wrap my legs around his waist.

"You're gonna turn my world upside down, aren't you, Scarlett," he says, his forehead leaning against mine.

"You better believe it," I say, grinning.

CHAPTER TWO

WHAT DREAMS ARE MADE OF

JAMISON

I laugh.

This girl.

I appreciate a beautiful woman, like any other hot-blooded guy, but Scarlett took my *breath* away the moment I laid eyes on her, and I'm not usually quite so rattled. She's not just beautiful, she's stunning and funny and she keeps on surprising me.

Her teeth stretch over her plump bottom lip and I grow even harder—I have been since she first looked at me—and I lower her slightly, clenching her perfect ass in my hands. Her eyes grow round as she feels me underneath her and I want to kiss her more than I want my next breath, but not yet. For now, I just want to look at her, memorize every expression that crosses her face, because I already know this experience will go by way too fast. My flight back to Boston is at godawful o'clock and I already feel out of time to worship her like I wish I could.

"Your turn," I whisper, enjoying the way she arches into me when I squeeze her cheeks. "Tell me something good."

"I couldn't tell how green your eyes were in that dark bar," she says. "Beautiful."

"Your eyes are really beautiful too."

"Just brown."

"Nothing about you is *just* anything…" I tell her, meaning it. God, do I ever mean it. Her breath catches when I lower her another inch and she can fully feel how hard I am for her.

"And *that…you.* You feel incredible," she whispers, her head falling back, just as the elevator dings.

I step off, holding onto her backside with one hand and sliding the card in front of the door with my other. Once we're in my suite, I toss the card to the ground and walk straight to the bedroom, the lights of the city from the open window and the full moon leaving the perfect light to see her.

With her still in my arms, I tilt her chin so she's looking into my eyes. "You sure you want this?" I ask.

She licks her lips and nods. "I really do," she whispers.

I grin, and again, she surprises me. She clutches my face in her hands and pulls my lips to hers, and she wasn't lying—she manages to turn my world upside down with just one kiss. I'm assaulted with a craving so profound, our kiss quickly gains momentum. She rubs herself against me as we kiss deeply, and I groan into her mouth when she whimpers. Her lips are soft and full and her tongue tastes like sugar and lemons and heaven. I reach up to run my thumb across the nipple that's been driving me wild as I thrust against her and her head falls back, her mouth parting in an O. She stiffens against me as she gasps and shudders, letting out the sweetest long moan before looking back at me in shock.

"Are you an orgasm whisperer?" she asks in awe.

"You tell me," I chuckle, holding onto her thighs and tossing her back playfully on the bed. She lays there looking like a fucking dream, her long dark hair splayed out, her tight skirt up around her waist, and a tiny scrap of pink lace wet between her legs.

"That was record time for me," she says.

"Let's see what other records we can set," I say, unbuttoning my shirt.

She slides her shoes off and they drop to the floor as she leans up on her elbows and watches while my shirt falls on the chair next to the bed. Her eyes widen slightly as she looks down my chest and stomach. She leans up, her fingers skating reverently over my abs before she undoes my belt and I unbutton the tiny buttons on her blouse, my huge fingers clumsy. She moves to her knees and once I've gotten two buttons undone, she lifts her blouse over her head and I hiss out a curse on a long exhale when I see her.

"What is this sexy thing?" I bite out, my dick surging toward her. I palm myself over my pants to try to calm down.

She's already undoing her skirt and slides it down, revealing the most amazing vision I've ever seen. Underneath that classy yet sexy professional outfit she was wearing, she'd been hiding this all along—a one-piece pale pink lace thing that plunges low on the top, the deep dip between her breasts catching my eye before shifting to the pebbled nipples straining against the lace, and rides high on her hips, spotlighting her flawless legs.

"I like pretty things," she says softly.

I reach out and rub the tips of my fingers against her nipples, swallowing hard. "I wouldn't have been able to have any resemblance of—uh, any semblance of—fuck…" I groan. "Any *sane* conversation with you if I'd known this was all going on underneath."

"I'm glad you like." She grins and lowers the zipper on my pants, gasping when she sees me. "You've got a lot going on here too," she whispers.

I can't take my eyes off of her as she lowers my boxer briefs and I spring free. She wraps both fists around me and I curse again.

"I can't even fit my hands around you," she says in awe.

"I love how you say exactly what you're thinking," I tell her, wondering again how the hell I'll get enough of her, and that thought alone is enough to send me sideways. Since I don't have time for a relationship and am nowhere near ready to settle down, it's a good thing we'll be going our separate ways in just a few short hours, maybe even after this one time.

And that sad thought snaps me back into action.

I don't want to waste another second.

She fists me up and down with just the right pressure to make me lose it fast if I'm not careful. I thrust into her hands twice, brushing my fingers across her neck and pushing her hair back before I put my hands over hers and bring them up to my mouth to kiss each finger.

She stares up at me and fuck, this woman is lethal.

"As much as I love this amazing thing you're wearing, how do I get you out of it?"

She grins and turns around, pulling her long waves to the side to show me the back view. I groan, swiping a hand over my face but unable to look away. A thin ribbon between her shoulder blades and another at her waist are tied in bows and underneath the lace high on her hips, her firm, full ass is on display.

"Scarlett, everything about you is something good." My voice is raspy and when she turns to look at me over her shoulder, her eyes shy again, I have to rub my hand over my heart because it's beating so hard it hurts.

I untie the bows, sliding the lace over her shoulders and down her body, my rough fingers trailing over her soft silky skin. The sounds of the city are faint below, but my ears are tuned in to the soft intake of her breath, the sweet whimpers she makes as my hands glide over her body before she turns around and faces me.

Her long, dark brown hair is still clasped in her hand and she drops it, letting her hair fall free. It's so long it covers her breast and nearly reaches her waist.

"I've never seen anyone so beautiful," I say, swallowing hard.

I rub my chest again and turn to my suitcase to get the condoms I keep in there.

Scarlett laughs when she sees the long strip I pull out. "Prepared much?"

I make a face, laughing too. "You might not believe me when I say I never considered this being an opportunity when I packed for this trip, but it's true. When I was around fifteen, my older brother taught me to tuck condoms in my nightstand, bathroom, glove compartment…suitcase. 'One in the wallet just won't do' was his motto and I have never been so glad that I listened." I'm saying it as I slide it down my length, my breath hitching when I watch her mouth part as she stares at me.

"Sage advice," she whispers.

"Lie back and I'll make you forget you were ever sad," I tell her.

And I spend every moment for the next few hours fulfilling that promise—if her cries of pleasure are any indication—until she falls asleep, a smile on her face, her head on my chest, arm draped over me and her thigh wrapped around mine.

I glance at my phone, wanting nothing more than to fall asleep with this gorgeous woman and wake up to do all of this over again, but it's already time to get up. I gently remove her arm and leg first and then slide out of bed, putting my pillow under her head to replace my chest. She whimpers but stays asleep while I shower and get dressed. I whisper her name to see if she'll wake up, but she's sleeping so hard. I smile at the picture she makes and zip up my suitcase, turning to find a paper and pen.

I write before I can talk myself out of it, knowing I can never put into words how incredible our night was.

. . .

Scarlett,
An unforgettable night with an unforgettable woman.
You asked me to tell you something good and you ended up
giving me something exceptional.
You will be forever engraved in my memory.
Jamison

P.S. I have an early flight and you're sleeping so soundly I
can't wake you up. It would've been too hard to say
goodbye anyway. I hope you wake up smiling, beautiful. Xx

I almost put my phone number at the bottom but don't. I know nothing about her and it's not like we could see each other again anyway. As much as we communicated throughout the night, neither of us even mentioned where we're from, and nothing was said to lead either of us to believe it'd be anything more than this one night.

I don't know why I'm even hesitating—I don't have a good track record with relationships, so at least we're ending on a high note, before we ever began. I turn to look at her and sigh, placing the note on the nightstand.

It's best to just leave it at this…like my note said, an unforgettable night.

But my heart is conflicted as I walk away, feeling like I left a piece of it there, with her.

CHAPTER THREE

LIGHT OF DAY

SCARLETT

The sun is bright when I wake up and stretch, feeling deliciously sore everywhere.

The ache between my legs is persistent enough that I think it will stay with me, reminding me of the night I just had. My body heats up as I remember all the ways Jamison worked my body over, and I smile and sit up, looking around.

"Jamison?" I call, my stomach dropping when I see that his suitcase is gone. There's no response and I feel kind of sick, the euphoria dissipating with the reality of the morning.

Something skitters to the floor when I fall back on my pillow. I lean over and pick up a piece of paper, pressing my fingers to my lips as I smile at his words. Turning it over, I'm disappointed to see the other side blank. I read what he wrote again and then close my eyes.

There's no way that level of intensity could've held up over the long haul anyway, I tell myself. Best to chalk it up to one of the greatest experiences of my life, a gift, and hope that I'll eventually meet a man that can come close to lighting up my body the way Jamison did.

At best, he did exactly what I needed him to do—made me forget the dumpster fire that is my life right now. At worst, I'll never meet another man like him again.

My exhale is loud in the quiet room. I force myself to get out of bed and pick up my blouse and skirt, the lace teddy that Jamison loved so much taking more time to find. I grin again, imagining his face when he saw me in it.

"Guess I'll be making more of you," I say out loud when I find the lingerie under one of the pillows on his side of the bed. Maybe it's time to get more serious about my sewing hobby now that my dreams of running our family resort are flushed down the toilet.

And the funk is fully back.

Landmark Mountain Lodge is no longer ours.

I've given my entire life to that place. It's the only home I've ever known, the only job I've ever had, and I'm the only one out of my four brothers who feels that way. They love the place and hated to see it go, but each one of them already has the career they love, all successful in their own right, and the upkeep of running the lodge to the extent it needs to return it to its five-star glory would take each of us giving everything we had…not just our money but our time, our passion. *Everything.*

My overachiever brothers have never imagined themselves running the resort, and for me, the baby of the family and the only girl, I'd never imagined doing anything else. From as far back as I can remember, I have craved any and everything that keeps the tradition and stability in our family. Our parents died in a car accident when I was two and our grandparents raised the five of us. We're like stairsteps—each three years apart. I often wonder if I was the last child my parents planned to have or if they'd lived a year longer, maybe another baby would've been born by then.

Theo is the closest in age and a livestock vet. Wyatt is a family practitioner, Callum is a rancher, and my oldest brother, Sutton, is a judge, divorced—thankfully—and has a little boy named Owen, who is the light of all our lives.

And then there's me, the only one who has the hospitality blood in my veins.

My phone vibrates and I pick it up and set it back down when I see that it's Theo. I'll call him on my way home. In the bathroom there's still a faint scent of Jamison, lime and sandalwood. I shiver, my skin remembering every touch from him, every sensation.

Still naked, I look in the mirror and point at myself. "Snap out of it," I hiss. "Time to figure out what you're doing with your life."

I take a quick shower, putting the same clothes back on minus the teddy but surprisingly okay with it. It's not like

I'm in Landmark, where I can't go anywhere without being recognized. Is it even the walk of shame if no one knows? This was the most spontaneous thing I've ever done and I can't even bring myself to regret it.

When I see the note lying on the bed, I pick it up and put it in my purse and then I get out of Jamison's hotel room quickly so I'm not tempted to crawl back into that bed and wallow. Once I'm in the car, I call Theo back and put him on speaker before I put the car in reverse.

"You okay?" he asks, skipping over the greetings.

"Oh, you know…I've been better."

"Where are you? I got worried when you didn't show up at The Pink Ski last night. Called you a ton," he grumbles.

"I told you I wasn't up for a family dinner. As much as I love you guys and would do anything for every single one of you, I'm just not up to celebrating yet." I make a few turns, on high alert with all the traffic. I'll breathe easier once I'm out of the city limits.

"I'm an idiot for not realizing what all of this would mean to you. We all are." Theo sighs.

"I would've just brought you all down last night. I ended up staying the night in Boulder after I left the real estate office. I wasn't ready to go home yet."

"Really? That…surprises me," he says. "I don't know what Granddad was thinking, but I've said that at least a hundred times since the will was read. And Grinny is worried sick about you. You need to call her."

A wave of guilt hits when I think about my grandma worrying about me. I should've at least let her know I was okay last night.

"I'll call her as soon as I get home. Did you see the

buyers at all?" I ask, my stomach already churning like I'm talking about the enemy.

"No, Sutton did, but since we didn't all have to, we just signed the paperwork and headed right back to town. Two weeks will come soon enough. I'm surprised you didn't stay to meet them, since you're the one that will have to work with them for the next ninety days. It was nice of you to agree to that, by the way…"

The first contract had stipulated that I stay on for six months to help with the transition. I might not be a consideration to own Landmark Mountain Lodge, but I at least have an iota of negotiating power when it comes to my time. Although lowering it to three months doesn't feel like much of a win for me.

"That should be a sufficient amount of time for everyone to adjust, and I plan on staying out of the way as much as I possibly can," I mutter.

"Well, I'll do my best to make sure I'm there on that first day. And just let me know what I can do to…help." He curses under his breath. "I'm sorry—I've gotta run check on a bloated cow."

"All right." Normally I tease him about all the ailments he has to tend to, but I don't have it in me today.

"Love you," he says.

"Love you back."

He ends the call and I turn on the music, now on the roads I'm more comfortable driving. I ignore Sutton's call, then Wyatt's, and after another twenty minutes go by, I ignore Callum's call.

Their time is in demand, so it means a lot that they're checking on me. Callum particularly despises the phone—I'm doing good to get a few one-word texts from him every other day—so the guilt stirs up again when I ignore his call.

But the tears started up within five minutes of hanging up with Theo, and they haven't stopped yet. My brothers are as crazy about me as I am about them, but they've only seen me cry two times—once when I was seven and broke my leg, and the second time was eight months ago at Granddad's funeral. The panic levels my brothers have gone to those two times I cried were enough to instill in me to never ever let that happen again. They doted and carried on like I was an invalid or so fragile that I might break, and I handle that about as well as a giraffe in an elevator.

When I pass the *Welcome to Landmark, population 4,504* sign, I can tell by the traffic near the quaint shops and then more accurately from the cars parked near the different sections of the lodge and the ski resort, that our town has somewhere between an additional 10-12,000 tourists today, which is up slightly from last year due to the snowfall we got last week, and down about 12,000 from our busiest season between Thanksgiving and the New Year. Spring break is just getting started and it will pick up even more around here over the next month.

The sprawling lodge is surrounded by snow-covered mountains, white peaks glistening in the late morning sun, and the beauty overwhelms me. I take it in the way I always do...with love and awe and pride that such a magnificent place has thrived in this tiny majestic mountain town named after family who came long before me.

I just don't know if there will be room for me here once the new owners move in. Even though no one is requiring me to, I'll move out of the condo in the back where I've lived since I graduated from high school, doing college classes online and working full-time at the lodge so I could know the pulse of the lodge better than I had living with Granddad and Grinny in the Alpine House. With the new owners taking over, it'll be too close for comfort.

I have no idea where I'll go.

My whole life has been wrapped up in the lodge, but it's all about to change.

And I don't know how to figure out where to land.

CHAPTER FOUR

NECESSARY INTRODUCTIONS

JAMISON

Two Weeks Later…

I take a deep breath and chug water from my Yeti, trying to combat any altitude weirdness. I didn't notice it much when I was here before, so I should be fine.

I arrived late last night and fell into bed, not bothering

to unpack any of the boxes that arrived before me. This morning, I was too excited to sleep, ready to meet everyone I'll be working with. It's been a long time since I've been the newcomer at work and it's never been in this capacity…as the boss. I help manage people's millions as their financial advisor and while that's rewarding, I'm looking forward to a new challenge. I step in through the back entrance, going through the offices. It's quiet and I'm glad to be the first here. I stop by the kitchen and am surprised to see a pot of coffee already brewing. I grab a mug from the cabinet above and pour a cup, taking a sip.

"Damn," I say with regret. It's barely coffee-flavored hot water.

I turn and a few drops of coffee spill onto my hand, but I barely notice.

Because holy fuck. It's *her*.

"You," she whispers.

"Scarlett," I say, my voice hushed to match hers.

She looks even more beautiful than I've imagined her and I've imagined her every single day since I left her in that hotel room weeks ago. I set the coffee down on the table and walk toward her, unable to stop smiling.

"I can't believe it." My eyes can't help themselves, they drink in every inch of her. "What are you doing here?"

Her lips part and she stares at me for a long moment in shock. I stop when I'm within a foot of her, wishing I could hug her but uncertain of what the protocol is for running into your one-night stand after thinking you'd never see them again.

"This is my—what are *you* doing here?" she asks, her eyes narrowing.

And it's then that I realize she's not looking as happy to see me as I am to see her. "Listen, I'm sorry for the way I left. I tried to wake you up…it did feel wrong to not say bye, but—"

"Jamison, what are you doing here?" she interrupts, crossing her arms over her chest.

I smile, despite the unease building. "I'm the new owner of Landmark Mountain Lodge." I sound like I'm ready to do jazz hands and tone it down when I add, "Technically, my brother and I are both owners, but I'll be the one doing most of the day-to-day as we transition…"

Her face has lost all color while I've been talking and I reach out to steady her, but she takes a step back.

"What kind of sick plan was this?" she asks, taking another step away from me. "Wasn't it enough that you'd taken my family business from me? How did you know I'd be at the hotel that night—did you follow me? Did sleeping with me add to some notch on your—"

"Wait a minute. What are you talking about?" I nearly take her arm, but the way she's shaking and the color is returning to her face in whatever shade *very angry* is keeps me firmly in place. "I had no idea who you were when we met…I still don't. Your family business—wait, does that mean—are you, you're a Landmark?"

I feel winded, maybe there is something to that altitude thing.

"Yes, I'm a Landmark," she snaps. "You can't possibly expect me to believe you didn't know."

"How would I know? Your name wasn't on anything. I would've remembered a name like Scarlett. I met Sutton Landmark, but the only other names on the contract were

Wyatt, Theo, and one other…" I shake my head, trying to remember but too confused to get there.

"Callum. The Landmark brothers, John Henry Landmark's grandsons. I'm their little sister and *I'm* the one who has run this place alongside Granddad all these years." Her voice cracks and I'm torn between trying to comfort her and getting the hell out of here to avoid her wrath.

"I'm really sorry for your loss," I tell her, meaning it with all my heart.

Losing my grandma was one of the hardest things our family has ever gone through. I wouldn't wish that on anyone. Every kind of emotion is at war on her face as she stands there, her chest rising and falling rapidly.

"And you're staying to help with the transition." The pieces start coming together. "Albert mentioned one of the family members would be my right-hand…well, he said man, but…" I chuckle and it dies a painful death when her eyes try to murder me with hateful, stabbing glares.

"You tried to prolong my stay from three months to six —I can't believe you're still pretending to not know it was me. Did you think sleeping with me would give you more time? My name wasn't on the deed, but it was on the contract saying I'd only stay ninety days."

"So was mine," I insist. "But the agent was in quite a rush, at least when my brother and I were there. I'd barely sign my…chicken-scratch signature before he had another form in place for me to sign. It all ran together. I swear to you, I had no idea you were part of the Landmark family, but now that I know…all the better, right?"

She doesn't say a word, her shoe tapping on the floor faster and faster.

"My brother and I have loved this place since we were young and came here on a family vacation. When I got the email saying the place was for sale, I couldn't believe my luck. I can't tell you how excited I am to get the property back to its former glory and even beyond—"

She holds up her hand. "I'll stop you right there. Save your sales pitch. Not all of the Landmarks are happy about this." Her lip trembles and she takes another step back, jumping when she runs into Albert.

"Hey there, little lady," he says, looking down at her fondly.

Her face softens when she sees him. She swallows hard and whispers, "Morning, Albert."

"I see you've met Mr. Ledger." He beams at me. "Nice to see you with the early birds." He motions between him and Scarlett. "It's usually just the two of us here at this time. Vera will be along shortly…in time for the meeting," he adds, winking.

"I'll be in my office until then," Scarlett says, moving past Albert and bolting down the hall.

I watch her go, feeling more than a little conflicted. How the hell did I sleep with the former owner's granddaughter and not even realize it? I want to go study the contract she's talking about, but Albert clears his throat.

"She's the heart behind this place," he says, nodding solemnly. "Put everything she has into making it what it is and not always with all the resources to back her up. I have a good feeling about you though."

He smiles big and his words would help a lot more if I weren't still in shock about Scarlett.

"It might take her a while to warm up to the idea of you," he says under his breath, "but she'll come around."

He walks me back to my office and stands in the doorway. The sun is blinding through the window.

"I'm going to do my morning walk-through before the meeting. Can I help you with anything before I go?"

"No, thank you, Albert. I'll see you in an hour."

He nods and backs out, whistling as he goes down the hall.

I sit down at the outdated desk, setting my laptop on the dark wood on autopilot.

What started out as an exciting new opportunity now feels way more complex. And all the fantasies I've been entertaining about Scarlett over the past couple of weeks will have to be filed away forever. There's not only no time for that with all the work that needs to be done, but it's obvious that she would rather jab her eyeballs out than ever see me again.

CHAPTER FIVE

UPSIDE-DOWN SMILE

SCARLETT

My pen hovers over today's list, pausing over the last line.

- *Skip the bakery this morning.*
- *Meet Lorena in the lobby, 7:30 a.m.*
- *Mtg with HP, 8 a.m.*
- *Let HP do the rest of my work since he wants this place so bad.*

I nicknamed the new boss Head Prick before I even met him, but now that I know Jamison Ledger is the new owner of my family's lodge, I wish I'd been meaner.

I pace my office, regretting not making the bakery stop. I could use a chocolate croissant right about now. I didn't want the HP to expect that from me every day, even though I've picked up coffee and treats from Happy Cow from the time I could drive. As with everything in this transaction, the joke's on me because Jamison doesn't know what he's missing. I'm the one who's left with gnawing hunger and a headache from not having my usual morning treat and caffeine fix. I purposely made disgusting coffee this morning just in case the HP was a coffee lover. But I didn't think that one through.

Jamison. A whimper escapes me and I put my hand over my mouth, trying to keep it in. The number of times I've wished I could see him again in the past two weeks... it's ridiculous. How could he be here? In my resort, probably in Granddad's office by now...*that man*, who has taken over every waking and sleeping thought since we slept together, is *here,* in Landmark. Population 4,505 now.

How am I going to work with him every day?

I groan and then jump when my timer goes off. I grab my planner and hurry out of my office, making a point to not look in the direction of Granddad's office. I refuse to call it Jamison's.

Lorena is right on time and comes in rolling a huge cart of flowers. I can barely see her behind all the flowers and feathers. I help her into the lobby and admire her work. Our front desk clerks are switching over—Doug is officially off for the night and Elsie is beginning her shift —and they both ask what they can do to help.

I give them the list of arrangement placements, checking to see if each arrangement is labeled as I asked. They are, which earns Lorena huge points in my book.

"Stunning, Lorena. I love what you've put together. And thank you for marking them—that makes our job so much easier."

"The rest is in the van," she says, beaming.

"I'll help you," I tell her, walking outside with her.

Lorena's not quite five feet and her voice is soft and childlike, her brown skin flawless. When I went in to visit her new shop, she shocked me when she said she'd been in business for forty years in Portland, and she had the pictures to back it up. The crinkles at her eyes when she smiles are the only evidence that she's not exactly my age, but the way she unfolds another cart and hauls these arrangements out of the van like they're nothing when some arrangements are nearly as big as her is impressive.

It's windy this morning, so we hurry to avoid anything getting messed up, guests from the resort slowing down to watch as we roll the cart toward the entrance. I stop abruptly, causing Lorena to squeak, when Jamison opens the door for us. He has his sleeves rolled up already, his tie loosened slightly, reminding me of that night when he took off his—

Heat floods my face. "I'm sorry about that," I tell Lorena, steadying a few of the arrangements before we move slowly toward the door and Jamison.

He grins at me tentatively and quickly moves his attention to Lorena when I don't smile back. He chats with her easily and has her eating out of the palm of his hand in no time, the bastard.

Grinny would be appalled at my behavior, Granddad

too. *I* would be too, if I thought Jamison was telling the truth about not knowing it was me that night.

I just can't buy the coincidence.

And yet, I never once noticed his name either. I was in too much of a fog, too upset about what was happening for it to register. Now that I think about it, Theo did go on about how cool it was that an NFL player would be part of the history of the lodge...

Lorena is giggling at something Jamison says and Elsie blushes as she takes one of the arrangements from him. Elsie is tall and beautiful and freshly twenty-one, so totally legal. My stomach clenches and I feel a pang in my chest at the thought of the two of them hitting it off.

"Are you an NFL player?" I ask Jamison quietly.

"Pardon?" he asks, turning away from Elsie to look at me. He's closer than I realized and I freeze. He blinks slowly and glances down at my mouth and seems to shake himself out of a stupor when he says, "Oh, did you say NFL player? No, that's my brother, Zac."

I can't explain the relief I feel when he says that. I don't know any professional athletes, but I know there are a lot of women involved...right? That's a thing?

"He's coming in a few weeks with his wife and daughter. You'll love—" He pauses and seems to rethink whatever he was about to say. He glances down at his watch, the large face looking too good on his arm. "If we're all set here, I'll head to the conference room so I can be there to greet everyone," he tells me. "Lorena, it was so nice to meet you. Scarlett made the right decision when she chose you." He grins at her and it drops when he sees my narrowed eyes.

He walks away, disappearing through the door to the offices.

"I'm sorry I don't have time to linger, Lorena," I tell her, still looking over my shoulder after Jamison. "You nailed the order, thank you."

Elsie and Doug continue to move the arrangements into place as Lorena fluffs and positions flowers here and there.

"I'm so glad you like everything," she says. "I'll be back with the small vases this evening at five thirty. They'll be ready before then, but until I can hire help, I'll have to wait until the shop closes." She smiles sweetly, her round cheeks lifting. "Are you still good with one hundred even?"

"Five thirty will be perfect. And yes, I believe one hundred is still right. I'll let you know if we have a bunch of surprise check-ins."

"Thank you, Scarlett," she says.

"Thank *you*."

I ask Bill, one of the porters who just came on duty, to help Lorena with her carts and hustle down the hall toward the conference room. Jamison is already there, placing the black and white boxes of pastries from Happy Cow on a side table, two industrial-sized dispensers of coffee next to that. He straightens a little bowl of sugar and creamer and then the plates and cups. How he managed to pull all of this off is beyond me. Who told him about Happy Cow anyway?

"Don't do that," I say, when he looks up.

"Don't do…what exactly?" he asks, his lips twitching. He thinks this is funny?

"Don't brown-nose me with our employees. It won't

win you any points with me. I can handle myself, thank you very much."

He studies me, his eyes drifting down my black pantsuit and lingering on my hot pink floral blouse so briefly, I almost think I've imagined it. I'm glad I dressed to impress this morning. I know I look good. I almost went the other direction and intentionally looked like a hot mess so the new management would worry about what he'd gotten himself into. I can at least be grateful I didn't go that route.

He nods slowly, his tongue dipping out over his lips making it hard for me to concentrate. "I have no doubt you can handle yourself just fine," he finally says. "In fact, I know you can."

Flustered, I turn and walk closer to the entrance, stopping in the doorway.

Jamison moves to stand next to me, and I second-guess my decision to not just go sit down and wait for everyone to arrive. My legs feel weirdly shaky.

"I'd like to run something by you," he says.

I don't respond.

"I'd like to have a cocktail party," he says. "By next Friday night if possible. We'll invite all the business owners here for a happy hour…let them know I'm here to help them in any way I can."

"We're already helping the business owners in Landmark," I say, folding my arms across my chest as I turn to stare at him. "They don't need a party to know we send business their way every chance we get."

He turns to face me, mirroring my stance. It's sexy as all hell.

"Okay, it'll be a chance for them to get to know me

and vice versa then," he says, smiling calmly.

I drop my arms and groan inside.

"Fine," I say through my teeth.

"Excellent."

Vera and Albert are the first to walk through the door, and Albert greets Jamison like they're old friends already. I don't know why that feels like a betrayal, but it does. I can't be mad at Albert though, he's as sweet as they come.

He introduces his wife Vera and she glances over at me, her eyes twinkling as she says, "Albert didn't tell me the new owner was such a looker."

I grit my teeth and laugh with the three of them, faking it even more when Jamison says, "You must be confusing me with my brother."

"And he's humble to boot," Vera cries, patting the top of Jamison's hand as they shake.

Since some of the staff has to watch the front and be available to guests, everyone isn't able to attend the meeting, but Doug comes in, and Bill and Andy are next. Deb, the head of housekeeping, also swoons when she sees Jamison. It's an epidemic. And then finally, my brothers trickle in, one after the other. They didn't have to be here today, but they promised me they would come to show their support, for the new owners and for me.

I pretend they're only here for me as I hug each one of them. But as they shake Jamison's hand and he handles them like a pro, I see them all relax, even Callum, the antisocial one, and I wish they'd just let me handle this on my own.

Jamison is entirely too smooth. I can't believe I didn't see right through him the night we met. No one this charming could be up to any good.

CHAPTER SIX

CONNECTIONS

JAMISON

The Landmark siblings are an intimidating bunch.

Attractive, smart, and confident...a couple broodier than others, but I've always loved a challenge. With the exception of Scarlett, our first meeting notwithstanding, I think I win them over fairly quickly. And from what I can tell, I really like them too.

The meeting goes well. Turns out the pastries are a

common occurrence around here in the morning, so that wasn't anything new, but they seem appreciative anyway. I tell them about the cocktail party and they seem excited about that, and I lay out just a few of my ideas for updating the resort and getting new guests coming in, but I go easy on them this first time. We'll get to know each other and maybe some of my ideas will go over better with a little time.

I can tell Scarlett is the one who will challenge everything, and that's okay. It's obvious she cares about the lodge, so it's understandable that she'd feel strongly about things.

I can't help but wonder why the resort didn't go to her. The brothers are here as a courtesy today—I'd be surprised if I see them at another meeting—but with each topic I bring up, Scarlett has a question…or statement.

Like when I suggest that we renovate the south wing that isn't getting as much occupancy as the rest of the resort.

"When you say renovate, do you mean to match the charm of the rest of the lodge?" she asks.

"I hope to keep the charm but to update…and I would like to eventually update the entire resort, so this would be the first wing to showcase that."

"So you *don't* want to maintain the integrity of the resort."

"I *do*," I insist, trying my damnedest not to smile too big.

My smiles seem to make her angry.

Everything I do seems to make her angry.

I just find her so entertaining. And still can't believe my luck or curse, whichever it might end up being, that she's here in the first place. I'm choosing to believe it's luck.

"I'll be happy to show you some examples of what I mean between now and our next meeting," I add.

She glowers at her large, fat notebook, writing something furiously.

I end the meeting by saying something I hope will convey how much this place means to me.

"My family and I came here twice, once when I was eight and the next when I was seventeen. The first time, my brother and I lived on the slopes and our parents could barely get us to stop and eat."

There's a rumble of laughter in the room.

"It was magical. I'd never been down such long runs and loved being able to ski right out of the condos...I could probably figure out which one it was if I go out and study each one."

Another pause while they laugh. Everyone but Scarlett.

"The second time, I remember thinking we weren't skiing nearly enough, but we hung out in town more because my parents insisted we spend time with our grandparents who were with us. I adored my grandparents, but skiing and girls were more important at the time, so I wasn't as happy about the arrangement. But man, the memories we made at The Pink Ski...I still remember their fries with that fancy sauce."

More chuckles.

"The bear sauce," someone calls out.

"And the one and only time I ever saw Pappy drunk was on that trip, at The Dancing Emu, to be specific." I smile, remembering it like it was yesterday. "He sang all the way back to our condo, with Gran giggling behind us, as my brother and I flanked him on either side."

Everyone cracks up, and even Scarlett looks like she's trying hard not to smile now.

"I can't tell you how happy I am that all these places are still here. Well, I hope all of them are. Is Sunny Side still here?"

"Yes," Albert says, sounding surprised. "Usually the tourists don't venture out to that one."

"Well, I think maybe your grandma told mine about Sunny Side." I direct my comment to the Landmark brothers, not wanting Scarlett to think I'm brown-nosing her with this one, but still wanting to tell the story. "Gran was very impressed with this lady, saying she had the cutest name, Grinny…" I laugh now, remembering Gran's joy at that.

"That's her all right," Vera says.

"I remember because Gran asked if it was too late for us to start calling her Grinny too."

Vera loves that, her plump shoulders shaking as she laughs.

"So, we went to Sunny Side and Gran hadn't had much of an appetite the whole trip, and even before that, but that day she ate the pancakes and eggs *and* the hash browns. She hadn't gone skiing with us that whole trip, but when we got back to the resort, we convinced her to go on the toboggan with us. Zac and I took turns taking her down the bunny hills and the way she laughed…"

I shake my head and have to take a couple of seconds to keep going. Throughout this process, my brother and I have found ourselves getting emotional when we think about owning the place that holds such incredible memories for us.

"I'll never forget it." My voice is hoarse when I add, "That was the last trip Gran made with us. We found out she was sick not long after that, and she died a year later."

Some of the ladies are wiping their cheeks and I feel bad that I made them cry.

"Sorry to get heavy on you. I only wanted to convey how special this place is to me…this town, and the places and people in it. My mom was even inspired by hearing Gran talk about Grinny and her cute name. When my niece was born, my mom decided she wanted to be called Daisy instead of Grandma and she expects us all to call her that. Her name is Tammy, so I'm not really sure where Daisy came in, but you don't argue with Mom or Tammy or Daisy."

They're laughing again and I'm relieved.

"I don't fully know the traditions or the legacy in these walls, but I want to learn." I look at Scarlett when I say my next sentence. "I'm not here to tear down the old but rather to enhance what's already here, to build on the shoulders of the ones who came before and make sure it lives on."

She swallows hard and looks down, fidgeting with her pen.

I wish I could start all over with her, tell her everything about me from the beginning, find out all I can about her, and then relive our night all over again, with eyes wide open.

My thoughts rattle me, and I have to focus on Albert as I wrap up the meeting.

"I'll let you get to work now. I'll include this in the email I send to everyone who couldn't be here today, but feel free to pass along this message. I've set up a schedule outside my office, and I'd like each of you to fill out a time to meet with me when it's convenient for you. I want to get to know each one of you, the sooner the better. Thanks, everyone."

There's a smattering of applause and everyone comes up to say something before they leave. They seem like a nice group of people. The brothers are saying something to Scarlett and then hug her before coming to me, one by one.

Theo, the one who seems the most chill, is the first one. I've always thought it was interesting how siblings can look so similar and yet so distinct at the same time. The brothers are all over six feet and their hair varies in shades of brown, but their personalities are what make them stand apart. Theo's eyes are wide open, no guile to them, as he shakes my hand.

"I love that your family has a connection here," he says. "That makes all of this really special."

"Thanks. I think so too," I tell him, grateful that he's not angry about it like his sister.

Everything about the next brother looks gruff. Callum. His voice is low and almost growly, but he shakes my hand firmly and says, "Welcome to Landmark."

"Thanks, man," I say.

Wyatt is the next one and he's not quite as laidback as Theo, but not as serious as Callum either. He's professional when he shakes my hand. "I think you'll be a good fit for this place," he says.

"That means a lot."

Sutton is the last one and he's got one arm around Scarlett when he reaches out with his other hand to give mine a hearty shake.

"And you already met the judge," Scarlett says, holding her hand out toward her brother.

"Yes, we met. Good to see you again, Jamison. Scarlett will keep you in line here until you figure out the ropes," he says, grinning. He lifts an eyebrow, his expression suddenly serious. "Step out of line even one inch and we'll send you back to Boston so fast you won't know what hit you on the way out."

Something tells me he's used to being intimidating, which makes sense if he really is a judge, I guess. I smirk and he starts laughing and pounds my back.

"I'm kidding," he says. "Well, not really, but Scarlett will keep me up to speed."

Scarlett rolls her eyes, and I let out a long exhale when they both walk out.

This is going to be a long initiation.

CHAPTER SEVEN

BOILING WATER

SCARLETT

If I thought it was hard to get Jamison out of my mind before, that was nothing compared to seeing him right here in my space…and don't get me started on being in his positivity cloud.

Granddad was a force to be reckoned with. He was a kind man, but he was also firm and old-school. I was the sunshine to his rain, the glass half-full to his *the glass doesn't even have water unless we wring the water into the glass in the first place.*

Being around Jamison, I feel like the Grinch…or worse, like I'm channeling Granddad after working so hard to snap him out of his grump most of the time. I'm just so angry. Angry that the lodge isn't mine. Angry that it's Jamison's. Angry at Jamison for *everything*.

Seriously, if I were to meet him today and he tried to give me five orgasms, I'd find a way to be angry at him about that too. In fact, I'm already angry at him about that.

Because how can it be that the one guy able to please me in bed to that extreme is the one guy I have to pass the reins to in three months? There is nothing fair about this.

Growing up, Grinny never let us say life isn't fair because *duh, no kidding, it's not*, her words not mine and she'd be whispering the sassiness but still mean it, and in the big picture, she's right. And there are so many more worse things in life than what I'm going through, I do realize that, but…since Granddad is not here and I can't take it out on the person responsible, I can still take it out on the guy who's taken what I wanted most right out from under me.

And why does he have to be so charming? He nearly made me cry in that meeting this morning. I can't believe his Gran met Grinny—and neither could she. I'm gonna dropkick whichever brother called to tell her about it because she's shown up now, eyes dancing.

She hugs me and pats my arm. "Come on, angel, won't you introduce me to this fella? You're not gonna believe it, but I remember his grandmother!"

"How is that possible? We get so many people through here," I tell her.

I'm groaning on the inside, wanting to lock my feet in place, but instead I'm leading her toward Granddad's office.

"You sure you want to go in here?" I ask before we knock.

The door isn't closed, but when Grinny nods, I knock anyway.

"Come in," Jamison calls. He looks surprised when I walk in and then his face splits into a wide smile when he sees who's with me. "You must be Grinny—I'm sorry, I mean Mrs. Landmark!"

"I am," she says, laughing and delighted. "And don't you dare call me Mrs. Landmark! I couldn't believe it when my grandson told me about your Gran. And I was just telling Scarlett here that I remember her! Beautiful, tall lady with the prettiest accent. North Carolina or South Carolina, if I remember right."

"North Carolina," he says, shaking his head as he grasps her hand in his. "I can't believe you remember."

"She was so lovely, talking about her grandsons and the cute things you said. We talked about my name, which is what made me first remember, but I've always remembered her because well…" She glances at me and I'm suddenly afraid of what she's going to say next when she winks. "I'll let it stay between two grandmothers, but let's just say, we covered quite a bit of territory in a short amount of time. Do you remember meeting her?" she asks me then.

Caught off guard, I quit fidgeting. "Me? I met her too?"

"Yes, you were about thirteen, and she saw you behind the front desk and said you were as pretty as a picture, and after one conversation with you, she could tell that even at your age, you were smarter than all the girls her grandsons had ever gone out with…combined." Grinny laughs and Jamison does too.

My face heats at the comment and with the realization.

Jamison says, "That sounds just like her," just as I'm saying, "I *do* remember her."

Jamison stops laughing and stares at me, the tension between us crackling like a live wire. "Really?"

The sun shining through the windows highlights the darker green in his eyes gradually turning into lighter shades until a ring of gold surrounds his pupils.

Absolutely captivati—*ridiculous*—absolutely *ridiculous* that I'm getting lost in his eyes.

I clear my throat and turn to Grinny, who's covering her mouth with her hand, her eyes all lit up like fireworks. I narrow my eyes at her and she laughs outright, clearly amused by something. When I've been over at her house over the past two weeks, she's grumbled more than I have about Granddad's will, wondering who's coming in here to take over, and how life will never be the same in Landmark. One conversation with Jamison and she's putty in his hands…and she's Team Scarlett all the way!

He's clearly highly manipulative and sketchy to have such an effect on the Landmark women.

"Well, it will be so good to have you here, Jamison," she says.

I can't keep the sigh from escaping. It didn't even take him an hour to win Grinny over. And it just gets worse.

"Has anyone told you that our Scarlett was the one who got the resort operating in the black again? She came up with the two nights, third night free idea before that was really a thing, like it is everywhere now, and once that happened, we were able to start contributing to the shelters in town and in the surrounding area. Who knows? You might find out that the two of you make a *fine* team."

My face feels feverish around her first sentence, but by the time she's wrapping it up with *a fine team*, I'd kill for a full-body ice bath. Maybe I could just step outside, strip, and lie down in the snow, see if that cools me off at all.

It doesn't help that Jamison's eyes have never once left mine. He is studying me like I am his science project and he'll be testing on me later.

When he says, "I have no doubt you're right about that," his voice all swoony rasp, I have to hold onto the edge of the desk. I'm sure it's just my imagination, but it's almost as if I can see the memories of our night together playing across his mind the way they are mine.

Somehow I manage to say, "See why I take her everywhere?"

Grinny waves me off. "She hates it when I brag on her, but I can't help it. You'll understand when you're grand-parents one day."

Jamison loosens his tie a little more, pulling his shirt away from his neck like he needs air.

Grinny clasps her hands together and Jamison's eyes slowly drift back to her. It helps me breathe a little better to have a break from his gaze. "I'll let you two get back to it, but I have an idea," Grinny says, beaming, and Jamison can't help it, he melts like butter.

It's the Grinny Effect.

He gives her a full-wattage smile back and her shoulders straighten in that way she gets when she's on a mission. I find myself gripping the desk again.

Heaven help us.

"I know the baton has already been passed over to you, but to seal the deal, I'd love to have you over for a little dinner party. What do you say?"

"That sounds like a wonderful idea," he says, glancing at me like he thinks I might shut the whole thing down.

And I would, but Grinny turns that beam on me, and what can I say? I've never been able to resist the Grinny Effect. I rarely even try anymore, and I really can't now, when she hasn't looked this happy since Granddad died.

"Perfect," she says. "Does next Friday night work?"

Jamison nods like he's about to say yes, still under her spell.

"The cocktail hour with local business owners is Friday night from 5-7:30," I remind him.

"Right. How could I forget?" he says, running his hand over his jaw. The cocktail hour was his idea and a damn good one, even I have to admit that. He turns to Grinny. "What time do you prefer to eat dinner?"

"I can go as late as you need, but how about we make it another night? Next Saturday?"

He glances at me as if I should answer that and my mouth falls open, shoulders lifting.

"Are *you* free Saturday night?" he asks.

My head tilts. "Uh, I think so, but I'm not sure I'll—" The words pour out of me quickly.

"Perfect," he says, grinning. "We'll be there."

"Oh, excellent. I can't wait," Grinny says, while I stutter some kind of nonsense. "And I won't invite the girls just yet, it'll be just us."

"I didn't exactly agree to a dinner party." I frown at Grinny. "And yeah, hold off on the Golden Girls."

I love her girlfriends, but they're a handful.

Grinny chuckles. "Okay, no Golden Girls. Just as long as you're there—we can't very well fully pass the baton without *you* there, angel." She smiles at me fondly.

"You said we'd already passed the baton," I hiss.

Grinny chuckles and taps her hand on Jamison's desk...*Granddad's* desk. "I'll see you Saturday at 5:30, if not sooner."

He nods and takes the hand she offers, patting it so sweetly, I just about die.

There's no way my heart can hate him as thoroughly when he's so kind.

CHAPTER EIGHT

NEW PLACES, NEW NAMES

JAMISON

The next morning I show up at Happy Cow an hour earlier than yesterday, wondering if I'll run into Scarlett.

But Lar and Mar are chatty today. They were yesterday too…until I told them I was there to get whatever a typical order for the lodge would be. When I'd picked up the keys from Albert the night before, he'd said the employees enjoyed things from this place occasionally, and I thought it'd be a nice gesture for the meeting. It wasn't until later that I heard Scarlett usually picks up pastries and coffee every day from Happy Cow and for whatever reason, hadn't yesterday.

"Landmark Mountain?" Lar had said.

And then their eyeballs practically waved visible red flags as they looked me over.

"You're the new owner, I take it?" Mar had sniffed, doing one more drag over my suit and from the look on her face, finding me lacking..

"I am." I'd reached out to shake her hand, glancing again at the name in red cursive on her apron and then his. "Hi, Mar, Lar. I'm Jamison."

Both waved their flour or powdered sugar-gloved hands at me like I should've known better than to shake a baker's hand, stupid businessman. And I mentally agreed with them in my head. It was stupid to try to shake a baker's hand. *Way to pass around the germs, dude. No one wants to go down eating a donut.*

"It's *Mare* and *Lare*," she corrects, scoffing. "Marrrr and Larrrr," she mocks, shaking her head. "*Mar* like Mary, *Lar* like Larry."

Just striking out right and left. I'd even consciously reined in my accent that first time and still got it wrong. "Mar and Lar, got it," I said, pronouncing it correctly this time.

"So Scarlett is gone, poof, just like that?" Mar's jaw clenched and I shook my head, raising a hand.

"Oh no, she's still working at the resort...as long as she wants to, as far as I'm concerned, but...it's ultimately up to her."

It was like the sun came out again and there had never

been a storm in this quaint bakery to begin with, the reception considerably warmer once I said that. Lar pounded me on the back—I guess that's okay germ-wise. Mar told me all the extra things she'd stuck in the bag for me to try out, on the house, and even waved when I backed out with my arms loaded down.

It was a little old lady with tight white curls who looked at me shrewdly and asked if I planned to walk out with the entire bakery on my back. I hadn't known what she meant or what she was doing when she patted around on my back until a cloud of white dust Lar had left on my back filled the air around us.

Today, Lar and Mar greet me like I'm their oldest friend.

"Jamison, how was your first day?" Lar booms.

"It was a great day," I say.

It was the most off my game I've been since—oh, middle school, but I keep that to myself.

"Glad to hear it," Lar says. His head tilts when the phone rings and he holds up his index finger before he turns to answer it.

"Did you and Scarlett get your wires crossed or are you picking up the order for her today?" Mar asks, grinning at me like I'm in on a joke.

"Uh, I don't—"

The door swings open, bell jangling loud enough to wake the dead, and I turn around to see Scarlett glaring at me.

Great.

It looks like she didn't have time to warm up to the idea of me taking over her family legacy overnight.

I brace myself and smile, taking her in. I could barely

look away from her yesterday. Today, it will be best if I only look away. The thoughts that run through my mind are X-rated.

She's in a short pencil skirt similar to the one she was wearing the night we met, only in fire-engine red. Another pretty floral blouse tucked in, the neckline of this one dipping down just enough to drive me mad all day long. I wonder if she's wearing one of those lacy one-piece things again and what color this one would be.

"Is there nothing left of mine that you *aren't* taking over?" she asks, coming to stand in front of me, her red heels toe-to-toe with my Oxfords.

I don't know why my lips curve up, but they do. "If I hadn't seen what a kitten you can be, I'd think you were all roar."

Her eyelashes flutter as she glances down at my mouth, her own parting slightly. She shakes her head, her eyes closing for a second, and when she opens them again, her hand goes to her hip.

"You don't want to see my claws come out, Wingtip," she hisses.

I snort, and I swear, sparks of fire sizzle off of her. "Wingtip?"

"You walk on ice in those things?" She bops her head up once before glancing down at my shoes.

"Ahh," I say, laughing. "I'd say they stand a better chance than those heels you're wearing."

"Oh, you *think*?" she asks, nodding briskly, her big brown eyes and full lips defying me.

I want to kiss the pout right off of her mouth.

I take a step closer to her and she gasps. "Yeah, I do."

She's breathing so hard, her chest brushes against mine as she inhales, drops as she exhales. I live for the inhale.

"I could run the lodge on an *iceberg* in *heels* all day long, Jamison Ledger."

"I have no doubt you could," I say. Then I lean into her ear and whisper, "And that's Orgasm Whisperer to you, beautiful."

She freezes and when I stand upright again, her eyes are wide, her teeth scraping over that plump bottom lip.

I smile and turn to see Lar and Mar's eyes bugged out, possibly struck speechless given the fact that they don't say anything for what feels like a solid minute. Scarlett seems to be under the same affliction, so I clear my throat right as the phone rings again. Lar looks disappointed when he has to answer it.

"I'd like a large cup of whatever coffee you have with the most caffeine," I say.

I feel Scarlett's shoulders slump next to me, her head bowed when I turn to her.

"Can I buy you a cup of coffee?" I ask.

She shifts her lips to one side, embarrassed or apologetic, I can't be sure. "No, thank you. I-I usually place an order for the lodge and thought you were—"

"I might've if you hadn't gotten here when you did." I opt for honesty instead of getting an apology I don't deserve.

Mar clears her throat. "So, the one cup of coffee? And I've got your order ready to go, Scarlett. Seems to me Mr. Wingtip can go ahead and foot the bill," she says, her eyes darting to the cash register. Her lips twitch with her effort to not smile. "Unless you're taking this one, Kitten."

When Mar looks up again, there's a staredown between

the three of us, Mar's tongue in her cheek as Scarlett and I face her incredulously.

"I suppose we asked for that," I say, placing my credit card on the counter.

"Welcome to Landmark," Scarlett says.

Mar picks up my credit card with a smirk.

Lar hangs up the phone and turns toward us. "What'd I miss?"

"Gotta pay attention the first time, Lar. Drama like this doesn't come free," Scarlett says lightly.

Lar chuckles, and I grin down at the receipt as I sign it.

Sparring before sunrise, I had no idea what a rush that could be.

CHAPTER NINE

OFF THE RAILS

SCARLETT

- *Don't look at him.*

It's bad when I only have one thing I'd put on my list and not a scrap of paper besides the napkins in these pastry boxes in sight to write it on.

Jamison helps me carry everything to the car, and as I open the door to get in myself, still all aquiver from his

Orgasm Whisperer comment and the way he says he has *no doubt* when he's about to say something that sends me sideways, he stretches his hand to the roof of my car.

Lord, have mercy. What am I going to do?

Everything about the way he moves and breathes and speaks reminds me of that night.

"Hey, I noticed you put someone else in the slot I'd set aside for our meeting on both yesterday and today's schedules," he says.

Since Danny and Regg both work at the ski resort and their common terms are *the powder's fresh, dude*, or *shit, it's a blue bird kind of day out there*, I never realized how sexy schedule speak could be.

"Can we sit down when we get back and go over a few things?" he continues.

Yes, I have some things he could go over. Some slots he could fill. I list all the cuss words I can think of in alphabetical order to bring my mind out of the gutter.

Ass, bitch, c-u-nex-t week, damn, and get stuck on the f-word, thinking about the way he said *fuck* so reverently as he slid his long, thick…shit, how could I have forgotten *dick* and *cock*? Or are those even cuss words? I think not. Except…the way he used his, I can see either argument.

I fan myself with my hand despite it being thirty degrees out.

"We have a lot to cover," he says.

We sure do. First up, I'll be needing to *get a grip*.

I try very hard not to look at him as I hold on to my car door for strength. "I've left detailed lists of every single employee, as well as instructions about the various vendors that will be calling this week."

I don't mention the extensive file I've created about

our regular guests, partly because I'd never want anyone to see the things I sometimes write…things like…

The Fergusons' suite always needs an extra cleaning due to all the lube. Besides the normal power clean, wash the ceiling fans and the walls, and while they're guests, wash the sheets in this order: once with bleach, twice with detergent, once with softener, and once more with bleach. Upon checkout, dispose of the sheets.

Housekeeping knows this nugget, so the secret won't be leaving when I go, but there are some things Jamison can learn the old-fashioned way.

"That's very helpful, thank you," he's saying when I pull myself out of my thoughts. "I'd still like to sit down with you and discuss—"

"We better go while the coffee's still hot," I say, moving to my seat. He frowns down at me when I reach to shut my door. I give him a little salute and start the ignition. He steps back and I make my escape.

When I pull into the parking lot, Bill happens to see me and comes to help me carry everything in. I grab my coffee and chocolate croissant and hurry to my office to avoid any more awkward chats with Jamison.

I manage to avoid him all day, instead resorting to email to pass along any information he needs to be aware of. But mostly, I take care of business like I would if he wasn't here. I walk through the lodge, greeting guests and going through the various checkpoints I typically oversee on any given day. I know I'll have to let these things go, even before my three months are over, in order to ensure the lodge has the best chance for success, but I'm not ready for that *today*.

I'm on the wing closest to the ski resort when Holly walks in, her cheeks pink from the cold.

"Hi. How did you know I needed to see you?" I sound kind of pitiful, but I'm just really glad to see her.

She looks like a dreamy ski bunny, tall, blonde, and beautiful, but the girl can out-ski everyone on this mountain. She slides her hands together to warm them up and then stretches them out as she walks toward me.

"I'm sorry I haven't been here sooner." She hugs me hard and leans back, looking me over. "The gift shop's been insane the past few days, so I only have a few minutes—Olivia's leaving soon. You haven't been calling me back or coming over to visit. How are you holding up?"

"It's been...something," I say, looking over my shoulder to make sure no one is close enough to hear me. "I almost told you and April in our group text but..." I feel my face heating and I try to fan it away.

She makes a face, her eyes widening as she leans in. "What is it?"

"It's too far-fetched to believe, but that's how life is, right?"

Holly waves her hand, trying to speed me along. "Spit it out. Olivia's going to kill me if I don't get back to cover the shop for her in three minutes."

"One-night stand guy is here."

Her head tilts as she stares at me, her mouth dropping open. She quickly lights up and grabs my hand. "He came to see you? No wonder you've been so quiet, you little freaky-deak."

"No, he's *here*." I point to the ground. She looks down

and then back up, confused. "*He's* the new owner of the lodge."

Her eyes get even bigger. "*Jamison Ledger* is your guy?" she hisses. "Holy hell. I had to miss the staff meeting, but I made it to my one-on-one with him, and he is fuh-reaking *stunning*. I'm going to need more details about that night now that I have a visual." She laughs and shakes my hand when I don't laugh with her. "What? This is incredible. It's a *sign*!"

I made a face. "A sign that I'm going to be punished for my night of"—I whisper my next words—"*incredible sex*? Put me out of my misery now." I moan and Holly puts her arm around my shoulder, walking me toward the door.

"Walk me back," she says. "Walk and talk. I can't believe you have been withholding this information."

I turn back to make sure everything seems okay and check that the volume on my phone is up before I walk out with Holly, the burst of cold air on my face feeling better than usual. The gift shop is between the lodge and the ski resort with an outside entrance, so you don't have to be staying at the resort to stop by and shop.

"Since you're not talking nearly as fast as I wish you would, I'll just throw in here that your hair looks amazing, I love this outfit on you, and I'd like you to take this as an opportunity. You can finish out your three months here with a bang, *literally*." She laughs at herself and this time, I join in but shake my head.

"It's not like that. I'm so mad at him. He claims he had no idea it was me the night we—"

"And why would it matter if he did?" she asks.

I frown. "Well, that would be weird and why would he lie about something like that?"

"Exactly, why would he lie about it? You said yourself, sometimes life is more far-fetched than movies. Or was that your point? I was trying to follow, but you were all over the place. Ow!" she says when I smack her arm.

We walk down the snowy path toward the gift shop. "The window display looks incredible."

"Thanks, I just finished it before I came to see you. And you're not changing the subject on me that fast, no matter how nice the compliment."

"We only had a few minutes anyway," I grumble.

"Drinks at The Dancing Emu around 8:30? Or should we venture over to The Gnarly Vine tonight?" she asks.

"I don't know, I have some work I need to—"

She shoots me a look and I nod sheepishly.

"Okay, yes. Let's do the Emu. Save the Vine for some-time next week."

"Look at you, attempting to not be a workaholic. I'll drop it in the group thread. No talking yourself out of it," she adds.

"Scarlett, hey!"

I turn and see Danny walking toward us. I grin and wave, and his smile grows. I'm glad he's stayed my friend. When he reaches up, he hugs me and then Holly.

"How've you been? I've tried calling and texting…you okay with all this?" he asks, when we're facing each other again.

"Oh, you know. I don't love any of it, but I'll be okay."

He nods and clears his throat. "Well, let me know how I can help. I've wanted to be there for you since Grand-dad…and know you're not big on sharing feelings," he laughs awkwardly, "but I miss him too and…well, I'm here."

"Thanks, Danny. I know you are. That means a lot. And I know you miss him too. He loved you so much."

His phone buzzes and he lifts it. "Better run, I'm on the clock. But call me." He points at me and hugs me again before hurrying off.

"He has got it so bad for you," Holly says.

"No, he doesn't. He knows we're just friends."

She rolls her eyes at me and I shake my head.

"He does," I insist.

We pause in front of the door of the shop and she opens it for the cute couple I helped check in last night. They smile when they recognize me.

"We went to The Pink Ski like you suggested," the girl says. "And stuck with the pizza." She laughs. "It was so good. Maybe we'll go back and get more daring with the bison or Rocky Mountain oysters…"

Her husband makes a face and shakes his head. "Or maybe just have the pizza again."

"It's your vacation—you shouldn't eat anything you don't want." I nod at Holly as she squeezes my shoulder and heads inside the shop. "I don't think I told you about The Gnarly Vine. If you enjoy fine wine and the most amazing charcuterie board selections, you'll love it."

"That sounds great. We'll give it a try. Thanks, Scarlett."

"No problem." I smile at them and walk back to the lodge, wondering for the millionth time what I'll do when I don't have this.

CHAPTER TEN

PROPOSITION

JAMISON

Scarlett pauses when she sees me standing outside her office and then reluctantly walks toward me.

"What's up?" she asks.

"Do you have time now to talk?"

Her eyes skirt past my shoulder, looking at everything but me. "I—" Her shoulders drop slightly and she motions toward her door. "Sure, why not."

I grin, nervous energy coursing through my body the way it does every time she's close.

"Great," I chirp and inwardly groan. I was going for nonchalant but still sounded way too excited.

I'm not gonna lie, it's got me shaken up. These nerves, the excitement I get when I see her, when I just *think* about her…it's confusing as hell.

And what's even more confusing is that she's not softening. She's not flirting back or smiling longingly…*she's barely looking at me.*

Not to be the world's biggest asshole, but I don't struggle with women.

I keep things fun and light, and always, *always* leave them wanting more. I make it clear that I'm not looking for anything serious, and sure, that's caused some tension when a woman thinks she'll change my mind and that I don't really mean it about her, but…I've never even considered changing my mind.

I didn't make up how good that night was. I didn't. She told me over and over how it was the best anyone had ever made her feel, and maybe that's just what she says in the heat of the moment, but I felt her pleasure firsthand on my fingers and my dick, watched her lose herself as she cried out my name over and over.

I adjust myself when she walks past me to sit behind her desk and sit down across from her, trying to school my thoughts. But fuck me, she's just so fucking beautiful.

She folds her hands in front of her and fixes her gaze somewhere around my chin. I clear my throat and lean in, my forearms on her desk. She swallows hard and her fingers twist together.

"Why didn't you take the lodge?" I blurt out.

Her brown eyes fly to mine, caught too off guard to hide her surprise. A tiny frown gradually deepens between her eyebrows.

"I wasn't given a choice. My grandfather's will was an old one and the option was it either went to my brothers or they sold it. All of them are doing well for themselves, but they didn't have the capital or the passion a project of this magnitude needs…" She shrugs. "And I've worked here for practically nothing for most of my life." She lifts her finger. "Not nothing. My grandparents covered my schooling and I stay in condo seventeen for free. As you've probably seen, I make close to what Albert makes, which was high praise in Granddad's eyes…"

"But he doesn't do even close to what you do around here from what I can tell," I jump in.

She shrugs. "It hasn't been about the money for me, ever. I love this place, it's something that belongs —*belonged*—to my family and therefore, it's been important to me." Her voice drifts off. "And now, it's yours."

"So why are you leaving in three months and where are you going?" I can't explain the rising anger I feel on her behalf or why her sudden monotone voice and shrugs set me off even more.

From what I've seen, everything about her screams that she cares, from her animated voice and expressions… when she's pissed at me or when she excitedly greets guests, so this blank, hollow expression she's wearing now is all wrong.

"Why would I stay?" she asks.

"Do you really believe Albert can do the job you do around here?"

A laugh sputters out of her and dies as she studies me closer, her brows once again creasing in a scowl at me.

I miss it when she handed out her smiles to me like free candy. I didn't realize what a gift that was.

"I love Albert and he does an amazing job, but he'll never be able to do what I've done around here, no." She shakes her head and leans back in her chair, folding her arms across her chest.

It's a struggle to focus on her eyes, but I don't dare let myself check her out now.

"Why would you ask that? It won't be Albert taking my place running the lodge...it'll be *you*."

"Well, yes, ultimately, I will be calling the shots, but..." I pause, wondering if it's possible that she doesn't know. "You do know I'm only in-house for six months and then I'll be going back to Boston and staying on top of things from there...right? That was the agreement."

Her face goes through a transformation, shifting from placid to stormy in a matter of seconds. I just thought I'd seen her angry before...that was nothing. She lifts her hand to push her hair out of her eyes and it's shaking.

When she finally speaks, her voice is deadly calm. "Please leave."

"Excuse me?"

She stands up and points to the door. And then she leans over, one hand on the desk and the other on her chest.

I stand up and nearly put my hand on her shoulder but leave it hovering. "Scarlett, what's going on—are you okay?"

"My heart is racing," she whispers.

I don't hesitate. I rush around the side of the desk and

help her back into the chair. I open the window behind her and cool air wafts in.

"Breathe," I tell her, crouching in front of her chair.

She takes a deep breath and then another. Her head falls back on the chair and she stares straight ahead, taking one more deep breath.

"*Pftt.*" She snorts. *"In-house."*

Another dismissive sound. *"O*kay, Wingtip."

She shakes her head, still not looking at me.

Another huge breath.

"I can't even believe this. So…you're telling me you've come in here acting like you *care about this place* and that it *really means so much* to you…" She goes into what I guess is supposed to sound like my voice, only much whinier and with a weird accent when she says phrases I said at the staff meeting.

"And you're not even sticking around?" She laughs, but it sounds like she's closer to crying. "I can't even begin to list all the—" Her voice fades and she shakes her head again.

She's quiet, staring into space and then shivering slightly. I stand up and close the window and then see if she has anything else to say. When she doesn't, I take a deep breath myself.

"One of the reasons I've insisted on meeting everyone and not just for general introductions, but to keep ongoing check-ins, is because I want to personally get to know every employee so well while I'm here that when I have to be remote and should problems arise, I'll know who I'm dealing with and how we can best handle the situation."

Still nothing from her.

"I realize it may not be ideal, but many resort owners,

in fact, I'd say *most*, have a manager who essentially runs the place while the owner comes in and out. I assure you, I'll still be very hands-on when I'm not here."

I take a ragged breath like I'm the one who was just struggling for air.

"I'm a financial advisor and I'm able to be here right now because I've established relationships with my clients and they trust me whether I'm sitting in front of them or not. That's what I intend to do here in the next six months, and I was under the understanding—an assumption that I should not have made based on his pay and title—that Albert would be that man. I haven't even been here a week and I know that's not the case. It should be you, Scarlett."

I pause, waiting for an indication that she's listening. She's staring into space and her chest is still rising and falling in a distracting and compelling way. Torture.

I clear my throat. "I've been going over the files, seeing how many changes you've implemented over the years, heard the respect the employees have for you...and I'd like to put together a compensation package that shows how valuable you are around here...or at least a good start on that...and for you to consider staying on as general manager for good."

Someone yells outside, but otherwise, it's utter silence in here besides the ticking from the small crystal clock that sits on her desk.

"No," she says softly.

"No?" I echo, clearly not understanding what's going on here because when she finally looks up at me, her eyes are unbearably sad.

Almost lost.

"But...you love it here. You never wanted to leave, and

you don't have to. I already have a plan for bringing in more revenue that will more than cover your compensation if that's what you're worried about. I can show you what I've already started drawing up."

"No, thank you," she says, her voice tired. She glances at the clock and leans up. "I have to go."

She stands and grabs her coat and purse from the hook near the door, and she walks out, leaving me wondering where the hell I went wrong.

CHAPTER ELEVEN

PERSPECTIVE

SCARLETT

I'm about to leave to meet Holly and April when I'm ambushed by my brothers.

Callum pokes his head in my office first, which is enough to make me race toward him, asking him what's wrong. It's rare that he leaves the ranch.

"Nothin', just figured you couldn't avoid us here." He

puts his arm around my shoulder and his cheeks lift with his smile.

I tuck into his soft flannel shirt, wrapping my arm around his waist to squeeze him.

"Us?" I ask.

My brothers tease Callum for never smiling, but he smiles at me all the time, and I always melt. My gruff brother is a softie underneath the growl, but I think Grinny and I are the only ones he lets it show. And Owen, our nephew.

Wyatt and Theo walk in next, and just like that, my office is loud. I hug Wyatt and then go for Theo but take a step back when I get closer, wrinkling up my nose. He's still in his long-sleeve coveralls from work.

"We should probably skip the hug. Sorry, it's been a day. You don't want to know," he says, making a face.

"It's probably too late since I've already inhaled your stank, but stay over there." Wyatt points at the space across from him. "I don't know if I'll have time to change before my shift."

Theo pretends to be offended while going to the farthest corner of the room. "How's that, little precious."

Wyatt's nose twitches. "I can still smell you, ya filthy bastard."

I hurriedly shut my door. It's not like they're a rowdy bunch…in public, they're more on the mellow, aloof side —or as April calls them, the sexiest enigmas of Landmark, ew—but when we're together, they're as goofy as anyone else. And wouldn't know the meaning of a whisper or using inside voices. They're the worst to watch movies with, especially Sutton and the way he dissects *everything*.

He's the last one to walk in, opening my door wide and holding his hands in the air like he's hot snot.

"Okay, the judge has arrived. We can call this meeting to order," Wyatt says dryly.

Wyatt takes his coat off and is in the mossy green scrubs that match his eyes. When I first saw him in them, I accused him of becoming a doctor at Pine Community just so he could wear those scrubs.

If there were degrees on a facial hair and apparel spectrum, Callum would be on the far left with his beard and all things comfortable, and Sutton would be on the far right side of fancy with his three-piece cashmere and wool suit and cleanly shaven face…with Theo and Wyatt somewhere between the two.

"What's up?" I ask, hugging Sutton and dropping back down on my heels to grin at my brothers.

I've been crazy about them my whole life and still get a rush of dopamine when we're all together.

"We wanted to give this to you sooner, but it didn't work out at The Pink Ski…and everyone had to rush off after the staff meeting," Wyatt says.

Everyone looks at Sutton and so I do too, and he pulls a long envelope from the inside pocket of his suit jacket. He hands it to me.

"It's only fitting that you have this," Sutton says. "We all feel terrible about you not being included in the will and we want you to have the freedom to do whatever *you* want to do next."

I smile even though I could easily cry just from looking at their solemn faces.

Callum lifts his chin toward me and the envelope. "Open that up and see if it helps at all."

I rip it open and pull out a check, gasping when I see the amount with all the zeroes. "What? *What?*"

"After we paid the ridiculous fees at Dunleavy & Smithson and we paid for the—well, it was actually a very reasonable list of repairs from the Ledgers compared to what it could have been, but it still took out a chunk—we divided what was left five ways and then each added more to yours since you're the one who's given your life to this place," Sutton says.

My eyes are wide and stinging with tears, and as hard as I try, I can't keep them in. They each look at me in horror and start talking at once.

"Aw, please, Scarlett, please don't cry."

"You deserve it."

"We still took some, don't think we weren't selfish too."

"Where are the tissues? She's leaking."

"We love you and hope this helps you do something you love…your own thing…"

"What did the goat say to the hound?"

I put my head in my hands and bawl and their buzz just intensifies, but they circle around me and envelop me in a group bear hug, Theo getting tossed out from Wyatt early on, and all the panic and uncertainty that's been pressing in on me from every side just alleviates.

I take a deep, shaky breath and wipe my face with the tissue they hand me, blowing my nose next.

When I look up, they're all staring at me like they're afraid to move.

"So what did the goat say to the hound?" My voice is all trembly, but I manage to get it out. I look around them and to Theo, who's standing by the window. I think he's the one who said that.

"Uh…I have no idea," he says. "Hold on..." He lifts his finger and grins. "He said, 'Leaf me alone. I've goat to go.'" He lifts his eyebrows. "Eh? That was pretty good, right?"

I laugh, but everyone else groans.

"I love you guys." I wave my hands in front of my face and they freeze again. "Oh, relax, a woman's tears won't kill you."

"You're not a woman, you're our little sister," Theo grumbles.

"Exactly," Wyatt adds. "Wait. Sorry. No. Not exactly…"

"Our hearts just can't take seeing you sad," Callum says quietly.

See? Melt.

Theo and Wyatt chime in like that's exactly what they meant.

"We love you too," Sutton says. "And we can't wait to see what you decide to do next."

* * *

The Dancing Emu is hopping when I arrive a few minutes late.

Mostly a bar but with a few delicious food options now that Pierre has taken over from his dad, it's one of my favorite places in Landmark. It looks like hobbits and fairies could coexist inside, the rounded arches and coved ceilings lit with twinkling lights. The plus or downside, depending on who's up and what a person's ears can handle, is that there are half-hour karaoke sets throughout the night.

There's a nice crowd, and I don't see the girls until April's in front of me.

"You better be so glad you didn't bail," she says, her smile and bear hug softening her words. "Holls and I were about to come drag you out of your office. Come on, we lucked out." She grabs my hand and leads me to our favorite table. "Can you believe no one beat us to it—it's been months!"

"Meant to be," Holly says, holding her arms out toward me.

"Sorry I'm late," I say as I'm hugging her. "I was in a meeting."

"With Loverboy?" she asks, her eyes all lit up as she does a little dance on her stool. She lifts her thumb toward April and they both speak at the same time:

"I haven't told her a thing yet, so get after it."

"Loverboy? Oh my God, you better spill."

"I've been dying to tell you," Holly says to April. "Dying. And you're going to die that she hasn't told us this before today."

April's doe eyes turn to me and I've never been able to resist her. The words are out in a rush.

"He's not Loverboy now." I hold my hands up. "Don't get your hopes up. The guy I slept with in Boulder is Jamison Ledger, AKA, the new owner of the resort, AKA, the new boss who is ruining my life."

April's too stunned to speak for a moment until Holly nudges her.

"Right?" Holly says.

April blinks and frowns. "How did this happen? And

what do you mean he's ruining your life? Is he being rude?"

I think of how he helped me calm down earlier, the way he hustled around my desk and managed to get me breathing steadily again. Even though he was the one who got me in that state to begin with.

"He's not rude, no. He's annoyingly nice while systematically dismantling everything I've built...Granddad built," I correct myself. "He plans to operate the place from across the country. He's not even staying in Landmark." My voice rises and I try to rein it back in. "It's *Landmark Mountain Lodge & Ski Resort*, where the foundation is family and community, not some amusement park in Orlando that he can make all nice and shiny and expect it to last. They tear down and rebuild something completely different every few months in those places. When he's done with Landmark Mountain, we won't even recognize it...I give it two years max."

April grabs my hand and squeezes it, and the joy looks punched out of Holly's face.

"I'm sorry. I'm a real ball of delight these days."

"You don't need to be sorry. This is a big deal. We need to get a drink in you..." April waves at Pierre and lifts up three fingers and he nods.

"So, what was this meeting about? He's really tearing the place down and rebuilding it?" Holly asks.

"No, I was saying..." I put my head in my hands. "I'm all over the place."

I take a deep breath and look up to see a lemon drop sliding in front of me. It's been our drink at The Dancing Emu since we could drink, but of course, my mind goes back to where it seems to be on default.

That night. That fucking night.

Literally.

"For my favorite girls," Pierre says. "Should I bring the artichoke dip out? Maybe the deconstructed steak tartare?"

"Yes," we all chime in.

Pierre bends his tall, lanky body into as much of a bow as he can in the crowded space and then hurries off.

"So back up," Holly says. "What is Jamison trying to do to the lodge?"

"He does plan to renovate, and he wants to show me a few ideas...he actually asked me to stay on as general manager and I said no."

They both gasp.

"Why?" April asks.

"I can't stay on and watch him destroy everything!"

"What if he...makes it better?" Holly says. "If he's willing to show you a few ideas, it sounds like he's open to your feedback. And general manager! That would be just as good as owning it, right?"

"No, general manager is doing all the work and *not* owning it, which is what I've already spent my whole life doing."

"That's fair. But is it also fair to say that if you did own it, you'd still be doing all the work anyway?" Holly says, lifting her eyebrows. "Like you said, Landmark Mountain Lodge is about family and community...and that hasn't changed, no matter who the owner is."

I don't say anything, choosing instead to take a long sip of my drink. I close my eyes and savor the flavors. Pierre's is the best. Finally, "I hate it when you make sense."

She laughs. "You hate it when I'm *right*. Give him a chance, Scarlett. Maybe he'll surprise you."

"I'm tired of being disappointed, you know?" I sniff, trying to ignore the tears trying to gather. "And I'm not used to being all over the map. You guys know me, I'm not so…" I lift my hand and wave it up and down in front of my face.

"You need a vacation. You're the most levelheaded person I know," April says.

I blink quickly and clink my glass to theirs. "Enough about me, what's going on with you?"

"We don't have to be done with this topic. You never let us dwell on you. I kinda like not being the one with the most drama," April says.

I laugh. "Well, it's making me itchy."

"Okay, well…there's this guy that's making it almost *impossible* for me to not break my tourist fast," April says. "He walked by a few days ago when I was shoveling the walkway in front of Toyland and ended up taking the shovel and finishing it for me. He's come in the shop every day and before he leaves, he asks me out to dinner."

"He sounds worth breaking your fast for," Holly says.

"I don't know. I thought that about all the others and look how they turned out," she says. "He's so hot too, you'd be proud of how I've kept it locked." She shakes her head. "But I'm so close to caving."

"What's his name and how long is he staying?" I ask.

"Well, that's the other thing." She makes a face. "His name is…" She glances around like she's afraid he'll pop out of the woodwork. "Barney." She winces again. "I'd almost go by Barn if I were him instead of invoking that purple monstrosity every time I said my name…"

We all laugh and the appetizers are set in front of us.

"Anyone ready for another drink?" Pierre asks.

"Yes," Holly announces for all of us, holding up three fingers again. "What? We all walked…you did walk too, didn't you?" she asks me.

"Yes. But only one more," I say. "I can't stay too late and it's cold out there tonight."

"If you decide to become general manager, can we go to Bali to celebrate?" April asks.

"I'm not sure I'd have the time if I became general manager…see? Another good reason why I shouldn't do it. What's got you thinking Bali?"

"Barney went to Bali last year and said it was amazing," she gushes.

This makes Holly and I lose it and when our second round of lemon drops come by, we're a lot lighter than when we started.

CHAPTER TWELVE

FOUR-LEGGED SURPRISES

JAMISON

After being inside most of the day and still feeling keyed up after that conversation with Scarlett, I decide to take a walk before calling it a night.

I'm still putting on my coat when I step outside and then I blow air in my hands to warm them up and head toward the twinkle lights. Every colorful shop and restaurant is covered with white lights, making it the quaintest, most charming little town I've ever seen.

I'm not sure how late everything stays open around here, but it seems at least during this time of year, the restaurants and bars are still going strong. I'm tempted to get a beer somewhere, but it feels too good to walk, so I wind through the streets, enjoying the crunch of snow beneath my feet and the sounds of people laughing and enjoying themselves.

I wonder what it's like to live here year-round, when for the majority of the residents, at least nine months of the year are spent serving someone else's vacation. Scarlett's exhausted face and the way she had what seemed to be a panic attack loop in my head. When's the last time she had a break?

A low growl catches my attention and I turn, trying to find where it's coming from. I've wandered behind a row of businesses where the garbage is kept. A raccoon lowers to all four legs from the garbage can he was raiding and a massive dog that could pass for a wolf—holy shit, *is* that a wolf?—bares his teeth. The raccoon turns and runs the other way, and the dog stands guard until he's out of sight.

It's then that I realize I should probably do the same in case it *is* a wolf, and I turn around to go back toward Heritage Lane, the main street. I've reached the front of the building on the corner when I look back and rub my eyes, certain now that I'm seeing things. The wolf/dog is leaning forward on his front haunches and it looks like a large rat/dog climbs up on his back.

That can't be right.

Familiar laughter rings out, snagging my attention because I'd recognize Scarlett's laugh anywhere. Circa two weeks ago, that laugh became the magnetic field to my dick, making it zing to attention in an attempt to get to her. She files out of the door with two other girls, one who works at the resort, arms flailing as she gets her coat on and tries to hug them at the same time.

I keep moving toward them and when I'm close enough that one of them notices me, I nod. "Evening, ladies."

Scarlett's head whips around so hard she nearly slips on the snow. I reach out and steady her, my hands on her waist.

"I've got you," I say.

She shivers and levels me with a look that's not as frigid as it was earlier, but it's still not warm fuzzies. My hands drop off of her.

"Figures you'd show up here too." She sighs. Her arm flings out and I smell sugar and lemons. "May as well get the introductions over with since he'll be trying to take over the town next. April, this is Jamison."

The petite girl standing next to…Holly, I believe her name is…gasps and then tries to quickly recover by holding her hand out. "Uh, h-hello. I…welcome to Landmark." Her eyes dart to Scarlett and she drops my hand quickly.

"Thank you. It's nice to meet you."

"We'll just get going," Holly says, staring at me. Definitely not as friendly as during our meeting, but not like she wants to run me over like the woman I can't seem to avoid. "Scarlett, you okay getting back?"

"Yeah, I'll be fine. It was fun. Thanks for forcing me to go out." She gives me one last lingering look before walking past me.

Holly tilts her head toward Scarlett and stares point-edly at me like *go on, what are you waiting for*…the last thing I expected. When I smile in thanks, she almost smiles back.

I turn and start the walk back to the lodge, the pretty girl with the long brown hair and the seductive sway a few feet in front of me.

I can tell by her exaggerated sigh that she knows I'm following and I don't know why it makes me want to laugh. I hate that my presence annoys her so much, but shit, she's funny and sexy and beautiful.

Just then, something runs past us and I nearly bump into her when she stops.

"You saw that too?" I ask.

"Yes," she breathes out. "That was the cutest thing I've ever seen." She starts walking faster and I keep up, both of us scanning the street to see where they went. "Where did they go? That little one shouldn't be out in this cold."

"Was that a wolf?"

She chuckles and I'm so happy to hear her laughing with me, I almost forget what we're looking for and just stare at her.

"Pretty sure that was a husky…and maybe a chihuahua? I didn't get a good look at the little one. We don't have many wolves around here, but they *are* plan-ning to reintroduce wolves to Colorado over the next few years."

"Really? I didn't know that. Right before I ran into you and your friends, I saw the little guy hop on the husky's back and thought I was seeing things."

She laughs again and I think I'll walk with her all night.

"How did they disappear?" she asks, turning to face where we just came from and then back around.

"They seemed healthy. Maybe their owner lives around here."

"I don't know anyone with those dogs…unless someone just got them. I haven't heard anything about that yet though."

"I forget you pretty much know everyone who lives here and…all that goes on around here too, it sounds like."

"Oh yeah, hang out at the front desk, especially when it's Doug's shift, or at Lar and Mar's for long, and you'll get filled in on plenty you don't *want* to know." She stops when we reach the end of the shops and her shoulders droop. "Maybe a tourist brought them and they're lost…"

I can tell she's not going to rest until we find them and I'd like to make sure they're okay too. It's also the least hostile she's been toward me in days, so I want to stretch it out for as long as possible.

"How about I circle around the back of the shops? Maybe they're where I saw them the first time. You could either come with me or stay right here in case they come back this way."

She runs her hand over her arms. "I think I need to move. I'll come with you."

We take a left at the corner and another left when we reach the restaurant patios and backs of shops, heading down the opposite end from where I saw them the first time. I point ahead.

"See that blue light by the dumpster? The husky and a raccoon were having a standoff."

"It sounds like the beginning of a joke, but I believe you. Never a dull moment around here, I swear," she says.

There's no sight of the two and we're almost at the end when I see them run from the dumpster and toward an old caboose on the next street over. I remember the caboose being here when I was a kid. I tried to peek in the windows and was disappointed that we couldn't go inside.

The husky leaps onto the back ledge and the chihuahua takes one step at a time, and once they're both up, the husky nudges the door with his nose and they run inside. The door closes behind them and Scarlett and I turn and stare at each other.

"Unbelievable," Scarlett whispers. And then, "I'm going in."

"Are you sure that's a good idea? The husky has a mean growl."

"You're scared of dogs?"

"No, but…I'm cautious. Are you wanting to keep them?"

"Well, we can't just leave them out in the cold."

"I think they've been doing this little routine for a while. They perform better than any dogs I've ever had." I haven't had many, but still.

"Same," she says. "I think we should see if they'll follow us back and we can look them over, make sure they're fed, take pictures to post in case someone's looking for them…"

"You're always five steps ahead, aren't you?" I tease, but it's the truth.

"You better believe it," she says, smirking, and then she bites her lip and looks away quickly.

When she said that to me the night we met, she rocked my world and then some.

"I haven't been disappointed yet when you've said those words."

She gets her bearings quickly, rolling her eyes. "Don't get your hopes up, Wingtip." She gets up on the back ledge of the caboose. "You coming with me or what?"

"That *is* my favorite way," I tell her, loving the way her eyes flare wider. I'm on the back ledge in the next second and she leans back into me for a beat before nudging the door open slowly.

"Hello," she says in a sweet, soft tone.

I turn on the flashlight from my phone and cast it through the space. There's a small hallway and then it opens up into a bigger area with a built-in couch on one side and a wooden bench on the other. The dogs aren't on either side and the only thing left is a small built-in desk and a bathroom. I turn to look at the desk and tucked in the space underneath, the husky is curled up and staring at us, and the chihuahua is between his chest and huge paw, sound asleep.

"Hi, big guy," I say in the same singsong way Scarlett did before. It seemed to work for her, and so far, so good.

"Oh my goodness. You guys are so cute," Scarlett coos. "What are they doing here?" she asks me, but doesn't wait for an answer. "Hold on, I think I've got something you'll love."

She reaches into her purse and pulls out something that makes the husky's nose start twitching. As soon as Scarlett starts unwrapping the package, the tiny one's eyes open and it sits up and hops over the husky's paw and straight to Scarlett.

"What kind of magic are you holding?" I ask her.

"A beef stick," she says, giggling.

That magnetic field is going to be a real problem for me.

She breaks off two small pieces and gives the smallest one to the chihuahua. That gets the husky's attention and he stands up and walks over, sitting down in front of her. She gives him a treat and then the two dogs look at her expectantly.

She holds a hand out without a treat and lets the husky sniff her, and I hold mine out next.

"You think they'll follow us out of here?" she says quietly.

"I couldn't begin to guess, but I'd say we stand a good chance if you have plenty of that beef stick."

"I have another one in my purse."

"Of course you do."

"Hey, they come in handy when I forget to eat," she says.

"It's brilliant. I want a purse just so I can carry beef sticks."

She laughs and it just doesn't get old.

"Okay, guys," she says. "We're gonna go someplace not too far and much warmer. Are you ready?"

"Yes," I say in a high voice.

She rolls her eyes at me, but she's grinning. "Why don't you go ahead and open the door, and hopefully they'll follow this." She holds up the beef stick.

I slowly move to the door, careful to not be too loud. When the door is open, Scarlett leads the dogs out and once we're on the street, they keep following her. Before we reach the busier street, she gives each of them a little bit, and then we keep going...all the way to the lodge.

"Oh…" She stops when we reach the back of the lodge and are near the condos.

"Are you okay?"

"Would it be okay if we take them to your condo, just for tonight? You're in ten, right?"

"Uh, sure…yeah."

"It's just…you're in one of our pet-friendly condos and I'm not. I don't have the little fenced-in area and…there should be a dog bed in one of your closets actually."

"I…haven't unpacked yet, so there very well could be."

She smirks and we head toward my condo. Once we're inside, she gives the dogs the rest of the beef stick and grabs two bowls from the kitchen, filling them with water.

The dogs lap up the water like they haven't had a drink in ages.

"Oh…look at that. Little guy is a boy," she says. She leans down to check out the husky and comes back up smiling wide. "And the big guy is a girl." Her head falls back and she cracks up, and the dogs stop and turn to look at her and then slowly crowd around her. Even the animals can't help but bask in her glow.

She sits on the floor and pets them and I join her down there, laughing when the little one's back side leans into my hand on whatever side I scratch.

"Well, you are full of surprises, Jamison Ledger," she says.

"So are you, Scarlett Landmark. So are you."

CHAPTER THIRTEEN

FOR THE RECORD

SCARLETT

I wake up to a tiny pink tongue licking my hand and then my arm.

I crack open my eyes and the little guy moves to sit on my stomach, his tail wagging furiously.

I look over at the other couch across from me, and Jamison is asleep on his side with the husky tucked up against him, her eyes alert. She's watching the little dog closely, like she doesn't really want to move, but if he needs her, she'll be over in a flash.

I didn't mean to fall asleep at Jamison's...didn't mean to do a lot of things last night. I drank just enough to let my guard down and get happy, spent enough time with him away from work that the fact that he's the new owner blurred along with my anger, and it felt like I was just with Jamison, the hot, charming guy I met and bonded with a couple of weeks ago. He ran to get dog food while I stayed with the dogs, and I fell asleep before he got back.

All of this is confusing and I need to get out of here before he wakes up...and never put myself in this position again. I scratch the puppy's ears and then set him down. He follows me while I grab my shoes and purse and sneak to the door, and I decide I better let him out just in case Jamison keeps sleeping for a while. I open the door to the small fenced-in area and that gets the husky's attention. I don't know if she needs to go out or is just concerned that I don't take the chihuahua away from her, but they both go out and do their business.

"Oh...yeah, we're gonna have to get some bags for that. Wow. Husky girl, you can do some damage."

"I'm not sure any woman wants to be called husky girl," a sleepy voice says behind me.

I smile but school it before I turn around. I can't be the easy-breezy person I was last night or he'll get ideas.

"You might be right," I concede. "What do you think their names should be?"

Confusion flits across his face. "Is it a good idea to name them if someone is going to claim them?"

"It's either name them or they're stuck being husky girl and little guy."

He nods like this is a serious issue and it's then that I allow myself to take in his grey sweatpants splendor. Geez, how did those get past me? If I didn't already remember the amazingness he has to work with, the sight of him in those pants brings it all back in vivid detail. I really have to get out of here.

"I've gotta go." I hurry past him and he grabs my arm, stopping me in my tracks. I stare straight ahead, afraid to look at him.

"Hey, it was fun last night," he says. When I don't say anything back, he adds, "And I think their names should be Lucia and Delgado."

"Lucia and Delgado?" I echo, turning to face him. He lowers his hand and I miss the warmth. "Those names just came to you out of thin air?"

"Lucia did. It seems like it goes with Delgado. And...I begged my parents to get me a chihuahua when I was little. I'd never seen a white one like this and it's a good thing, because he's the cutest thing I've ever seen and I would've really been disappointed when they didn't get me one. But his name was gonna be Delgado. My puppy that never was." He flushes slightly and bends down to pick the little guy up, nuzzling him with his cheek. "But here you are now," he tells the puppy.

Be still my throbbing ovaries.

Husky girl weaves between his legs like she's staking her claim while he's handing out the love, and I don't blame her.

"Delgado...and Lucia it is then. It feels...meant to be." I swallow hard, knowing I need to bolt but finding it hard to do it.

I never knew seeing a hot guy with dogs would do it

for me the way that Instagram account of guys reading in the wild does.

"It does feel meant to be," he says softly.

His eyes fall to my mouth and the space between us tightens.

And that's when I find the strength to move.

I'm at the door when he says, "Scarlett?"

I stop and look back.

His hand moves near his chin and then extends out toward me, almost like he's blowing me a kiss but...not. I must be seeing things that aren't there.

"Thank you," he says.

I don't know what he's thanking me for, but I nod. And right before I step inside, I look at him once more. Between him and the dogs, it's like a rope tugging me back toward the three of them.

"I'll call Theo and see if he has any supplies on hand. He's a vet for large animals, but he has a dog and occasionally takes in strays that come through. Once I have leashes, I can take them to my place so you're not stuck with them...until we see if anyone claims them."

"I don't mind keeping them here. But it would be nice to have leashes to walk them and so I don't have to carry them both to work. Don't want them to pull a runner."

Both eyebrows hike up. "You're taking them to work?"

"Yes." His voice tilts up at the end, but he says it like it's a given.

I try but fail to hold back the smile this time. "Okay, well, I will see you guys at work. I can handle the Happy Cow run today since you...have your hands full."

"Tell Lar and Mar hello."

"Will do."

Lucia follows me back inside the condo and when Jamison sets Delgado down, Delgado runs after me too. "Oh, you guys. You're impossible to resist."

I pet them both and Jamison holds onto them while I walk toward the front door.

"Careful, box to your right," he says, saving me from bumping into a box.

I glance down and clench my teeth when I see an open box of books—*novels*, not just boring books on how to run businesses or how to watch the stock market.

I *did not* need to know that Jamison is an avid reader.

My shower is done in half the time I usually take, and there's no time to blow-dry my hair, so I braid a small section in the front and pull it into a low ponytail, dividing it into two sections and then twisting them together before securing it into a bun.

It takes three minutes to do the bare minimum on my makeup, but with the updo, my short cream sweater dress, and camel-colored over-the-knee boots, I look like I've made way more of an effort than I really have.

I'm at Happy Cow five minutes earlier than usual and back at the lodge, unloading everything into the kitchen and managing to avoid seeing anyone as I take a coffee and chocolate croissant to my office. I take a big bite and call Theo, which is a mistake, because he answers right away and my mouth is too full to speak.

"Scar, you there?"

I gulp it down. "Sorry, yeah. I should've chewed before I called. Hey, got any dog supplies you could spare?"

"Sure. What's up? Whatcha need?"

I tell him about finding Lucia and Delgado, avoiding

the names because I'm trying to not even mention Jamison in this conversation. And the names are just the kind of thing my brother would latch onto…he knows me far too well and would be able to hear how stinking clever and endearing I found that whole story about Delgado.

"Text me their pictures and I'll post them in a few groups and on the board at the co-op. I've got a stop to make this morning before work and could bring some stuff by."

"That would be great. Thank you."

"Sure. How are you holding up? I'm sorry I haven't been back over there before now."

"It's okay. It's been busy and you know…it's weird, but…just trying to get through it."

"Grinny invited me to dinner Saturday night…"

"Yeah…she warmed right up to Jamison, let me tell you."

He laughs. "She did call and talk him up pretty good."

"Funny, she's been awfully quiet with me since she made that dinner plan."

He just laughs harder. "Honestly, you sound better than I thought you would."

"Well, I still hate the situation, but it's hard to be mad at Grinny. It was nice to see her excited about something. She's been so sad."

"I know. I thought that too."

"I better let you go so you can get over here."

"I'll see you soon. Love you."

"Love you too."

I hang up and turn my chair away from the window, facing the door. Jamison is standing in the doorway holding both dogs. The sight of him in a suit looking good enough to lick is already something I'm struggling with—add these two adorable dogs in his arms? I can't take it.

I burst out laughing and rush over to at least take Delgado off of his hands. Jamison smiles, but he looks more serious than usual.

"Do you have a boyfriend?" he asks when I hold Delgado up to my face and bury my nose in his fur.

I frown. "No? Why?"

He visibly relaxes but then has to regain his hold on Lucia. "No reason," he says. "Okay, not true. I've wondered if that's one of the reasons you've been so…"

"Hostile?" I fill in when it seems like he's unable to finish his sentence.

He tilts his head like *you said it, not me.*

I want to be livid with him, but it was a short night, and I was exhausted before I ever even met Jamison Ledger…still, I feel that feverish fury burning under my skin the way I have since I realized *he* is the one taking over.

And last night was just a good reminder that I need to stay far, far away from lemon drops when I'm anywhere near this man.

"I don't know about *your* moral compass…" It's hard to pull off a cold voice when you're holding the world's tiniest chihuahua, but I #nailit. "But if I had a boyfriend, I wouldn't have…spent that night with you. *I* am loyal, *not* a cheater."

His eyes flash with something as close to fire as I've been able to get out of him. So far he's mostly seemed amused or flirtatious or concerned by my anger toward him. He steps forward with Lucia and shuts my office door behind him with his foot, setting Lucia carefully on the ground.

I have to bite back the laughter at the insane amount of fur left on his dark suit. He glances down and winces but doesn't whine about it.

Damn it all, why does he just keep on being awesome?

When he looks up, there's something else in his expression that has me gulping and taking a tentative step back. He advances toward me, swallowing up the space between us in two long strides. He lowers his face until his mouth is barely an inch from mine and I stop breathing, my heart rate thumping violently.

We stand there suspended in time, and his hand comes up near my face, just barely breezing over my skin in a caress before he drops it.

His voice is low and raspy when he finally says, "That makes two of us. When I spent the night buried as deep inside of you as I could possibly get, it was with a conscience free and clear."

My insides tremble, the deepest part of me craving him to fill me up again.

He takes a step back and nonchalantly rubs the spot between Lucia's ears like he's not one bit affected by what just happened. Meanwhile, my legs feel like they might go out. I wrap one hand around my waist and give my side a pinch to snap me out of this lust haze.

Three months cannot come soon enough.

CHAPTER FOURTEEN

LOGISTICS

JAMISON

A knock on Scarlett's office door comes at the perfect time.

I nearly kissed the curl of contempt off of her lips just a second ago and should've bolted then, but for some reason, I'm still standing here.

"Come in," Scarlett says, her voice shaky.

She's so fucking hard to figure out. Just when I think we're getting somewhere, she slaps those walls up again.

Her brother Theo pops his head in, holding a big box. He grins when he sees me and then his attention goes to the dogs. He sets the box down and then gets on the dogs' level with his hand out. They both circle him curiously and sniff him and then he reaches out and pets them.

"Hey there," he says. "Look at you. All-white chihuahuas like this are rare." He laughs when Delgado prances back to Scarlett. "So cute. And you," he gives Lucia's neck a good scratch, "are such a beauty. Yes, you are."

He reaches into his pocket and gives her a treat and Delgado circles back over to get his too.

He chuckles and looks at Scarlett and then me. "It's hard to believe someone wouldn't be searching all over the place for them, but you never know what people are gonna do. I've seen too many horror stories over the years to be surprised anymore."

"Everything seems so idyllic here, but I guess things like this happen everywhere," I say.

"Not that it couldn't be someone from here, although I can't imagine anyone we know abandoning their dogs, but my guess is that it's either a tourist that lost them or someone drove through and dumped them." When they nudge him for another treat, he takes the opportunity to check their teeth and then their paws. "They're well-behaved and don't seem fearful of people, so they don't appear to have been mistreated."

"How old do you think they are?" Scarlett asks.

"It's hard to be sure, but I think this little one—"

"Delgado," I say, feeling a rush when I look over and see Scarlett trying to hide her smile.

"Delgado." Theo grins. "Nice. I think he's maybe a year and a half or two, and have you named the husky?"

"Lucia." I reach out and pet her.

"I think Lucia's maybe a year at most. And I don't think they've been on the street long. Their paws aren't too bad and Delgado would've been showing signs of distress more than Lucia." He stands up and looks at me. "I told Scarlett I'd post about them in some of the groups I'm in and if you guys put the word out around the lodge and at the businesses on Heritage Lane, we should be able to get them back to their owners in no time…if they want to be found."

Scarlett nods and leans down to pick up Delgado. He looks over at me smugly. *I know it, buddy. I'd be happy leaning my head against her chest too.*

"Brought you some things. Best dog food I know of is what Sally Shire makes, but I wouldn't recommend giving them that unless that's all you plan to ever feed them." He grins and rocks back on his heels. "I've gotta run. Call me if you need anything else. I can't tell whether to hope you find their owners or that you don't. Which one of you is keeping them?"

There's something a little sly in the way he asks, and I can tell I'm right by Scarlett's pointed look and his attempt at innocence.

We both speak at the same time.

"Me."

"I can now that I have the leashes."

"Lots to figure out around here," Theo says.

Definitely a little shit-stirrer. He reminds me of myself when I'm trying to get under Zac's skin. Scarlett looks down at Delgado, but her jaw is clenched. I stifle a laugh and pretend like it was a cough.

Theo reaches out to give Delgado one last pet and walks to the door. "I guess I'll see both of you at Grinny's dinner party on Saturday night."

"Yeah, see you there," I respond. "Thanks for bringing all this over."

"Sure." He knocks on the doorframe twice and leaves.

"Well, I'd better get to work," I tell her. I lean down to pick up the box. "I can come back for them once I get this out of here…"

"It's okay," she says, shaking her head. "They're good here."

"Are we fighting over custody of our dogs now, Scarlett?" My lips curve up.

She sniffs. "We don't know *who* they belong to yet… but if we don't find their owners, I think they should be with me."

"And why is that?"

"You're not even planning to be a Landmark resident. Do you plan to take them back to Boston in six months?"

I shift the weight of the box to my other side. "You're looking pretty far ahead…what's wrong with enjoying these dogs while I'm here, figuring the rest of it out as we go?"

"Because you'll leave them brokenhearted when you decide you can't be tied down to small-town living," she spits out, her face flushing.

The only sound in the room is Lucia sliding into a sprawl across the floor.

"Does that mean you're planning to stay too?" I stare right back at her, and she squirms, crossing those sexy as fuck boots in front of her.

I want to lift that sweater dress and see what lacy surprise is underneath.

If she's wet for me.

"I have more resources for finding them a home around here than you do, and you're busy running a lodge." She lifts her hand around the room and dips her head, offering an annoying yet valid point.

I reluctantly set the box down where Theo had left it. "Okay. If you really want to keep the dogs, that's fine. But let me know what I can do to help."

"We'll be just fine, won't we, guys?" she says.

Lucia gets up and sits next to her, thumping her tail. But when I walk to the door, Lucia moves with me, and I lean down and love on her a little bit.

"Sit," I tell her.

She doesn't until I say it about four more times and then I hustle out of there, closing the door behind me so she doesn't follow.

The rest of the day is spent finishing up the meetings with the staff and a few Zoom calls with clients from home. My focus is torn between work and checking on Scarlett and the dogs. But she was right about one thing—there's too much to do—and I figure it's best to give Scarlett some space.

Maybe she'll realize she needs my help more than she thinks.

She doesn't need my help.

When I leave for the day, I knock on her door, but there's no answer, and all is quiet throughout the rest of the night. I finally unpack the boxes of clothes I'd shipped ahead.

After touching base with the family, I call it a night, checking my phone like I expect Scarlett to reach out. I've given her my number in our work emails back and forth, but she hasn't given me hers. I need to remedy that tomorrow.

Before I can talk myself out of it, I pull up her email and send a quick one with Bonnie & Clyde in the subject line.

How are my furry friends and their temporary/possibly new owner?
~Jamison

I refresh a dozen times before an email comes through and there's a picture of a floral comforter with Scarlett's long legs on top. Lucia's head is resting on Scarlett's knee, and Delgado is on Scarlett's stomach and his eyes look bigger than normal at this angle.

Her response simply says:

Peachy.

I laugh and look at that picture far longer than I should. Scarlett's toenails are painted pink, and there's what appears to be a scar on her left knee. Fuck me. Is this what happens when you move out of the constantly moving pace of city life? I've been fairly busy since I've been here, but still nothing like home.

Something tells me even if we switched locations and Scarlett and I were in Boston, I'd still be zooming in on the details of this picture for a closer view of her.

CHAPTER FIFTEEN

A UNITED FRONT

SCARLETT

I manage to have minimal contact with Jamison until
Friday night.

He's tried—still showing up at Happy Cow in the
mornings to help and sending an email every night to
check on Delgado and Lucia. I've been busy working and
taking care of the dogs.

Any guilt I have about his apparent desire to be a pet

owner is dulled by the need to keep as much distance between us as possible.

I've been nervous to leave the dogs in my condo alone. So far they haven't gotten into mischief while I sleep and they're good at the office, but I don't know if it'll be different when I'm not around. I've heard horror stories about huskies, in particular, the downfall of googling everything I can to learn more about the two breeds. Lucia's leveled up my exercise in a short amount of time. We go on a lot of walks so I can wear her out, and I usually end up carrying Delgado the last half. I took an extra-long walk this morning and wish I could again now to be sure she doesn't have too much energy. She looks innocent now, but…those videos of mass destruction at the paws of a husky have me concerned. I leave a large and small rubber toy filled with peanut butter for them when I leave and hurry to the banquet hall later than I'd planned.

And the surprise is on me.

When I left at four to potty the dogs, take a quick shower, and change into my favorite red dress, the new arrangements from Feather Whims were in place, and the caterers from The Pink Ski were already setting up food. But when I arrive right at five, the banquet hall is already full and buzzing with people, and there's a live band playing in the corner. A band I didn't arrange to be here tonight. I think every business owner is here and then some, judging from the attendees. I've never considered elementary school teachers business owners per se, but hey, maybe there's something I'm missing since all the single females from Landmark Elementary are here and looking great.

I recognize the piano player from The Gnarly Vine, but

I've never seen the soulful flutist playing with him. How did Jamison pull that off in such a short amount of time and without me knowing it?

Unease rumbles through my body and I take a glass of champagne from one of The Pink Ski's catering staff.

"Thanks," I say over my shoulder, distracted as I try to find Jamison.

"Of course," he calls, moving to the next person.

"Hey, beautiful." A hand wraps around my waist and I look up at Regg as I peel his hand off of me.

"Hey, what are you doing here?"

He frowns. "I'm a business owner."

"Really? I didn't realize you have another job besides working part-time at the lodge's ski rentals."

He's nodding along with me and jumps in as soon as I'm done. "Yes, *and* I have recently started selling this highly effective CBD oil that is the purest of any on the market." His hands start moving as his excitement builds. "I actually wanted to talk to you about making it available in the gift shop…"

"Yeah, no. It's not that kind of shop, Regg."

It actually might be something we'd sell in the gift shop, but I wouldn't want to take away from the local dispensary or our spa. I also don't want to work with Regg any more than I have to.

I take a step back to keep moving, and Regg says, "Well, I'll mention it to the actual owner and see what *he* thinks."

He looks too pleased when I look over my shoulder to glare at him and I walk right into Jamison. I come close to spilling my champagne all over him, but he steadies me and then takes a long look at me, his gaze taking inventory from head to toe.

My body catches flame and I take a long sip of my champagne so I don't say something stupid.

"There's the guy of the hour," Regg says. "Hey, man. Regg Parker here. I'm sorry I missed our one-on-one this week. Maybe I can set up a new time to talk with you. I've been an employee at Landmark Mountain for a long time...the Landmarks and I go way back."

He tilts his chin toward me, and his flirty smile makes me roll my eyes. It was definitely a weak moment that made me ever go out with him. And I don't think he'd appreciate it if I mentioned how many times Granddad nearly fired his ass.

"I've got some CBD oil that I really think would be a good fit in the lodge gift shop—" Regg says, winding up his pitch.

"As Scarlett said, it's not that kind of shop," Jamison cuts in, his expression nowhere near as warm as I'm used to seeing from him, his tone all business.

And I kind of wish I could love him. Or at least high-five him and laugh about this.

Regg stutters something else, I think maybe reminding Jamison about their one-on-one, but Jamison's focus is back on me. We shift away from Regg and suddenly we're the only two people in the room.

"You look incredible," he says.

His eyes wander down my body again and even though this dress doesn't have a plunging neckline and it covers my arms and almost hits my knees, he makes me feel like he's never seen anything more beautiful.

I remember him saying that the night we...met.

"Does your lace match your dress tonight?" he asks softly.

I know he's talking about the one-piece I was wearing. He never knew what to call it, but he sure as hell liked it.

I take a sip and look away, too stirred up to look at him. "Yes, it does. How did you know? I had a vision of something new to try and whipped it up late last night."

He mutters a curse under his breath and it pleases me entirely too much.

"You've been busy around here. Nice band," I admit begrudgingly.

"I didn't want to make you do all the work...or have all the fun," he says, smiling.

I lift my glass and clink it to his.

"Would you mind introducing me to a few people I haven't met yet?" he asks. "I've tried to make my way around town this week to introduce myself and make sure they were coming tonight, but I missed a few."

I nod, surprised that he's put that much thought into this event. "Sure."

He points out Jo, the owner of Sunny Side, and Cecil, the owner of the grocery store of the same name.

"Oh, two of my favorite people. Let's start with Cecil since he's closest."

We walk in the older man's direction and he hollers my name when he sees me, pulling me in for a big bear hug.

"I haven't seen you in ages," he says.

"You're hiding every time I come in to shop. You're not keeping secrets from me, are you, Cecil?"

His round belly lifts as he rares back and laughs.

"I should hope so," he says.

He sobers when he sees Jamison standing behind me.

"I was real disappointed to hear the lodge wasn't going to you, Scarlett," he says, his tone completely different.

"Well, this is the new owner, Jamison Ledger, and he wanted to make sure he met you. Jamison, Cecil owns Cecil's and it's a one-stop shop. You'll find things you didn't even know you needed at his grocery store."

Cecil chuckles and then scowls at Jamison.

Jamison reaches out his hand and they shake, but then Cecil's hands land on his hips afterward. Uh-oh. When Cecil's hands are on his hips, there's some old man sass about to drop.

"It's nice to meet you, Cecil," Jamison says, obviously used to winning people over with his smile. "I shopped at Cecil's yesterday, and Scarlett's right—I left with a lot of things I didn't know I needed. Like hand warmers and a really nice shaving brush and razor stand…"

"You doing right by this one?" Cecil cuts in, tilting his head toward me.

"Doing my best," Jamison says. "But you'll have to ask her."

Jamison looks at me, but Cecil is just getting warmed up.

"This girl is as good as it gets," he says. "I remember when her grandpa said she'd talked him into adding this room we're standing in right now, and John Henry wondered if the space would be useful…"

Cecil shakes his head and scowls.

"Sometimes that old coot was too stuck in the old ways to see what a gift he had right under his nose." He points at me.

I put my hand on his arm and squeeze. "Thanks, Cecil.

Jamison clears his throat. "I think you're absolutely

right about Scarlett, and I wish I'd known Mr. Landmark personally to have a word or two with him about it."

Cecil mutters something under his breath, not ready to let Jamison off the hook so easily.

"Well, now Jamison's just trying to get on my good side." I try to make light of it, suddenly desperate to get the attention off of me. "I'll come in to see you soon, Cecil." I lean in to kiss his cheek and then turn to Jamison. "Should we catch Jo before she heads out? She isn't planning to stay for the whole event."

"That would be great. Again, it was a pleasure to meet you, Cecil."

"Yeah, yeah," Cecil grumbles.

Maybe a smidge more conciliatory than before, but there's a ways to go before he'll be won over by the newbie.

Who knew Cecil would show more loyalty than Grinny?

We catch Jo as she's putting a wonton in her mouth. She holds up her hands, face flushed as she looks at the man next to me. Once she's done chewing, she reaches out and squeezes me.

"Hey, girl. Been missing you," she says. "I heard you've got some dogs—any takers yet?"

"No, not a single word. And I miss you too. I'll try to swing by sometime next week." I hold my hand toward Jamison. "I wanted to make sure you met Jamison before you left tonight. Jamison, this is Jo, she's the owner of Sunny Side. Makes the best…"

"Pancakes," Jamison finishes. "I thought you looked familiar, but it's been a long time. My gran loved your restaurant when we visited years ago."

"Oh, I'd forgotten about that," I say.

"Well, I love to hear that. I'm not on Heritage Lane, so most of the tourist crowd misses my place. I love that my little place stuck with you," she says, her smile wide.

"It absolutely did. In fact, I need to get over there soon. I'm still getting settled in, but I'll make it a priority to come to Sunny Side this week. Maybe I can even talk Scarlett into joining me."

Jo's eyes light up and she looks at me, her smile even bigger.

"Yes, Scarlett. I think this past week might be the first time you've ever not come around. Please *do* join Jamison." Her eyes widen at me pointedly—I love Jo, but she has the worst poker face in the world.

It's impossible to live in a town like Landmark and not have everyone in your business. I'm used to it, and especially with being a Landmark, the gossip my family and I generate around here just seems to come with the territory.

I would've never been able to get away with that night with Jamison if we'd been in Landmark. If nothing else, the glow on my face from finally having earth-shattering sex would've told the tale. The whole town would've known by morning that I'd slept with him.

Jamison shoots his sexy smirk my way and I give him the driest look I can muster.

"Sunday morning, ten o'clock?" he asks, pushing me while he has an audience.

"I'll have to check my calendar."

Jo's head tilts like *what is wrong with you, girl?*

And when someone calls Jamison and he excuses himself, she leans in and whispers, "Wowsers, he's even more handsome than everyone said he was. The Golden

Girls were in this week and Grinny warned me he was a looker. Helen said she dusted off his back and he had shoulders like a Viking, and you know Helen doesn't compliment *anyone*. But I *still* wasn't prepared."

"You know better than to listen to all that," I fuss.

She laughs like I'm ridiculous. "Honey, this fifty-two-year-old is living vicariously through you. I'm doing good to get Mark to realize I've even walked into the room. He's so tired when he gets home from the restaurant and so am I. The least you can do is give me some good stories about your love life."

Oh, if she only knew.

I turn and Jamison is surrounded by women. The Thompson twins from Hooked, the knitting shop; the owner of Hit the Slopes, the ski apparel shop; the sisters from The Great Divide, a combo of ski gear, kayaks, and hiking equipment. Their brother is nowhere to be found, and he's really who I'd consider to be the owner of The Great Divide. And let's not forget our teacher representation.

Seems like the whole town—heavy on the female side—has turned out to see the new bachelor of Landmark.

And is he ever making a splash.

"There's a pool going on over who can catch him the fastest," Jo says. "You better get in there, girl. My vote's on you."

Sounds like my cue to move to Timbuktu or maybe a huge place like New York City…a place where no one knows my name.

CHAPTER SIXTEEN

WAX AND FLESH

JAMISON

The cocktail party was a hit last night.

It went much later than scheduled, guests lingering until eleven even though the food and drinks were long gone. Scarlett made her escape around 8:30, looking gleeful to use the dogs as an excuse.

Around mid-afternoon, I email her asking what the dress code is for dinner at Grinny's, and she responds with:

A Hawaiian shirt and khakis.

I'm surprised by that and more than ready to give the suits a rest, but I've never owned a Hawaiian shirt in my life and besides my suit pants and jeans, I only have one pair of pants that will have to suffice for khakis. I venture out with only an hour to spare, and start with the lodge's gift shop. No Hawaiian shirts to be found. There's still snow on the ground, for crying out loud.

So I head to the strip of shops on Heritage Lane and come up with nothing. My last stop is Cecil's and I go in there to buy flowers to take to Grinny, and Cecil is on the far left side, hanging up several Hawaiian shirts.

No way.

"Cecil, you're saving my life," I tell him, taking one and holding it up.

There are some fun and even classy Hawaiian shirts out there—I've bought some for Pappy before—but this is…something else. A mountain and jungle scene combined, so many colors…and flamingos. Lots and lots of them. Too many to count are flying, and then two large ones face each other, front and center. Four smaller ones stand in the water below.

It's a lot. Unfortunately, it's the only one in my size.

There's a smaller shirt with tacos, palm trees, and tropical flowers all over it that isn't bad and Bigfoot with a surfboard that's actually the best one, but the parrots sipping cocktails is one of the tackiest shirts I've ever seen.

"It's my lucky day," I say under my breath.

"Well, all right then," Cecil says.

I'm pretty sure the man hates me.

"You missed one." He holds up the last Hawaiian shirt, and this one...

I bust out laughing and Cecil's mouth twitches as he tries to keep a straight face.

"Oh, that's...wow."

"I think it might be your size," he says, holding it toward me.

It's got the blue water and green palm trees, but then there's Jesus walking on the beach, Jesus walking on a wave in the ocean, Jesus with a lei headpiece, Jesus on a motorcycle...

I hold up the flamingos next to the Jesuses and lift an eyebrow at Cecil.

"You're asking me?" he asks, rubbing his hand over his thick beard.

I nod, wishing like all hell that my brother was here for this. The shit he'd give me. I'd make him wear whichever one I didn't buy.

"I mean, is there any question? You gotta go with Jesus," Cecil says.

I crack up. "You're right. As if I could pass this up." I start to hang the flamingo one up and pause. "I think I've gotta get this one for my brother too."

"Suit yourself," he says.

I pick out a pot of orchids rather than a bouquet and head to the counter. Cecil shuffles behind me and goes behind the counter.

"I'm the only one on tonight," he says, ringing me up. "Everyone's still yammering on about that party last night. You'd think you'd served prime rib or somethin'..."

I chuckle. "I'm glad you came, Cecil. Maybe next time we can have prime rib..."

He puts the shirts in a bag and holds it up, and I take it, thanking him.

"Don't forget your flowers," he grumbles.

"Saving me again, thanks."

"Yeah, yeah." He waves me off and trudges back to the shirts.

I jog home and take a quick shower, grimacing when I put on the shirt. I hope Grinny has a sense of humor.

Pride be damned, I'm going to Grinny Landmark's house, and after taking over their family business, the least I can do is follow the dress code. Even if I do look like a sacrilegious middle-aged man on vacation.

I put on my jacket and step outside, looking around in case Scarlett's walking over too, but I don't see her. I've spent a lot of time outside since we found those puppies, watching for Scarlett walking them, but I haven't seen her yet. I'm ninety-nine percent certain she's doing everything she can to avoid me.

It's a pretty walk, and when I get closer to the house, I notice all the cars in the driveway. More than I expected.

The door opens before I can knock, and it's Wyatt. Black sweater and jeans.

"Hi. Come on in," he says, opening the door wider.

A boy comes running up. "Hey, are you Jamison?" he asks.

"Yeah, that's me. You must be Owen."

I've heard about him a few times now, and the kid is pretty cute. He seems to be around my niece Ivy's age, maybe a little younger.

"My aunt does not like you," he says, eyes wide.

"Owen," Sutton says. "Mind your manners." He holds out his hand to shake mine. White button-down and jeans.

"Come on back, some of us are in the kitchen and some are in the great room. Can I take your coat?"

I shrug it off and the three of them freeze, taking in the shirt.

I put my hands in my pockets and nod slowly. "Yeah, I have a feeling Scarlett was pranking me about the Hawaiian shirt dress code."

Sutton laughs and Theo wanders in before we reach the hall. Grey long-sleeve shirt and jeans. I hold back my laugh.

"Hey, man. Lookin' like a vayy-cation," he says, tipping his chin toward my shirt. He tilts his head when he gets a closer look. "Oh, and Jesus. Bold, okay."

The house has beautiful craftsmanship, a cozy living room with hickory built-in shelves next to the stone fireplace, but when we step into the great room, it's even better. The ceiling is high with beams going across, and the back wall is all windows, showing the most incredible view of the Rocky Mountains.

"The place is gorgeous."

I hear giggling and turn to see Scarlett taking in my outfit. I point at her and she gives a little shrug.

"That is some kind of shirt," she says. "Grinny will be so pleased."

"Mm-hmm." I pretend to be more annoyed than I am by her trickery.

Grinny walks in then, setting a big dish on the table, and then she makes a beeline to me.

"Jamison, I'm so glad you could make it. Don't you look handsome. I've always been partial to a Hawaiian shirt. Such a happy print." She starts laughing. "Oh my. What on earth is Jesus doing in a hula skirt?"

I smile and hold the orchids out for her, trying not to laugh at Scarlett's told-ya smirk. "Thank you. Scarlett thought you might appreciate the shirt. And Cecil helped me pick it out."

"Is that right? Cecil's a hoot." Grinny giggles. "And my girl knows me well." Grinny presses her hands together in delight and then takes the orchids, setting them in the middle of the table. "These are just lovely. Thank you so much. Have you met the rest of my family yet?"

"Owen was the only one I hadn't met yet, and we said hello." I grin at the kid and he smirks back.

Callum walks in and stands next to Scarlett. "Hey. Sorry, I'm late."

She leans over and hugs him and then he walks the few steps it takes to kiss Grinny on the cheek.

"So glad you're here, honey," Grinny says.

He takes in my shirt, but he doesn't say anything, just studies me from across the table. If I hadn't seen how he smiles at Grinny and Scarlett like they hung the moon, I'd have trouble deciding if he's one of those hipster lumber-jack models or a serial killer.

Grinny motions for me to take the seat next to her and everyone else sits down. Grinny hands me the serving dish closest to her and I tell her I'll hold it while she gets hers first.

"That sounds just like my John Henry," she says softly. "He had a few backward ideas about some things. He wanted to be the one to provide for us and for me to be here when our kids came home from school and when he got in from work, but he was a gentleman through and through, always made sure I was served first, that I never had to open my own door when he was around…" She laughs, her eyes filling with moisture. "That man was such a contradiction, and do I ever miss him."

She nods when I hold up another serving dish toward her and takes a helping of mashed potatoes.

"What made you decide to go into the hotel business?" she asks.

"My brother and I have invested in a few properties the past couple of years, mostly backing friends of his who are buying restaurants or revamping vacation properties here and there that we buy and then sell. Zac's wife, Autumn, has an interior design business—so she's worked on the projects we've been involved in. Nothing of this magnitude though. Honestly, I'd never considered being a resort owner until I heard about Landmark Mountain being for sale."

"Must be nice to just"—Scarlett snaps her fingers—"snatch it up on a whim."

The table grows quiet and I feel all eyes on the two of us as Scarlett stares me down.

I'm not sure I'll ever get on the good side of this girl again.

CHAPTER SEVENTEEN

ANOTHER LAYER

SCARLETT

I can't seem to go a full thirty minutes without hating Jamison Ledger.

Or it would be more accurate to say I *wish* I could hate him. He has a way of oozing charm and all this sexy hotness that has me drooling while also making me want to dropkick him back to Boston.

Like right now.

Before tonight, it would have been impossible to convince me that anyone could look as hot as Jamison does, in a fucking Jesus Hawaiian shirt of all things. The level of agitation I'm feeling should be evident in my use of fucking *and* Jesus in the same sentence, Grinny would be horrified if she could hear my thoughts, and so am I, but these are special circumstances—it is cool Jesus in the surf and sand after all.

Jamison looks so hot tonight that I've had trouble getting a full breath to reach my lungs and my legs have been squeezed together as tight as they'll go, like that will keep me from soaking the slate blue lace teddy I made this morning…something else that I can't stop doing since our night together. I probably have twenty new lingerie pieces that I haven't even worn yet, and I'm putting in a lot of time at work and with the puppies. But every time the dogs are sleeping and I should be, I end up tiptoeing back to the sewing machine and starting another new creation so my hand doesn't try to recreate what Jamison did to me that night.

I'd gotten in the habit every morning and night in the weeks after our night, but now that I have to see him every day, I just haven't felt right about pretending my fingers are Jamison's.

Of course, all of these thoughts are running through my mind as I'm staring at him, wanting to hate him, and I feel my face flame. His eyes take on a gleam and he licks his lips slowly, drawing in his lower lip with his teeth afterward. I swear he knows my mind is in the gutter even when I'm glaring at him.

"I've been trying to talk Scarlett into staying on as general manager," he announces to the table.

And now I'm really mad.

Because everyone erupts at once, talking about what a great idea that is, and how that is so wise of him to make that judgment call so quickly, and...

"What about it, Scarlett?" Sutton asks. "Did you say yes?"

"Of course, I didn't say yes," I snap.

I push back from the table and toss my cloth napkin on the plate I haven't filled yet since I've been so busy staring at Jamison.

The room goes silent as everyone turns to me. Jamison looks conflicted as his jaw tightens, his eyes unreadable as he looks at me, and it catches me by surprise when he stands up and turns to Grinny.

"Grinny, thank you for inviting me to dinner. It's an honor to be in your home. I'm so sorry I can't stay. I know when I'm not welcome."

His eyes fall back on me, and I want to wither into the ground.

"I never wanted to come in and take the place of your grandfather." His voice is calm and yet it does a number on my heart. "I've tried to come in and include you, make you feel a part of this, but you've resisted every step of the way. Moving forward, it's for the best that we *don't* work together."

He looks around the table, giving my brothers a cursory nod, and walks out of the room.

My hands are shaking, every part of me is shaking, and I don't know whether to run after him or go hide in Grinny's bathroom until I can catch my breath.

"So things *haven't* been going smoothly between the two of you," Wyatt says dryly.

I roll my eyes and Theo laughs.

Sutton clears his throat. "You know, we're the ones you should be angry with, Scarlett," he says. "We basically pulled a Granddad and left you out of the decision about the place when you weren't in the will, thinking we were 'saving' you by giving you that check, giving you your freedom."

"Most owners would have come in and started tearing it up by now, hiring a whole new staff..." Callum says, looking down at his plate.

"You're taking it out on Jamison when it was all of us who made this decision," Wyatt says.

"None of us realized how hard you would take the sale," Theo adds.

"I kind of thought Granddad must've known you didn't want it...that's what I get for assuming," Sutton says. "Point is, it's on us that we didn't ask what *you* wanted."

I look around the table incredulously, surprised I've never looked at it this way. Why haven't I been mad at them? I fall back in my chair, appetite completely gone and a sick feeling taking over my stomach.

"You're right," I say softly. "I thought everyone knew how much I wanted to run the resort, but Granddad might've been the only one who knew how deep my love for this place went. You guys have been busy establishing your own careers and I've almost been grateful for that because I thought it was the only thing that paved the way for *me* to have it. Deep down I always felt like Granddad discounted what I did around here." I take a deep breath and hope my voice isn't shaky when I add, "Maybe I didn't want to risk experiencing the same reactions from all of you if you knew just how much I wanted this."

Six sets of sad eyes stare back at me.

"I really wish we'd known. Wish I hadn't been so caught up in my own shit," Theo says.

"Same," Callum says.

"Language," Grinny says, motioning toward Owen, who is reaching out to take my hand.

"I don't like it when you're sad, Auntie," he says.

I lean over and hug him. "I don't like it when you're sad either, but we all get sad sometimes, don't we?"

He nods solemnly.

I push back from the table and give Grinny an apologetic smile. "You know I live for the times we're all together, but I think I need to go too," I tell her.

She nods and when I stand, she gets up and meets me, hugging me. "We all let you down, angel. Can you forgive us?"

I sigh, my eyes filling with tears. "There's nothing to forgive."

When I step back, I wipe my eyes and put my hands on my hips, rolling my eyes as I try to laugh.

"I'm not ready to make it so easy for the rest of you," I say, getting a relieved laugh from my brothers. "But the truth is, even though it stings that Granddad didn't include me in the will, even if he *had* given me full rein, I don't think I could've saved the place either, not with all that needs to be done."

"I think you could've—if Jamison already wants you to be his general manager, I think you could've," Wyatt says.

The rest of them nod and start to pipe up.

I hold my hand up and they pause.

"No, really. I haven't been able to admit it to myself,

but it's true. I'm seeing things through a new lens now that we have new eyes on the place, and we need a *lot* of updates. I'm still not fully sure what Jamison is capable of, but he already has the charter helicopter schedule filling back up."

"No kidding," Sutton says in shock.

"Yeah, George has flown maybe once in the past four months, but we had two flights today and at least a dozen new bookings. I'm surprised Jamison was even able to get our other two pilots back. So that's something that I wouldn't have been able to do…at least not in the foreseeable future."

I help Grinny back to her seat.

"Who knows," I say. "Maybe Jamison will be able to take this place to the next level, the place Granddad always envisioned it being."

I pat Grinny's back and get out of there. I've already said way more than I ever have about my feelings about the lodge. Maybe I should've done that a long time ago.

My phone and keys are in my sweater pocket, so I rush through the house and out the front door. I'd normally walk over here since it's a mile and a half between Grinny's door and mine, but I drove tonight so I could hurry home to the dogs once I was ready to leave.

When I pull up to my condo and walk inside, Delgado and Lucia are cuddling together on the couch. Delgado's tucked back against Lucia's chest, and their heads pop up when I walk inside. They jump down and come over to say hello, Lucia weaving through my legs and Delgado doing these cute little twirls that I haven't seen him do yet.

"Did you guys miss me?" I ask, feeling lighter already.

I take a shaky breath and dab the corner of my eyes with my sweater.

"You sure know how to make a girl feel good," I whisper, nuzzling both their faces.

The knock on the door makes me jump and Lucia growls. Delgado starts barking and then Lucia chimes in and I stare at them in shock. I haven't heard them do that yet either.

"Whoa, I didn't know you had it in you." I walk to the peephole and Jamison is standing out there, his cheeks bright red.

I groan and Lucia and Delgado amp up their barking. "Okay, girls and boys, that's enough."

I pick Delgado up and hold Lucia by the collar as I open the door.

Jamison runs his hand through his hair and it falls back into the messy, sexy, perfect placement it was in before.

The dogs are excited to see him and I can tell he wants to pet them, but I'm still holding onto Lucia and she's trying to rush toward him and Delgado is squirming in my arms.

"You can come in," I say, stepping back for him to enter.

"This won't take long," he says, his tone different than I've ever heard it.

Colder.

He walks in, leaning down to scratch behind Lucia's ears and the side of her face as she leans into him. I let Delgado down and he skids across the hardwood floor to Jamison's side and starts that twirling thing he did for me. Jamison smiles down at the dog and dammit, here I go wishing it was me.

I try to school my wistful expression when he turns his focus to me.

"I know our...night together has made this complicated." His jaw clenches with each pause between his words. "Maybe this...tension...is just how it would've been with you no matter who came in here to take it over, or maybe you specifically want *me* to crash and burn, but I'd love it if we could come to some sort of peaceful place for the... less than three months you're staying on."

Delgado is still twirling around his feet, and when Jamison leans down and scoops Delgado up, I die. The cuteness factor is so blinding I have to turn away from them.

"But until then, I'm not going anywhere. If you'd like to share what your vision of this place was before...I stepped in and ruined everything, I'll welcome the input. If not, I suggest you don't stand in my way."

His phone buzzes and since he'd set it on my side table while the dogs mauled him, I see what the text says.

> AVA
>
> You left Boston?! I hate you, but I also thought we'd have our chance...

"Looks like I'm not the only one who gives you a hard time."

Fury flashes across his eyes when he sees I'm referring to his phone, and he sets Delgado down and picks up his phone, reading the text.

"I shouldn't have said that and I shouldn't have read your text," I admit under my breath. "I'm not normally this—"

"Tell me this, Scarlett," he jumps in.

Between here and Grinny's, he's turned into cold businessman mode, and for the first time since I met him, I feel the loss of how he looks at me when he's not flirting or smiling that sexy smile or trying to charm the panties off of me.

My stomach clenches, a pang that physically hurts.

"Would you rather just handle the daily responsibilities you have now, you and Albert? He can be our go-between, if that's helpful. And I'll put my focus on implementing the changes as I see fit."

I'm still so stunned by the difference in him that I'm quiet for too long as he waits for me to respond.

He lifts his eyebrows. "Do you need more time to think about it?" he asks.

"Uh, sure. I mean…no. I-uh, yes, yes, that works. No, that will be…fine." The disaster just keeps on pouring out of my mouth.

He either pretends not to notice or he really has shut off all feelings toward me as of tonight. He bends down to give the dogs equal attention and when he stands upright again, they're both panting after him, wanting more.

You and me both, guys.

"Okay, I'll see you on Monday morning then," he says.

He walks to the door and the dogs follow him there.

He sounds a little more like himself when he adds, "Let me know if you ever need a dog sitter."

And then he walks out that door, and I want to call him back inside, tell him I want to know everything, all his ideas, and not just that, but what's his favorite color and does he like oatmeal and when he's not in a hotel taking me in several positions, what side of the bed does he sleep on?

But I don't. I crawl on the couch with the dogs, and later, when they're in my bed and I can't sleep, I make more pretty things and try not to imagine him seeing me wear them.

And the next morning, when ten o'clock rolls around and my calendar is totally clear, as I knew it was when he asked me, I wonder if he went to Sunny Side without me, and I regret missing out on having those pancakes with him.

CHAPTER EIGHTEEN

IMPROMPTU

JAMISON

It's been two weeks since Scarlett and I had that conversation in her condo, and while things are definitely more peaceful around the lodge, I fucking hate it.

We barely talk to each other and when we do, it's so polite and strained, it's fucking miserable. But it's just the way it's gotta be. I'm here to run a business. Any lingering attraction I may feel for this woman has to be pushed aside.

I've run into her a few times when she's walking the dogs, and that's the only time it's slightly easier to be around her. She's more relaxed around them and I guess being out in the open air helps us both.

The rest of the time, it's almost like a constant state of claustrophobia, the desire mixed with tension so thick every time I see her in her office or break room or talking to guests in the lobby. Hell, it's there when I run into her at Sunny Side or Happy Cow too, so scratch my theory about the great outdoors.

I've immersed myself in work, not just around here, but with Zoom calls about lodge renovations and keeping up with my clients' accounts, so I've had more than enough to keep me busy, but this weirdness with Scarlett is getting to me.

After a Sunday morning breakfast at Sunny Side, something that's quickly become a tradition, I decide to take advantage of the snow we got last night, knowing there can't be many more perfect opportunities to ski before the season is over. I bundle up and head over to our ski rentals, surprised to see Danny working on a Sunday. I've met with him a few times to discuss some ideas he'd like to implement and I like him, nice guy.

"I didn't think you were on during the weekends," I say.

He shakes his head, going straight for my size boots and the skis he knows I like after helping me only once before. "Sam's got the flu and I had to call in backup already to cover the lifts. It's slowing down now, but it's been a busy one with the fresh snow."

He freezes and his face breaks out in the biggest smile I've seen on the guy. "Hey," he says.

I turn around to see who has him so excited and it's a gut punch to see Scarlett smiling back warmly at him.

It doesn't help that she looks better than fucking Catwoman in her black one-piece ski suit. It's belted and fits every damn curve like it was made for her. She's wearing a pink hat with two loose braids on either side. New fantasy look that I didn't even know I was into. She keeps them in supply.

"Thought I might see you out here today," he says, moving to a locked cabinet above the rest of the gear.

He pulls out a pair of black skis with pink detailing and matching ski boots and places them on the counter in front of her.

She glances at me reluctantly, and I tilt my head up in her direction. No smile for me, but I'm pretty sure my face has been in a permanent scowl since the night at Grinny's.

The whole thing pisses me off.

"Jamison," she says, reluctantly.

"Scarlett," I bite back.

"Couldn't miss this snow." She turns back to Danny. "Might be the last one we get," she says, completely animated when she talks to him.

My stomach churns. I've had about enough of this.

Danny hasn't stopped grinning since she came in here and I decide I was a little too rash in my estimation of him. He's totally forgotten I'm here...that's not great for customer service.

"Wish I was out there with ya," he says.

It's totally obvious that he's into her. Did they date before? *Are they dating now?*

"Well, come on out. It's almost final call. No one's gonna start skiing this late before we close…I mean… except for us." Her eyes dart to me and back to his quickly.

"Wish I could. Remember when you tripped on someone's lost boot getting off the lift and skied down the top of the mountain backwards?" He laughs. "Once I knew you were okay, I've never laughed so hard in my life."

She laughs. "Always laughing at my expense."

"Always giving me a good reason to," he says, looking at her with such unabashed affection I want to hurl my Sunny Side pancakes and sausage.

"It takes skill to ski down a black diamond backwards." She shrugs.

He shakes his head in awe. "Damn straight, it does. Just more proof that you're good at everything you do."

I can't take any more of this and once my boots are on, I get the hell out of there. The line is winding down and there's probably only a half hour left before the lifts close. It's the perfect time to be out here.

I feel Scarlett when she skis into place behind me, can smell her sweet scent, and Bo grins when he sees the two of us. He pauses the lift since the last people in front of us are about five cars ahead and we're still not quite to the chair yet.

"You mind going up together?" he asks. "I just got a call from Regg asking me to check on something."

I look behind us and we're the only ones in line. Scarlett is avoiding looking at me, so I answer for both of us.

"I guess we can manage that."

"Great, come on. No backwards skiing today, Scarlett," Bo says, chuckling.

Scarlett rolls her eyes, but she's grinning good-naturedly at him too. What does it take to get that kind of smile out of her? Her squirming against my fingers, the sweetest smile on her face as she looked up at me, comes to mind, and for the millionth time, I try to put the memory of that unforgettable night aside...at least until I'm alone in my bed or shower.

We get in place and Bo gives us a big grin and a salute as we take off. It's silent for the first minute, and I appreciate the incredible view as we climb up the mountain. The slopes here are unlike any I've ever skied before, and next year, I plan to get out here earlier in the season to enjoy them more.

Maybe there's a way to keep our sides from touching, but with skis, I don't know how.

"You come out here often?" Scarlett says.

I stare straight ahead, surprised she's started a conversation.

"Not as much as I'd like. I've been out twice before today. You?"

"Not as much as I'd like either."

I chance a look at her, trying to read her mood. Her cheeks are rosy from the cold, and I resist the urge to jump off the lift and avoid such close proximity.

"One run is better than none...which is why I'm taking this one." She motions up the steep hill we're taking.

"Sounds like you're a pro. Danny and Bo sure think so," I say, trying my damnedest to avoid the edge in my tone but failing.

She chuckles slightly. "My brothers and I used to spend every chance we got out here. I'm rusty now compared to how often I skied as a kid."

"I bet this was such a great place to grow up," I say, looking out at the beauty in every direction but hers.

"It was the best," she says, her tone wistful. "The very best."

There's something about the way she talks about Landmark…it's different. Something much deeper than the way people usually talk about their hometowns. I love where I grew up, but it was more about my family, not my abiding love for our home or city.

We ride up and up and up, and the expanse of snowy mountaintops on either side of us is breathtaking.

"This view…it doesn't get old, does it? Wait until you see it in the summer and fall…if you…come back for that," she finishes awkwardly.

I glance at her and she's starting to fidget.

"Jamison, I'm not the mean, angry person I've been with you. I've been so frustrated and sad and…just a *mess* about this whole situation. I hope you'll forgive me for taking it out on you. I really am sorry. I've tried to show the professional I'm capable of being the past two weeks, but I sort of neglected the overdue apology." She makes a face, looking so uncomfortable that I soften.

"I…you're forgiven," I say, and it's surprising how easily I mean it. "I know you're not mean…well, I haven't seen you be with anyone but me."

"Ow," she says, laughing. "I deserved that."

"You think I don't see how everyone in this town looks at you? You're like royalty around here."

Her eyes are shy as we look at each other. Damn, she's stunning. *Keep it professional*, I tell myself.

"I've appreciated the peace, but talking is nice," I admit. "Definitely better."

She lets out a shaky, relieved sigh and looks so sweet, my stomach lurches and flutters like a lovesick traitor. I'm not going down that disastrous road again, so I tear my eyes away from her. It's best I don't look at her for long stretches.

"What was your favorite part of growing up h—"

A screeching noise interrupts me and we come to an abrupt stop, swinging back and forth. Scarlett's eyes double.

"That didn't sound right," she says.

CHAPTER NINETEEN

OMINOUS SWINGS

SCARLETT

Jamison and I look forward and then behind us, seeing if there's any indication of why we've stopped.

We're not far from the top of the mountain, but not high enough to see the terminal. No one is behind us, and the lifts in front of us are empty, swinging ominously.

Wind kicks up and we're still rocking slightly from

that quick stop. I keep thinking we're going to start moving any second, but…we keep sitting there.

"Does this happen often?" Jamison asks.

"If someone had been closer in front of us, it wouldn't be weird to stop if they had trouble getting off, but…not this long. It's getting weird…"

I reach around in my pocket, feeling around for my phone. "Dammit, I think I left my phone at Sutton's. My nephew is obsessed with Lucia and Delgado."

The concern on Jamison's face eases and he smiles. "How are my favorite dogs?"

I'm about to answer, but it's like the heavens suddenly part, and the fattest snowflakes fall on us at a rapid rate.

"What the hell is happening?" Jamison says, laughing.

His hair is covered in white within seconds, intricate snowflakes landing in his long eyelashes.

"I thought the snow was done for the weekend," I say, glad I wore a hat.

I shiver and Jamison shifts closer to me, his body making me heat up in more ways than one, but with the wind picking up, it's still cold out here.

"Let me see if I can find out what's going on." He shifts his poles to the side.

"I can hold those." I take them from him while he tries to find his phone. It's buried under his coat and he unzips his pants' pocket to get to it.

"Next time, I'll keep my phone in my jacket," he mumbles, making a silly face at me.

I bite the inside of my cheek to keep from laughing at him. "You look like Jack Frost."

"Do we know what Jack Frost looks like?" He frowns.

I point at him and he laughs, easing some of the tension between us.

"I guess I walked right into that one," he says.

He takes off his glove to call Bo and curses when there's no reception.

"I was afraid of that," I admit.

"You don't think they forgot we're up here, do you?"

"No, they wouldn't forget us. Bo was doing something for Regg, wasn't he? But Danny wouldn't leave us stranded out here…"

"Right, good ole' Danny," he says between his teeth.

I frown. "You…have a problem with Danny?"

"No. No problem." He sighs. "They wouldn't play a prank on us, would they?"

"They wouldn't mess around with something like this, especially not when the snow is picking up."

"I hope you're right."

"I am. At least about that," I add in a softer tone. "I'm sure we'll start right back up soon…"

He takes his poles back and tries his phone again, attempting a text to Albert this time, but it doesn't go through either.

We sit there for a few minutes, quiet except for the wind howling, and it starts to set in that we might really be stuck.

I look behind us again, down the steep incline, and run my hands down my arms, faster and faster. *Do not panic, do not panic.*

He keeps checking his phone every few minutes and the snow is not letting up. We yell for a while, but it just gets lost on the wind.

It's getting worse up here, and amping up the concern

is the fact that we're off to the side of where skiers are going down the mountain, so with the visibility decreasing as the snow comes down, I don't think anyone skiing down is going to see us sitting here, stuck.

If we have been forgotten.

And eventually, we're not seeing any skiers going past.

We go through stretches of quiet, stretches of yelling, stretches of trying to act like we're not stuck up on a cold mountain.

And then…I get beside myself.

"Okay," I say somewhat hysterically. "I can't believe this is happening. I thought we'd be going within like a *minute*, but this is…what has it been…forty-five minutes? An hour?"

I shake my head wildly and he turns to face me, making us rock.

"*Careful*," I shriek, reaching out to hold onto the side. "Steady. Okay, that's better. We're slowing down. It's not that cold out here, right? I can't believe out of the—has it been hundreds? I think probably so—out of the hundreds of times I've skied, this has *never* happened. Oh my God, what if they did forget us out here? They wouldn't, right? But it's snowing and technically, we're closed. It was so crazy to come out right before closing. That wasn't smart of either one of us. It is really, really cold…"

My eyes blur from the wind and my face is numb.

"I'm not crying, I'm just cold—"

"Scarlett." Jamison's gloved hand reaches out to grip my shoulder. "Breathe, beautiful."

When I just stare at him, he puts his arm around me and takes a deep breath himself. I try to copy that, inhaling and exhaling slowly until eventually I'm breathing calmly again.

"Sorry," I whisper. "I didn't know how much it would bother me to be stuck out here. I love riding the ski lifts… getting stuck, not so much."

"It's not my favorite either," he says. "But I have to admit, if I have to be stuck out here on this mountain, I'm happy to be stuck with you."

He pauses and looks over at me, our faces much closer now that his arm is around me. My heart rate is picking up for entirely different reasons now.

"That sounds horribly selfish of me," he's saying while I get lost staring into his green eyes. "I hate that you're cold right now and that you're miserable out here and…I even feel bad that you're stuck with *me,* your least favorite person ever, but," he smiles and my heart trips all over itself, "it would really suck to be out here alone."

"Agreed," I say, shivering into him. "If you weren't here, I'd have either passed out from panic or I'd be frozen." My arm is around his waist now, as we huddle to stay warm. "And you're not my least favorite person ever."

"Hmm. Not buying that yet, but noted."

"What's the story with Ava?" I ask.

He looks at me and I shrug.

"I need a diversion."

"I'm just surprised that's what's come to mind—a text you saw a couple of weeks ago. Ava…I don't know why she texted that. We talked a few times but never…" He shakes his head, frowning. "One of our mutual friends tried to set us up and when I found out she was a cheer-leader for my brother's team, I said it'd be best if we didn't go out. I didn't want any bad vibes if it didn't go well and then I'd be running into her at my brother's events." He makes a face. "But it backfired on me because *that* made her mad and now I still have to see her and her bitterness."

I feel a strange solidarity with Ava, knowing how she must feel. But it makes me entirely too happy to hear his explanation.

I play it cool and lift a shoulder. "Didn't seem to bother you much when you first got to Landmark Mountain and saw me here. Bad vibes if it didn't go well…"

"Yeah, I probably should've proceeded more carefully from the get-go there, right?" He lifts an eyebrow at me and I make a face.

I deserved that.

"I'd already had way more with you than I ever had with Ava," he says. "There's no comparison. I'd regretted not getting your number—seeing you was such a happy surprise."

"Really?" I whisper.

"You were haunting my dreams for weeks, I was so happy to find out who you were, where you were…I still can't believe you're here." He laughs and I shiver.

His hair is full of snow and he shakes a bunch of it off with his glove.

"Do you need to borrow my hat for a while? Is your head freezing?" I ask.

"No, I'm not going to put you through that torture when I should've worn a hat. It was practically balmy when I decided to come out here. What happened?"

"The sun went in and…I can't believe I didn't realize it was going to snow. I usually can tell and it didn't cross my mind. I've been a little…distracted. What if…what if they did forget us?" My voice cracks and I take a shaky breath. "I'm glad the dogs are safe with Sutton and Owen."

"Let's talk about them. Maybe it will help us not think about how cold we are if we think about Lucia's warm coat."

"She sheds like crazy. If I don't brush her twice a day, there are huge clumps of hair around the condo. She wasn't sure how she felt about the whole thing at first, but now she falls out every time I start brushing." I mimic her on her back, her paws up to her chest, Jamison's laugh like a reward. "I have to make her sit upright so I can get her back…otherwise, she'd have me brush her belly all day." I smile just thinking about them. "And Delgado gets cuter all the time. He lives for these chicken treats I give them. Lucia likes them, but Delgado *really* likes them. I've taught them both to sit and Lucia can shake…"

By now, we're cuddled up and shivering into each other.

"I'd love to see that. Are you teaching them any other tricks?"

I go into detail about the tricks I'm trying to teach them and how they end up tricking me by getting more treats out of me without even doing the tricks.

It's almost another hour before we hear the sound of a motor running. We sit up and look around to see Bo on a jet ski.

"I'm so sorry, you guys," he says. "So sorry. Harry thought the people in front of you were the last and I was helping Regg with something on the opposite side—sorry, you don't want to hear all my reasons. I'm just—I feel terrible about this and hope to God you don't fire me, boss…es…"

He waves his hand, jumping off and gathering his supplies. A few minutes later, Danny and Regg pull up and help Bo.

Danny apologizes profusely too, blaming himself for not coming to look for us when we didn't return our gear. Danny and Bo help Regg get all hooked up and then he goes to the closest pole and climbs up to the top, while Danny acts as the belayer below.

Once Regg has hooked all the appropriate things to each other, he starts the gradual slide down the rope toward us. He helps me into the sling, checking that everything is attached where it should be several times.

His eyes are full of mischief when he says, "It's been a while since you've held onto me like this."

"This'll be the last time too," I tell him.

If I wasn't relying on him to get me down and we weren't up so high, I'd strongly contemplate punching him.

I hear Jamison laughing and Regg smirks and rolls his eyes. I'm lowered slowly down and once my feet touch the ground, Danny detaches the hooks from me and the sling is sent back up with Regg. Bo wraps a warm blanket around me, and I watch as Jamison is lowered.

As happy as I am when we're off of that lift, it's strange to get on the back of Danny's jet ski while Jamison gets on the back of Bo's. We just endured something traumatic together and it doesn't feel right to just go our separate ways once it's over. Danny drops me off at my condo, lingering like he wants to come in. I'm sure Bo did the same for Jamison.

"I'm really sorry I didn't come looking when you guys didn't come back within the hour," he says again.

"It's okay. Just glad you came when you did."

He starts to say something else but stops when I lift my hand in a wave.

"I'm going to take the longest, hottest shower I can stand."

He nods, his smile still apologetic. "Let me know if you need anything, Scarlett," he says.

I nod and hurry inside, groaning when I remember my phone and the dogs are at Sutton's. I send him a quick message from my laptop, telling him what happened, and he says he'll bring them over in an hour or so.

Half an hour and a hot shower and my warmest pajamas later, that time out in the cold with Jamison doesn't seem so bad.

Not so bad at all.

CHAPTER TWENTY

LOVE CONNECTION

JAMISON

Since our crazy experience on the ski lift a few days ago, things have been much better between Scarlett and me.

I've still been keeping my distance, which has taken willpower I didn't know I had after what we went through together. But I've been busier than ever myself, getting ready for today.

Zac, Autumn, and Ivy are coming, and so is Pappy.

They're also bringing Magnus, their favorite contractor, and I've been talking to Lar's cousin, Steve, a local contractor whose work I love. Both Magnus and Steve say they like the idea of working together on a project of this size, so we'll see how it goes once they meet in person.

My parents have a wedding and an anniversary party to attend this weekend, so they'll be coming in a couple of weeks instead, but I wanted to get things moving forward with hotel plans and need Zac and Autumn here to do that. And I've missed my niece so bad I can hardly stand it.

They flew into Denver a little bit ago and I arranged for a helicopter to bring them the rest of the way. I would've given anything to have seen Ivy taking in that view, but there wasn't room for all of us. George, one of our charter pilots, said he would make sure everyone got to the lodge too. He's been a fan of Zac's since college days and I trust him—he's not scary fan material—so I agreed to it.

I've been looping around the lobby for the past half hour, excited for them to arrive.

"Are they here yet?" Vera asks, rushing in with one of the arrangements from Lorena's shop. "I want to go put this in their condo really quick before they get here."

"I haven't seen them. I think there's time." I laugh when she takes off jogging.

Now that I take a good look around, there are more people than usual hanging around the lobby today. I purposely told Zac to come on a day and time when it would be quieter because I didn't want him to be bombarded with fans. Looks like word has gotten out. It's like ninety percent of our staff, some who I would've sworn aren't even working today, have suddenly decided to congregate in the lobby at eleven on a Sunday morning.

Scarlett walks through the front door, the dogs on leashes next to her, looking like a movie star in her white yoga pants and fitted white ski jacket. Her hair is in a high ponytail and swishes across her chest, a dark splash against the white. I'm all about her short skirts and sexy blouses and the black pants that make her legs look a mile long, but I nearly lose my mind when she turns around and I see the back view of her in those white yoga pants.

Fuck me.

I try to school my face into nothingness and call my dick back into submission, but he's not going down without a fight.

Scarlett walks toward the offices and disappears for a few minutes and I hope for that old adage, *Out of sight, out of mind*, but no go. She's back in no time, without the dogs this time. And dammit, I was so dazed by her, I missed a chance to pet them.

It's weird how much I miss them.

And her.

She pauses when she sees Olivia from the gift shop and that bastard from ski rentals, Regg, who tried to pawn off his CBD oil…and okay, the guy who also got us off of the ski lift…

I just hate the way he looks at her. Probably a mirror to the way I look, gaping at her ass. I drag my hand across my face. Being this close to her and knowing what she looks like when she comes, what that body looks like underneath…it's a fucking torture I've never experienced.

"What's everyone doing here?" she asks, turning in a slow circle.

Kill me now. And go a little slower so I can get a better look…

"Doug? You're not on until tonight," she says. "What's going on?"

He flushes and glances back at me, hurriedly looking away, but not fast enough for Scarlett. She spots me next to the bookshelves and walks over. I pick up a book to subtly fan myself before she reaches me.

"What am I missing?" she says.

"I'm not sure. I just realized myself how many people are hanging around. Could it be because my family is coming?"

"Your brother Zac, the guy who recently won the Super Bowl?" She snorts. "*Yes,* pretty sure that's it. I don't think anyone will be obnoxious and hound him for autographs or anything, at least not the locals, but they're still a nosy bunch."

She lifts her hand.

"Hold on, I'll take care of it." She clears her throat. "Listen up, everyone. Guests of the hotel, I apologize. You can ignore me."

She smiles at an older gentleman who's been staying since Friday and he smiles back. She's so good with the guests.

"This announcement is for the Landmark Mountain staff. I know all of you are excited to meet our new co-owner, but I need all of you who aren't on the schedule today to clear out, and all of you who are to get back to work. Don't make me regret telling Jamison we'll be cool about his brother coming in. I'm sure you'll all get a chance to meet Zac in the next few days, but let's not overwhelm him by being here all at once when he's bringing his family for the first time, okay?"

The room starts clearing out immediately, by about eighty-five percent, when it's all said and done.

"Impressive. Thank you."

"Sure. I hope you have a nice visit," she says.

I don't tell her they're here for more than just a visit, because when she agreed to having Albert be our point person and to not be a part of the renovation discussions, I began to consciously keep her out of the loop.

Not because I ever wanted to. It's been hard every step of the way, not only because I like her way more than I should, but I also value her input and would love to have her be part of this process.

"Thanks," I'm in the middle of saying as the doors open and my family walks in.

Scarlett turns to see where my attention has gone just as my niece spots me and yells, "*Uncle Jamison!*" as she runs and leaps into my arms.

I hug her hard and then dance around the lobby while I'm still holding her. She laughs so hard, her little hands on my cheeks.

When I come to a stop, I set her carefully down, making sure she's not too dizzy before I let go of her. She looks up at me and signs, *YOU. I MISS.*

I point at her and sign the same thing back to her. She wraps her arms around my waist and squeezes. God, I love this girl. We text frequently and are on Zoom calls every other day, but it's not the same as seeing her in person.

Zac gets her attention and grins. "Are we going to get any attention over here or is it all about Ivy?" Zac says, signing as he speaks.

My niece has been deaf since she was three, and although it was challenging for our family to learn American Sign Language when we found out, we've become pretty fluent with signing in the past five years. Even Pappy, which is damn impressive for a man his age. For the most part, we still speak out loud while also signing, for the benefit of those who don't know the language, but we even do that when it's just us, so I guess it's really out of habit. Ivy speaks too and is shockingly good at lipreading, which can make people think she hears more than she does.

I hug my brother and reach out for Autumn to come in too. "It's so good to see you guys. Can't even tell you how good."

"I think he missed us," Autumn teases. "We've missed you too. Ivy's talked about this trip nonstop since she found out we were coming."

She makes a silly face at Ivy when she signs about her, and Ivy ups the silly-face ante and then does a little happy dance next to me.

"Where are Pappy and Magnus?" I look around, expecting to see Pappy chatting with someone at the front desk or maybe still outside.

But no Pappy, just Scarlett standing over there, watching me with an expression I haven't seen from her before. She flushes and turns back toward the counter.

"Scarlett, come meet my family." I motion for her to join us and she makes her way over, looking a bit shy.

"Pappy and George hit it off and George asked if he could bring him back in an hour. He wanted to show him the Sikorsky XR-4," Zac says before Scarlett reaches us. "Magnus wanted to see it too."

"Damn…I was planning to take Pappy over there to see that…"

Scarlett stops in front of Autumn and smiles warmly at her. "Hi, I'm Scarlett. There's been a lot of excitement around here about your visit."

"Oh, Scarlett. It's really nice to meet you," Autumn says. "How do you spell your name?" she asks, still signing the whole conversation to Ivy.

"S-C-A-R-L-E-T-T," she says.

Autumn nods and spells out the letters for Ivy, pointing at Scarlett. "Jamison has told us so much about you."

The color on her cheeks deepens, her eyes jumping to mine. I haven't said a word to my brother or sister-in-law about our night together, only that Scarlett is the grand-daughter of the owner and we work together, but I'm pretty sure Autumn will make a few assumptions based on Scarlett's expression right now. Sure enough, mischief is written all over Autumn's face when she directs her atten-tion back to me.

"And this is my niece, Ivy, the best little girl in the world," I say, grinning at Ivy as I sign the last part.

Scarlett watches my hands in fascination and then waves at Ivy, her smile wide. "Hi," she says. "I wish I knew sign language…"

Ivy smiles back. "Hi."

Scarlett's smile widens. "Beautiful family," she says, looking at Autumn again.

Autumn is thanking her when I pound on my brother's back. "And this is my big brother, Ballzac…I mean Zac… and Zac, this is Scarlett Landmark."

She laughs and Zac shakes her hand.

"Don't encourage him," he says, but he's laughing too.

"I have brothers, so it feels like I'm in a room with them right now," she says. "Nice to meet you, Zac."

"It's really nice to meet you. Jamison says you're the heart of this place…and that he wouldn't have been able to do this whole transition without you."

Scarlett looks at me in surprise.

"Well, he's settled in surprisingly fast," she says, and I'm returning her same look of surprise.

She leans in like she's confessing something.

"You better be glad you have a beautiful wife." Her eyes are flashing and I have no idea where she's going with this. "Because I just left Sunny Side and there's a wager going on in town that just keeps growing—who will capture the heart of Landmark Mountain Lodge's eligible bachelor?" She winks at Autumn, and I can tell my family already likes her because they all laugh and lean in like they're drawn to her. "I've put my money on Claudia."

"Who the fuck is Claudia?" I scowl.

I sign everything but the word *fuck*, but I know I've still blown it by the way Ivy's eyes grow wide. I make a funny face and she giggles.

"Don't tell me you've got a trail of broken hearts around here already, Little Squirt," Zac teases, and I cringe, knowing he's giving Scarlett more ammunition.

"I've never even met a Claudia," I mutter.

Zac laughs. "Notice he didn't say anything about the broken hearts…"

I glare at him and his laugh dies down when he sees I'm serious. He puts his hand on my shoulder and pulls me in.

"Best guy I know, right here," he says, backtracking. "He's apparently lost his sense of humor since becoming a resort owner, but it was bound to happen sometime…" He looks at me, his eyes apologetic despite his light tone.

I'm the one who's always stirring up shit with him, teasing him mercilessly and able to take it when he hands it out, so Zac is all kinds of lost right about now. I'm lost myself, playing catch up to why I care so much about what Scarlett thinks of me.

"Well, I just want to know who Claudia is," Autumn says. "If Jamison is finding a love connection, we've got to give our approval first. Me and Ivy, right?"

"Right," Ivy says, signing emphatically.

Scarlett shrugs and lifts her eyebrows. "Did you keep your receipt from Sunny Side this morning?" she asks me.

"Uh…maybe?"

She smirks and I dig in my back pocket, pulling out the receipt. The first thing I see is a phone number scrawled in huge numbers on the bottom, and above that says:

I love our talks. Call me sometime. Claudia

There's a heart by her name.

"*Oh*," I say, recognition dawning on me. "Is Claudia the waitress with dark hair and tiny hands?"

"Tiny hands?" Zac says, laughing.

Ivy cracks up both times we sign it.

"Yeah. We talk about how hard it is for her to carry everything," I add.

Everyone loses it at that, even Scarlett.

I'll be the brunt of every joke if it makes her laugh like that.

CHAPTER TWENTY-ONE

THE ODDS

SCARLETT

"Your family is wonderful."

We're walking back to our offices after showing Zac, Autumn, and Ivy their condo...which they went on about like it was a palace.

It was the proudest I've felt about this place in a long time. I'm as loyal as they come about the lodge, but I'm not oblivious to the ways it's showing its age.

I didn't expect to be part of the Ledgers' visit, especially with the way it's been between Jamison and me, peaceful truce or not, but I've already had so much fun with them. And Autumn invited me to go to The Pink Ski with them in an hour…that's part of the reason I waited to walk back to get the dogs with Jamison—I want to test out how he feels about me going. Things have been so much better since we were stuck on the ski lift together, but I wouldn't say they're footloose and fancy-free, as Grinny likes to say.

"Beautiful and so down to earth…" I add.

"They are, aren't they?" he says. "You'll love Pappy and my parents too. They're hilarious and so damn lovable."

"I had no idea Ivy was deaf. Now that I think about it…I've seen you use sign language before…I just didn't realize that's what it was until I saw you do one of the same signs. This…" I lift my fingers to my chin then extend them toward him.

"Thank you," he says. "That's the sign for *thank you*." He smiles and the easiness we've had between us…usually until I mess it up…is there.

I want to roll around in this warm feeling and never go back to his cool, blank looks, the steps of precaution I take, and the sadness that I feel to know he works hard to avoid me.

Granddad's voice rumbles around in my head. *You're putting too much time into this place, angel. Women are meant to keep the home fires burning, to fill up that home with children and so much love. Don't you want that?* He'd said that when I'd broken up with Danny, a guy he'd liked heaps more than Regg.

His words are a wet blanket that I try to shake off, for more reasons than I can delve into while walking next to Jamison.

"I wish I'd known about Ivy," I tell him. "I don't know any signs, and I hate not being able to say everything I want to say to her…"

His gaze is so warm when I look up at him, my heart tumbles down around my feet.

"That's really sweet, Scarlett. She likes you already and will be chatting up a storm by the end of the night, trust me. You can still say everything you want to say… she makes it so easy," he adds, shaking his head. "She's truly remarkable, the way she adapts to every situation. But one of us is always interpreting so she doesn't ever feel left out of the conversation."

He frowns. "I can't believe I didn't tell you. I really thought I had. She got meningitis at three and lost her hearing, and it was such a part of our every thought the first couple of years, trying to learn what we needed to make her life the best it could possibly be. To be the support system Zac needed…the guy is my hero. His career was taking off with the NFL, and he was a single dad, raising his little girl who suddenly needed something different than he'd ever imagined."

"Wait, Autumn's not Ivy's biological mom?" We stop in front of my office and I lean against the door.

"Don't get me started on Ivy's birth mom," he says, jaw clenching. "No, Zac met Autumn when Ivy was five and she's the best thing that ever happened to the two of them. As soon as she met Ivy, she started learning sign language, and she's better at it than all of us…well, not Zac, but right up there…"

His love for Autumn is more than apparent and now I can see why. I mean, she's obviously great, but wow.

"That's incredible. Well, show me a few—"

There's scratching on the door, and Jamison grins and cracks open my office door. Two snouts stick out and we both laugh.

"Scoot back, you two." They back up enough for us to walk in, and Jamison squats down to pet them.

"Ivy's going to love you guys," he says.

"I think Lucia will be gentle with her, don't you?"

"Oh yeah. Because you're just a love, aren't you?" He nuzzles into Lucia and she can't get enough. Meanwhile, Delgado is twirling himself dizzy and Jamison cracks up. "Stand still, little dude, and I'll pet you too."

Delgado finally calms enough to be petted and Jamison does for a few minutes before he stands up.

"I better go watch for Pappy and Magnus. They should be here any minute. Want to meet in the lobby at 6:45? We can all walk to the restaurant together..."

"Are you sure about me coming? I-I don't want to intrude on a family night..."

He studies me for a moment, those green eyes pulling me in. I keep expecting him to shift into polite business mode, the way he's been any time we've had to speak to each other lately, but his eyes never leave mine as he says, "I'd love for you to come."

Of course my mind goes to the dirtiest places even though that's not what he meant...

He smirks then and I'm left to wonder.

I call Grinny to tell her I won't be at dinner tonight. I've had several dinners with her since the one with Jamison, so it's okay that I miss this one.

"I want to hear all about it," she says, excited that I'm going out with the Ledgers.

"I'll call you later," I promise. "Or in the morning if it's too late."

I call my nephew, Owen, because he's the only one that will be truly bummed to miss seeing the dogs, but he's been invited to a friend's and my not going is the deciding factor for him to go to his friend's house.

"Just…make sure I still see you this week," he says. "I don't want Lucia and Delgado to forget me."

"Okay, it's a deal. But they won't forget you, buddy. You're impossible to forget."

"Love you, Auntie," he says.

"I love you, Owen."

I hurriedly get ready and let the dogs out one more time before I venture to the lobby. The entire group looks like they belong in a movie or a photo shoot for the world's most beautiful people.

I start smiling the moment I see Pappy, his face pure joy as Jamison lifts Ivy's hand and she does a pirouette. Pappy lifts both his hands near either side of his face and waves them and Ivy beams, doing another.

Jamison motions to Ivy when he sees me walking toward them and she turns and waves shyly.

I reach Autumn first and she smiles when she sees me. "Hi, Scarlett. I love your dress."

"Thank you. I love yours. Gorgeous and looks comfortable too."

"I never imagined I'd wear a short dress in the snow,

growing up in Charlotte, but Boston has warmed up my blood," she says, laughing.

Pappy walks over and Jamison puts his arm around his shoulder. "Scarlett, this is Pappy. Pappy, Scarlett Landmark."

Pappy gives me the sweetest smile, taking my hand in his and patting the top. He's the cutest old man I've ever seen, his shoulders stoop a little bit, but he's still so tall, like Zac and Jamison. His eyes light up with his smile, and seriously, the cutest.

"I am absolutely delighted to meet you, Scarlett Landmark," he says. He looks over at Jamison. "You didn't tell me she was such a beauty."

Jamison grins. "I knew you'd pick up on that soon enough."

I don't even need my coat after that, I'm so warmed up.

"Pappy, I'm warning you now, the ladies in town are going to swoon so hard over you," I tell him.

He throws his head back and lets out a loud laugh, and the rest of us can't help but join in. Zac's been signing our conversation to Ivy and she pretends to faint, which makes us laugh again.

"Ahh, there he is," Jamison says. "I have a feeling whoever doesn't try to snag Pappy will move on to Magnus."

A tall, blond, Viking-looking guy strolls up to the group, rounding out the model photo shoot with his striking looks, and chuckles. "Pappy definitely has more swagger than me." He holds out his hand when he notices me. "Hello. Magnus Evensen."

"Scarlett Landmark."

His eyes spark with recognition as he checks me out. Not in a gross way, but for sure appreciative. "Beautiful place. The architecture is incredible, amazing bones."

"On behalf of my grandfather and great-grandfather, thank you…" I say, feeling even more flushed with everyone's kindness and all the eyes on me.

He's the only one who hasn't signed while he's talking even though Zac has been signing what we're saying, so I'm surprised when Magnus looks at Ivy and his hand forms into a half circle as he drags it down his chest and looks like he's about to fall over. Ivy laughs and motions for all of us to follow her to the door.

Jamison is watching me when I look up, his expression impossible to read. God, I miss that guy I first met. How can my heart trip me up so much, making me build all these walls one second and then be willing to tear them down the next…over and over again? It's no wonder he's shut off all his feelings for me.

"Please teach me some words so I can talk to her," I say, my lips jutting out to the side in frustration.

His whole demeanor softens, and he puts his hand on my shoulder, his head tilting over to mine. Every nerve ending in my body jolts to life.

"I knew you were good people the moment I saw you, Scarlett Landmark."

He drops his hand and leans back and it's probably for the best because my heart was going to explode out of my chest if he kept touching me.

He points at me and then puts his open hand in front of his face and does a clockwise motion with his hand until his fingers and thumb meet near his chin. And the look on his face…I feel like Delgado after he does his nightly laps.

"What does that mean?" I ask, breathless.

"You." He points again. "Beautiful." And he repeats the second sign.

He smirks. "Sign that to Ivy and she'll teach you whatever you want to learn."

Oh, right. He was teaching me something to sign to Ivy.

"We better hustle. Looks like everyone's hungry tonight," he says.

I look around and the whole group is staring at Jamison and me. There's a tiny beat of silence and then Jamison and I are moving toward them. Autumn's eyes dance as she reaches out and takes my arm, looping hers through mine.

"Walk with me?" she says.

"Absolutely," I say, smiling back like I'm not a nervous wreck.

We step out into the cold and it feels so good to my poor fevered body, I breathe in the fresh air.

Zac and Pappy flank Jamison on either side, and it looks like they're all talking at once. Magnus walks slightly behind him, laughing at whatever they're saying and Ivy dances between the two groups, with Autumn and Zac both reminding her to be careful in case there are any slippery areas. The snow is mostly melted from the sidewalks, but they've been predicting a big snowstorm in a couple of days.

"I'm really happy you're joining us tonight," Autumn says. "I've been so busy with work, trying to wrap everything up before we made this trip, that I haven't gotten in on all the Zoom calls Zac and Ivy have had with Jamison. I haven't had a chance to grill him about everything going on here, and now I can see that I've missed out." She looks over at me and winks.

I smile and then when she keeps looking at me expectantly, I laugh. I like how comfortable she seems to be around me already, and I think I would be around her too, if I wasn't still in the Jamison lust fog.

"What do you mean?" I finally ask.

Her smile spreads across her face and she's truly so beautiful. And absolutely has a mischievous streak.

She leans in, her tone conspiratorial. "Well, if *I* were betting in the town's wager about my brother-in-law, and I won't since that would be an unfair advantage because I know him so well," she gives me a pointed look, "I'd put all my money on *you*."

CHAPTER TWENTY-TWO

CHEERS AND VISIONS

JAMISON

Zac and Pappy start in on me at the same time, one in either ear.

I knew I was asking for it the moment I signed that she's beautiful, but I wanted Magnus fucking Evensen to back the fuck off.

I saw the way he was looking at her.

I love the guy, but hell no.

And bottom line, I wanted to tell her she's beautiful. I would've signed a lot more, about what she's doing to me in that dress, how the way she wants to learn signs the moment she meets Ivy means everything to me...

"He's ignoring us, Pappy. Can you believe this guy?" Zac says, jabbing me in the gut. I yelp and they both cackle.

"Had I known you had a girl you were courting, I'd have come the very night you called," Pappy says under his breath.

I'd called him after the dinner at Grinny's, telling him things weren't going so well.

"It's not like that," I tell them. "And I'm glad you're here now. Are your eyes still feeling good? Seeing better and better?"

"Don't change the subject on us, you little whipper-snapper," Pappy says.

We all three laugh and then Zac starts in on me.

"What do you mean it's not like that? From where I was just standing, it very much looked like that," he says.

"From my angle too, yes, yes, very much, same," Pappy adds.

I laugh and slide my hand down my face before rubbing my hands together. "Oh, you guys. You wouldn't believe me if I told you. And I *cannot* tell you right now while she's within hearing distance."

"What if we talk in this tone right about here," Pappy says, going even softer.

I crack up and his eyes crinkle as he laughs back at me. "I'll say this much and that's it. She hates me for buying her family's resort..."

They wait for me to say more and when I don't, Zac frowns and shakes his head. "Try again, brother."

"That's what it all boils down to," I tell him. "We've barely spoken for the past two weeks. It's better than it was for a while there, but that's more recent. There's a lot of avoidance going on. I've tried to get her to stay on as general manager, and she's set on leaving when her contract is up in less than two months."

We reach the entrance of The Pink Ski and Magnus steps up to open the door for everyone. I turn around and Scarlett and Autumn are farther back than I thought.

"Well, it's good we came when we did," Pappy says.

"Slow your roll, Pappy. You know I've never needed help with the ladies. That was this guy here." I pound Zac's back.

Pappy and Zac both snort.

"No, you've never had trouble finding a willing *body*," Zac says. "That's something altogether different."

"That's right," Pappy says. "It's entirely different when you meet the one who sets your heart afire."

I groan and point at both of them. "Enough. Zip it. I might be off my game with her, but I'll figure it out. No meddling."

They both look like they want to say something else, but I do the sign for *zip it,* drilling them looks that show I mean it, and Zac sighs.

"Oh, all right," Pappy says. "For *now*."

"I never thought you'd be the boring, cantankerous, *humorless* one out of the two of us," Zac mutters.

"At least I'm the cute one," I tell him.

He shrugs. "Looks like I'm still the one getting laid more."

I crack up and so does he. "I'm glad you're here," I tell him.

Scarlett and Autumn reach us, and Scarlett looks a bit shell-shocked.

"Are you okay?" I ask her as we walk inside.

"Yeah," she says, nodding. She places her hands on her cheeks and takes a deep breath. "Yes."

The hostess takes us to a big round table near the back, and there are eyes on us the entire walk there. Several people greet Scarlett along the way, some smiling and waving at her from across the room. A few say hello to me too. And then they see Zac and it's obvious when recognition hits them.

Ivy sits between Autumn and me and Scarlett on the other side of me. Ivy immediately opens the package of crayons and starts coloring the bunnies snow skiing on her menu. While we're looking at our menus, a blonde petite lady comes to the table, bending to hug Scarlett from behind.

"Hi, Sally," Scarlett says. "I've been meaning to call you. It involves your dog food." She laughs. "But first… I'll let you do what you came over here to do. This is Sally, everyone. She's the owner of this amazing place."

"Aw, thank you, Scarlett. This girl is the sweetest," Sally says to the rest of us and then gives a little wave in greeting.

Ivy looks up from her coloring, so I start interpreting.

"Hi, everyone. Welcome to The Pink Ski. Jamison, it's always good to see you."

I smile at her. "Good to see you too, Sally." I introduce her to everyone and fumble a little bit with signing, glancing down at Ivy to make a face.

OUT PRACTICE, Ivy teases, signing it for me only.

We all laugh and I glance at Scarlett as I sign, "She's giving me grief for being out of practice."

"Guess you'll have to get your practice in while you teach *me*," she says.

Ivy's eyes light up when I sign that and she peers around me to grin at Scarlett, nodding excitedly.

"Sorry, Sally, we're easily distracted," Zac says. "Your restaurant is beautiful. Jamison has been bragging about your food."

Sally puts her hand on her heart and gushes. "It is such an honor to have you here. Big fan of yours. *Huge* fan. Congratulations on that Super Bowl win. It was an amazing game. And an amazing season."

"Thank you so much," Zac says, grinning. He's such a natural with all this.

"And your write-up in the last *Architectural Digest* was phenomenal," Sally tells Autumn. Her fingertips move to her lips and then spread wide. "Chef's kiss. Actually, I think I've seen every single one of your spreads in there over the years."

"Oh, wow, thank you," Autumn says. "I'm still pinching myself that this is my life."

Sally shakes her head, a bit starstruck. She snaps herself out of it though, before it can get weird, and I'm glad. I've had some intense experiences with Zac where the fans just couldn't keep it together and I'm glad that so far, it seems like the people in Landmark will be a nice balance.

"I'll get water right out. Shall I bring out a couple bottles of wine? A cocktail for anyone? Soft drink for you, sweetheart? Aren't you darling."

Ivy's eyes get wide when I sign *SODA* and she smiles sweetly at Sally.

"Thank you," she says.

She then signs *SODA* to Autumn, her eyebrows lifted.

"Sprite," Autumn says, fingerspelling it out.

Ivy pretends to pout, but she's grinning too hard to pull it off.

"Shirley Temple?" I ask, looking at Autumn for her mama go-ahead.

Ivy's nodding and doing *please* signs.

"Okay, okay," Autumn says, laughing. "Shirley Temple for her, and you know what? That actually sounds good to me too. No, wait…what is this drink with lychee?"

"Oh, that's our signature drink," Sally says. "It's delicious. Pink grapefruit, gin, lychee, and a hint of watermelon."

"Yes, please," Autumn sings.

Sally laughs and nods, waiting for the rest of us.

Scarlett pauses and then seems to make up her mind. "Lemon drop," she says.

Just hearing her say the words makes my mouth water. I think I groan out loud because she turns to look at me in shock.

"Haven't forgotten the way you tasted," I say under my breath, and she freezes. "Sweet lemons and heaven," my voice is husky as I look at my menu.

Pure sweetness. I think about it every time I look at her full lips, which is way too often.

Her hands tremble as she picks up her menu and I look up at her and smirk. Her mouth parts.

"Hope it's okay that I tell the truth," I say, lifting my shoulder.

She lifts a shoulder, mimicking me, but her eyes are glazed over as her eyes skate down to my mouth and stay there. Damn. Am I imagining this or is she drastically thawing?

Everyone else places their orders and I add a couple of appetizers to the list.

"I've been seeing you walk by with those adorable dogs," Sally says to Scarlett. "No word from anyone yet?"

"No, and at this point, I'm hoping with all my heart for none," Scarlett says.

Sally nods. "It's so easy to get attached, isn't it? I'll go drop this off in the kitchen and be back to take your order in a few minutes."

For the next hour and a half, I'm amazed by the way Scarlett handles all the questions my family throws at her. Questions about the resort, life in Landmark, her family… and she answers it all with humor and honesty. She also finds a way to quickly turn it around on everyone else, keeping her answers brief and then asking her own questions. The only time she falters at all is when Zac asks her what we can do to convince her to stay on at Landmark Mountain.

She swallows hard and takes her time answering, her expression more serious than it's been all night.

"My parents died when I was two and while I don't really remember them, there are things that stayed with me. My brothers took longer to bounce back, and I was too little to know that's what was going on, but when I was older and would hear the things they'd say or the way my grandparents would comfort them at different times when they were still grieving, I'd wish I had those memories of my parents even if it made me sad. But I didn't. I was told that I cried for my mom for months, but I didn't remember any of that. All I knew is I loved my life, and Grinny and Granddad and my brothers were everything." She smiles and takes a deep breath.

I want to take her hand, encourage her to say more, tell me everything, but I wait and she finally keeps talking.

"I loved our home, our land, our view, but what I loved most of all was the lodge. Some of my favorite memories were of us skiing on these mountains and decorating the trees around the lodge for Christmas. I wanted to hear the stories of my parents' wedding in front of the fireplace over and over again, or the way my mom didn't make it to the hospital with me and had to deliver me in…well, I'll keep the room number to myself in case that creeps you out."

We all laugh, spellbound by her words.

"Landmark Mountain became what I had of my parents and grandparents and brothers, and I felt like it was my calling to keep that alive forever."

She looks down at her hands and seems glad when they come around to pick up our dinner plates. She takes a sip of her drink and glances up to find all of us still watching her, waiting to hear the rest of her story.

"But it wasn't," she says, her face clouding over as she lifts a shoulder.

She smiles, and my heart breaks a little more.

"It's not…my calling," she adds. "The one person who saw everything I put into this place didn't think I had what it took…"

She takes another deep breath, tapping her fingers against the table. It takes everything in me not to take her hand and kiss each finger, to pull her against me, and try to take some of this pain from her.

"Anyway…I've realized my granddad was right. I have plenty of ideas, but I don't have what it takes to keep it going. And…lately, I've been thinking that sometimes the best way you can keep something alive is to pass it on to someone who can make it better than you ever could." She looks at me. "Maybe Jamison has told you that I haven't exactly been on board with this transition. The truth is, I've made things exceptionally difficult for him and…while I've tried to do better…"

She smiles and mouths *hopefully* to me, and I smile, happy to see some of the tension in her shoulders relax.

"Well, after today, meeting all of you and seeing what incredible people you all are, I want to let you know I'm not going to be that way anymore. I think the best thing I can do for the resort is to let it go into your capable hands."

She lifts her glass and numbly, I lift mine up, everyone else quickly following suit.

"To the Ledger family and the new Landmark Mountain Lodge and Ski Resort…or whatever you end up calling it…" She laughs and I rub the burn in my chest. "I'm wishing you huge success, a vision that far surpasses anything we've ever seen."

CHAPTER TWENTY-THREE

LACY PLANS

SCARLETT

You know you're with exceptional people when you can go as deep and melancholy as I went and no one makes you feel dumb or anything but heard and respected.

The desserts come and save me from myself. I don't know why I let myself go there. Damn lemon drops.

Everyone groans over the desserts, practically every bite someone saying how good it is, as they did with our dinner too, making them officially the funnest people I've ever eaten with.

Is funnest a word? I think so. If not, it should be.

My brothers love a good meal, but you don't hear them analyzing the flavors. The hint that they love it is that they barely look up from their food and then give a satisfied sigh as they push back from the table.

"Scarlett, I want to thank you for sharing your heart with us tonight," Pappy says, as our dessert plates are carried away. He starts out signing and then says, "Zac, can you take it? We all know my signing gets sloppy when I've got a beer in me."

Our laughter rings out through the restaurant, Pappy the loudest.

"It's such an honor to be here with you," he continues. "It wouldn't have been the same if these boys had taken this property without you being a part of it. And it's not up to me to change your mind about staying, but...well, I sure wish I could."

He laughs and my face heats from his praise.

"You might think you don't have what it takes, but I assure you, the love you expressed for your family and the business you helped build is more than most will ever understand, and that's why Landmark Mountain has always been a special place to our family. You can feel the love in its foundation." He grins and just when I don't think my heart can get any fuller, he says, "Your parents would be so proud of you. Your grandparents too. *I'm* proud of you and I just met you tonight!"

"Wait until you meet her grandma," Jamison says. "She's proud enough for twelve grandparents."

He looks at me with such affection, I feel panicky, like I might cry. I don't know how I've held off this long.

"Oh, I didn't realize she was still here," Pappy says.

Jamison reminds him of Gran meeting her, and Pappy shakes his head in shock.

"Well, I'll be. I do remember Gran talking about her." He looks at me. "She made such an impression on my wife. You come from good stock, child," he says, making me laugh all over again.

"She would *love* to meet all of you," I say.

Oh my goodness, would she love this family.

"I think I need a do-over dinner with her," Jamison says, lifting an eyebrow at me.

I make a face. "Yeah, she's mentioned that a few times, trust me. Name the night."

"How about we take her out to dinner while we're here?" Autumn says. "We could come back here or…you can tell us all the places we need to try." She leans in, her eyes bright. "I can't wait to show you what I have in mind for the lobby…I think you'll *die*…"

Jamison not so subtly shakes his head, and Autumn frowns.

"No?" she says.

"Uh…" He glances at me apologetically. "Scarlett's chosen to not be part of the renovation discussions—"

"Say no more, I get it. I'm so sorry I brought it up," Autumn says.

"Well, I didn't know you were working on lobby plans…or that you've had multiple spreads in *Architectural Digest*," I manage to get out somewhat calmly.

I'm practically frothing at the mouth to see what

Autumn thinks should be done to the lobby and kind of sick that I've been missing out.

"I'd love to see what you're thinking," I add.

"Autumn has such a phenomenal eye," Zac says proudly, and the rest of the table nods in agreement. "And she has this gift of expanding a person's vision so that it's even better than they imagined it could be."

"I paid him to say that," Autumn says, laughing. "Thank you, love."

"It's just the truth, Little Sass," Zac says, leaning over to kiss her.

I need to fan my face. They are so cute and so sexy, the wow factor combined with the love is intoxicating to be around.

"Get a room," Jamison coughs.

"Got one," Autumn says, shimmying her shoulders.

"Gotta get this girl home, Pappy," Zac says. "She's like you, a lightweight."

Pappy chuckles and everyone starts to stand. I look around, wondering when the bill came.

"I got it," Jamison says softly.

"Oh, thank you. I would've…thank you."

We walk through the restaurant and out the door, everyone else already ahead of us.

"Thanks for coming with us tonight…for everything," he says.

"I had such a good time. Thank you," I say softly and then I sign it, uncertain if he even sees it since it's dark outside now. The white lights on the structures and the cute streetlamps are enough light to guide our way.

He smiles. "You're a quick study."

"Your family is beautiful." I sign *beautiful* too and the way he looks at me sends flutters throughout my chest.

He takes a step closer and leans into my ear, and I stop walking, certain my shaky knees won't hold me up.

"Your beauty is a revelation every time I see you. And it's not just the way you look," his lips brush against my ear and I feel them lift with his smile, "although it is a constant challenge for me to even think straight when I'm near you. It's everything about you. Tonight, the way you opened up, it meant so much. Made me want to be more open myself."

His smile is tentative when he takes a step back. I reach out and take his hand, squeezing it once before letting it go. We start walking again.

"I'm sorry I've been such a bear to work with. My grandpa used to call me Little Bear because I can be pretty blockheaded."

"Are you kidding?" He shakes his head. "You've kept me on my toes. If this has been your bear, I can take it…as long as we can still talk like this. The hardest part of this has been losing that. We were able to…talk from the very beginning."

He looks over at me and I'm glad for the dim light so he can't see me flushing and breathing heavier.

"I've missed talking to you," I admit. "I know we haven't known each other long, so sometimes it feels like it doesn't make sense, but…"

"We covered a lot of ground in a short amount of time," he finishes.

"Yeah," I say, laughing.

"Can I ask you something?"

"Of course."

"Besides the resort and Landmark…and your family, what excites you?"

"Like hobbies?"

"Hobbies…passions."

I will not think of him naked, I repeat a few times in my head.

"Okay, I'm afraid to even say it out loud, and I've tried to keep it all—" I press on my heart and look over at him. He stops walking and turns to face me.

"What?" he asks, all focus on me.

"I'm kind of obsessed with Lucia and Delgado. And now that a little time has passed with no one claiming them, I'm allowing myself to hope…which is absolutely terrifying because I could still lose them. And I just really…love them." I finish in a whisper.

"You've lost a lot that you love, haven't you?" he says it simply, without pity, but the compassion is still there.

"I guess I have," I admit.

"It's okay to let yourself love them. The odds are looking better and better that no one will claim them, but even if they did…would you regret this time with them?"

"No. But I'd be really, really sad."

He smiles. "I would be too."

He takes a step forward and then wraps his arms around me, hugging me. I lean my head against his solid chest and feel his warmth, and it's the best feeling I've ever had. Peace courses through me, my chest filling with calm assurance that everything will be okay.

When we hear laughter in the distance, we break apart, looking toward his family. They're almost to the lodge.

I rub my hands together, chilly now that I'm not against his heat.

"Let's get you inside," he says. "Although I love this. I don't want you to stop talking to me."

"I won't," I tell him.

"What do you like to do around here? Do you ever take time off?"

"Rarely. But I love to ski…hike. I love to visit my brothers and take my nephew ice skating. I love to sew…"

I hear his quick intake of breath and look over at him. He looks at me sheepishly.

"You have a real gift at sewing," he says, his voice hoarse. "It's hard to not sound like a fucking asshole whose head is only in the gutter while also confessing that I *am* a fucking asshole whose head is in the gutter about that pink lacy thing I saw you in…"

I laugh. "I'm not sure that made any sense."

"I know. See? That pink thing knocked me senseless."

I crack up and try to ignore the pulsing between my legs. I take a deep breath and try to play it cool. "I've been thinking about pursuing something with my lingerie," I admit. "It would be such a different direction than how I saw myself spending my future, but maybe that's okay."

"I have an idea." He sounds excited and starts talking faster. "There's room for a little shop near the spa, that little alcove right before. The seating area there is unnecessary if we expand the lobby, and those rooms used for storage near there would be such a great space if we added windows. The storage could be added elsewhere—there are so many great options to making more effective use of space."

We've almost reached the others, but I put my hand on his arm and stop him. "You'd be okay with that? Me opening a boutique in the resort?"

He looks at me as if he's unsure if he's overstepped, and I feel bad for the roller coaster I've put him on.

"If that's not something you're interested in, don't give it another thought."

"You've only seen one thing I've made…"

"It made quite an impression," he says, his eyes dropping to my mouth.

CHAPTER TWENTY-FOUR

UNEXPECTED TIES

JAMISON

I should be dragging when I get to the office the next morning.

I barely slept. It was hard to tear myself away from Scarlett last night when it felt like something had finally shifted between us. Even harder to say goodnight without kissing her face off, but I still wasn't 100% sure she was up for that with me ever again and I didn't want to rock our newly steady boat, and Ivy was waiting patiently for me to read her a few bedtime stories and tuck her in.

Zac came back to my place after we hung out with Autumn for a little while, and then he and Pappy and Magnus wouldn't stop grilling me until I told them the whole story about the night I met Scarlett.

Well, I didn't tell them *everything*.

But enough for them to get the gist of why it's been so complicated between us...and enough for them to think I need to, in each of their words:

Make a move. You're Jamison freakin' Ledger. When have you ever been hesitant about anything? (Zac)

Just kiss her. If she kisses you back, you'll know she's still into you. (Magnus)

Woo her, my boy. It's time to woo. (Pappy)

They're all sleeping in this morning, and when they're up, we'll start going deep with the renovation plans. I got a little bit ahead with everything else, knowing I'd be busy once everyone got here and could've slept in myself, but I couldn't wait to see Scarlett. I'm about to go to her office —I have to know if she'll be back in her shell today or if it will be the Scarlett from last night—when there's a knock on my door.

"Come in."

Scarlett steps inside and the air whooshes out of my chest. First of all, she looks like a goddamn goddess. Her dark hair is down and straighter than usual, falling over a black double-breasted jacket and short black skirt.

And she's not wearing a shirt underneath the jacket.

It's not obscenely low—she's the consummate professional and wouldn't do that at work—but it's the perfect tease to make me lose my fucking mind.

The best part? She's smiling at me.

"Scarlett." Her name sounds like a warning. Didn't mean for it to, but holy fuck.

She shuts the door and leans against it, her chest rising and falling, the peeks of cleavage whispering my name. I run my hand through my hair and breathe deeply, willing my dick to chill.

No go.

"This is hard," she says finally.

I glance down, thinking she's talking about my cock, but I think my suit jacket is covering it for the most part.

"What is?" I ask, my whole body rigid.

"I don't know how to act around you." She laughs and it dies quickly.

She clasps her hands together and I have to force my eyes to stay on hers. *Don't drift.*

"There are times it's so easy, but most of the time, with us being so…um, *intimate*…from the beginning…it's—" She licks her lips and I think I groan.

Her eyes widen and she bites her bottom lip like she's nervous.

"And I…" She laughs again. "I don't think I've ever found it so difficult to get anything out, but I wanted to try after we had such a good night last—"

She drops her head in her hands, her hair all swooshing forward.

"Ughhhh," she says, groaning, her voice muffled. "I'm sorry I've been so mad. I haven't been fair to you at all. I believed you when you say you didn't know it was me when we met and I never really hated you at all and—"

"Scarlett?" I say, moving to stand in front of her.

She peeks through one of her hands and I move her

fingers enough to expose one eye, as her other hand falls to the side.

Her scent is intoxicating and a flood of too many things to identify, one minute I think it's cotton candy and lemons, the next peach or jasmine.

I tilt her chin up and we stare at each other, my clock's *tick, tick, tick*, the only sound in the room.

"This is hard for me too," I tell her. "And completely new. I...don't know what to do with all these feelings and also be respectful of what you want."

"What do you want?" she asks.

"I want you." The words rush out of me and the act of saying them out loud underlines them in a way I haven't been able to fully admit even to myself before now.

"I want you too," she whispers.

We crash into each other, our lips frantic. Her hands go in my hair and mine are on her face, her hair, down her back, and then on her waist, where I tug her as close as I can get.

She moans into my mouth, her soft, full lips and sweet tongue my decimation.

Our kiss is savage, all the pent-up tension from the past few weeks taking control, our bodies remembering all the favorite hot spots from our night together.

I thrust against her and she moans, her head falling back and my hand slides between us, cupping her between her legs. She looks at me, eyes glazed over, and I drop my hand, taking a step back, breathing hard.

"We can go slow. I don't want you to regret any of this later," I tell her, my chest heaving.

"I don't think we're capable of slow," she says. "Part of this *frustration* has been that my body remembers how

you make me feel and…trying to shut that off has been—"
She shakes her head, eyes wild.

I loosen my tie and unbutton the top buttons of my
shirt before undoing the knot and taking my tie off.

"Go sit on my desk," I tell her.

So much for wooing. I'll have to do that later. We've
gone about this backwards from day one.

Her eyes widen, but she doesn't waste time moving
into place. She sits, back-to-back with my laptop, and after
I lock my office door, I stalk toward her, moving her hands
behind her back. She gasps when I wrap my tie around her
wrists and knot it.

I smirk like the devil I'm feeling. "You want me to
stop, just say the word. Do you have the word?"

"No, I won't need a word," she says, her voice raspy.

I lean in, my nose against her neck, inhaling her before
lifting up to kiss her, this time so slow that she starts
squirming.

"How much time do you have?" I whisper.

"A-an hour before my first meeting. And my friend
April is walking the dogs until around that time too."

"Good."

"I want to touch you," she whimpers.

"Next time." I kiss down her jawline and down her
neck, stopping to bury my face in the dip that was driving
me crazy just a few minutes ago.

"You're killing me," I say against her skin.

Undoing her buttons one at a time, I open her jacket
slowly and slide it off her shoulders, and then I step back
so I can fully appreciate the picture she's creating. I'll
never look at this desk the same way again.

My head explodes with every swear word I know, so it's a fucking miracle that what comes out is, "Stunning."

"You haven't seen the best part," she says, smirking.

"Let's see," I say, lifting her off of my desk by the waist.

When her feet are firmly on the ground, I unzip her skirt and glide it down her hips, where it then drops to the floor.

"Fuck me," I whisper, walking around to see her from every angle. "I—speechless. What *is* this?"

"You really want a description right now?" She giggles.

"No, but I'm trying to prove I can take it slow," I tell her. "It's torture, but I'm trying."

"How about *you* describe it to *me*," she says, her voice turning into pure seduction.

"I've changed my mind about taking our time," I tease.

"Nuh-uh. Start talking."

I slide my hand down my jaw. "Okay. I can see through that black material, which I love, but then you've covered the best parts, your perfect pink nipples and that sweet pink pussy—"

I glance at her and her lips have parted, her eyes gleaming with lust, but she lifts an eyebrow for me to keep going.

I groan. "With a pink…flower…section—"

"Embroidered floral panel—" she corrects.

"Embroidered floral panel," I groan again, which just makes her laugh and sit up straighter, her nipples standing at attention under the pretty flowers.

"You love torturing me," I growl.

"I do." Her eyes are all lit up and those lips, her teeth stretch over her bottom lip, tugging slowly.

She leans forward. "Keep going. And lose the pants."

I lift an eyebrow and undo my belt buckle, letting it crack as I slide it off.

"Uh…this embroidered floral panel—there should be a sexier word for that—around the low…part covers your nipples but not how fucking full your tits are, which was generous of you, thank you. And then that goes down the center, farther down than I wish it would."

I undo the top of my pants and she watches my every move.

"But this part here at your hips is a really nice touch…"

"A ruffle trim," she whispers.

"Right…pretty. But then the back is even better because…well, I like these little ribbons that you do, but the best part is that the pink embroidered shit isn't covering anything up back here. It's all that black sheer stuff and I can see every bit of that glorious ass."

She starts laughing when I say embroidered shit, and I tug her against me, finally touching her again.

"Okay, that was slow enough," I growl.

"You're still wearing your pants," she cries.

"Patience."

She scowls and I grin, loving every second of this. I undo the ties in the back and slide it off of her before I set her back on the desk.

"Even better," I whisper. "God, you're beautiful."

When I lower my knees to the ground, her eyes widen in surprise, the anticipation in her eyes making me so hard I hurt.

I bury my face between her legs and inhale, getting my own rush. My first taste of her sends her buckling toward me and I don't go easy on her. I do several long swipes against her slit and dip inside, needing the taste of her and already craving more.

I spread her legs wider and flick her clit with the tip of my tongue over and over until she's whimpering my name, her sounds nearly making me lose my mind. When I wrap my lips around that spot and suck, her head falls back and she presses into me, greedy.

I give her what she wants and thrust a finger inside, one to start since my fingers are big, and then two when she takes it all, so wet she's dripping. I slide in and out, in and out, and she convulses against me in no time, her flutters against my fingers and tongue making my cock twitch in my pants.

"I want to lick you all day," I tell her, wiping my mouth with my free hand. "Keep you perched right here and see all the ways I can make you come with my tongue and fingers alone."

Her eyes squeeze shut as she clamps down around my fingers again. I press down on her clit with my thumb and she falls apart again.

"Jamison," she whimpers. "Get in me, *now*. Please. I don't want to go slow anymore."

"I don't have the heart to tell you that wasn't very slow," I tell her, kissing my way up her body.

"Show-off," she says.

I laugh against her stomach and she shivers. When I slowly withdraw my fingers from her, I lick them clean and wrap my tongue around her nipple, running my hands down her arms to warm her up.

"You cold?" I ask.

"Yes, get inside and warm me up," she says.

She squirms, her chest arching into me.

"Oh, I've missed you so much," I tell her. "How could one night with you completely wreck me for anyone else?"

Her eyes flare with surprise and we stare at each other.

"I mean it," I tell her. "You've ruined me for anyone else."

I untie the knot around her wrists because I want to feel her hands on me and all attempts at making this last longer are going out the window. I'll go slow later…in a bed.

I grab a condom out of my wallet and she unzips my pants, shoving them down. Her silky hair hits my chest as she takes the condom from me and slides it on, her hands on me making me hiss.

"Turn around and bend over," I tell her.

Her feet drop to the floor, and she turns to face my desk, her eyes daring as she looks at me over her shoulder. I slide my hands over her full cheeks, squeezing each side in my hand.

"This ass has threatened to undo me many, many times. You have no idea." I move one hand to her hip and take her hair in my fist. "Sure you don't want a word?"

"I won't want you to stop. I can take whatever you give me," she says. "I already want more."

I curse as I plunge into her with one long thrust. She's so wet there's little resistance, more of her giving way around me as I keep pushing inside, but she's still so tight, her walls clamping down on me.

"Best thing I've ever felt," I say, watching as I pull out of her slowly and drive back in.

"Mmm, so full," she moans. "I've missed you too, Jamison. I've missed you so much. Don't stop. Please don't stop."

She lays flat against the desk, the angle sending me even deeper, and I pick up the pace, my balls slapping against her clit. When she starts tightening against me, she leans up on her elbows and meets my thrusts, her head turning to look at me.

"If you could see the way you look right now, taking me, and those eyes. Fuck, Scarlett," I moan, wishing I could stretch this out, but too damn close.

She flutters around me, just a hint of it at first and then her walls are squeezing me like a vise.

"Come with me," she cries out.

My arms and legs start tingling and I jerk violently inside her, which seems to take her pleasure to another level. I thrust deeper, the sensation indescribable and lasting forever.

I think I might blackout for a second and then I see fucking stars.

I lean my chest against her back, my hands on her perfect tits, my lips on her ear and in her hair, kissing her. Her hands clutch mine against her, holding on as we try to catch our breath together.

I'm still hard and ready to go again, especially when she angles her head and kisses me while I'm still deep inside her.

A knock on the door has reality crashing in quickly.

CHAPTER TWENTY-FIVE

DOWNSIDE

SCARLETT

My body is limp, all the endorphins I've experienced in this little office visit knocking me out.

Wow.

Every time with Jamison has been mind-blowing, but that was—

I jump when I hear a knock on the door. Jamison's

hand caresses my hip, lulling me back into that drowsy peaceful place.

"Was that—" I whisper. "How loud were we?"

"Yeah, someone's at the door. It's locked. Maybe they'll go away," he whispers. "I think we might've been…loud enough." He chuckles.

We both whimper at the way he slips out of me slightly.

"Noooo," he whispers, his lips lifting against my neck. "I'm not ready. I now know the downside of office sex."

"You've never—?" I start to ask but stop myself.

I don't think I want to know.

"No. Have you?"

"No. But I'm surprised. I would've thought a guy like you, hot, successful…in a place like Boston…this kind of thing would be the norm."

There's another knock, making me jump again. I'm so lost in him that I've been having a conversation with him *still inside me while someone waits to see him.*

Who am I?

I lean up and he puts his hands on my hips, sliding the rest of the way out. The ache where he's been feels so good, but I wasn't ready for it to end.

He disposes of the condom and hands me my things, holding up the lacy teddy last, like he wants to help me get it back on.

"We'll never get out of here if you touch me right now," I hiss, snatching it out of his hands.

But I start laughing and clamp my hand over my mouth, certain that whoever is out there will know exactly what's going on if they're still there.

I try to put my feet in the sheer material, but I'm not

steady enough and keep missing, which just sends me into another fit. The more I try to stop, the harder I laugh. And Jamison is not helping. He's laughing right along with me, laughing harder when there are tears running down my cheeks.

"Ow," I whimper, clutching my stomach and trying my hardest not to lose it again.

I wipe my face and step into my skirt, giving up on the teddy, and barely manage to get my jacket on, fingers fumbling as I try to button it up quickly.

"I can't decide which is better," he says. "Knowing you're naked under that or knowing you were wearing this."

He waves the teddy in front of him and then holds it to his face, inhaling. "Mmm. You smell so good. Taste so good. I can't wait for more."

I fan my face, embarrassment and awe at him being so…into…*that* sending a flash of heat over my face and neck. I've only had one other experience with oral sex… Danny did it once and it was so awkward. I didn't come and it never happened again. A little blow to the self-confidence of everyone involved.

But Jamison…he's got skills.

The Orgasm Whisperer indeed.

"Come back later," Jamison yells, and then yelps when I swat his arm. His laugh fills the room, not bothering to be quiet any longer. "I don't think I can let you go just yet."

"Shush, I've gotta go. Everyone's gonna know exactly what we're doing in here."

"I guess that would put an end to the wager." He lifts a broad shoulder.

I take a moment to fully appreciate him in the light of

day. Muscled perfection. He sees me checking him out and his smirk is on full display. All of the watchful reservations from the past few weeks wiped away.

"Oh, you're all cocky now that we've done this, I see." I've barely stopped laughing, so my voice is hoarse and I can't stop smiling, so it doesn't matter what I say, he's not threatened at all.

"I'm feeling pretty good about things, yes," he says. "*Really* good." He steps into his pants and zips them up and walks over to me, his hands on my hips. "Are you okay? No second thoughts?"

"Better than okay," I tell him, smiling shyly. "This is our first real morning after…I like it so much more than waking up alone."

He leans his forehead against mine. "It's so much better than leaving you in my bed, I can't even begin to tell you. It physically hurt to walk out of that room with you there."

Emotion wars within me. A see-saw of contradictions.

I wish I'd known who he was from that very first night.

I'm glad that night was exactly how it was.

I wish I'd not wasted a second with him when he got here.

And I know that it had to go exactly the way it has.

"What are you thinking?" he asks.

But I haven't *completely* changed overnight. So much about this is already unlike me. Sex at work? With a guy that I have no idea if I'll even see again in a few months?

I've said more than I've ever said to anyone, opened up in ways I wasn't sure I could, and while that may not seem like much more than baby steps, to me, it's everything…and more than a little unsettling.

"I'm happy," I tell him, smiling.

I can be happy and unsettled at the same time.

He smiles and kisses me, and I'm willing to work through all my mess, including the unknown, to have whatever this is with him right now.

―――――――

When I open the door to head back to my office, Jamison right behind me, trying to convince me to stay a little longer since it's still early, I'm shocked to see Danny, of all people. He's leaning against the wall, arms folded, and glaring in our general direction.

"Danny? Hey. What's up? What are you doing here?" I ask, getting antsy the longer he doesn't say anything.

I haven't seen much of him since Jamison got here— come to think of it, maybe only that one day with Holly and when Jamison and I got stuck on the ski lift. He did call again after that and I never called him back…which was rude.

I should be a better friend to him.

He doesn't look happy with me. Or happy, period.

He pushes away from the wall. "I'm giving my two weeks' notice," he says.

"*Really?*" I ask, shocked. "You've always loved your job."

He stares over my shoulder at Jamison. "I'll send an email with my official resignation by tonight."

"Okay," Jamison says. "I'm sorry to see you go. I enjoyed the times we spoke, thought you had good ideas to implement on the skiing side of things. Are you sure this is what you want?"

He lowers his chin once, acknowledging what Jamison said. "I'm sure, yes. It's time." And then he points at Jamison, his next words rushing out. "I love this place. See that you give it the love and attention it deserves."

He flashes one last look at me, and I stare after him as he stalks away.

"Oh," I whisper, my face falling along with my heart. "That's such a loss."

I glance at Jamison and he's watching my reaction.

"Danny's an excellent employee, and it's hard to find new hires that are full-timers."

"I'm more worried about you," he says simply. "Are *you* okay?"

"I'm surprised and…really sad to see him go. I wish I knew why he was leaving, but…I'm okay. That was weird. He wasn't acting himself at all."

"I think maybe he heard us," he says, crinkling his face. "I'm sorry about the position that puts you in. He clearly has feelings for you and doesn't like this," he says, pointing between the two of us.

"*No*…you think he's the one who was out here and just never walked away?" I hold my hand across my forehead. "Oh, that's so awkward. But no…he doesn't have feelings for me like that." I shake my head. "I-we've been friends for a long time. I don't know what's going on with him, but I'll try to find out."

"Were you and Danny ever—"

"Yes. He was my first boyfriend. Half the time, I canceled on him. He hated how much I worked and how consumed I was with the resort, even though he's worked here since he was sixteen. After we tried dating for a while, we decided we were best as friends." I shrug.

"*You* decided," Jamison says.

I tilt my head, nodding eventually. "Yeah, I guess it was more me in the beginning."

"How do you have no idea that Danny is in love with you? I saw him with you for two seconds and knew, and I'm a guy. I'm supposed to be the oblivious one," he says, laughing.

"Ugh, you sound like Holly." I shake my head.

And Granddad, but I keep that to myself.

I don't think Granddad really thought Danny was in love with me as much as he thought Danny would be a nice, safe option for me. He was so ready to marry me off that I always thought he was exaggerating Danny's feelings to get me to reconsider dating him.

"Oh, Holly thinks he's in love with you too?" He smirks. "Interesting."

I press my lips together. "I'm going to work now. *Someone* has distracted me long enough."

"I think your work ethic is sexy," he says as I walk down the hall. "Your sway is too," he adds, softer.

I turn and stare at him with wide eyes over my shoulder, trying to shush him again. "Do you want the whole town to know about us before noon?" I say under my breath.

He lifts both hands, palms up. "Why not? Nothing could make me happier actually. This...you and me...it feels pretty fucking awesome."

I press my finger to my lips, but I'm grinning when I turn around and go into my office. I shut the door and lean against it, my hand against my chest as I inhale and exhale a huge cleansing breath.

We do feel pretty fucking awesome.

CHAPTER TWENTY-SIX

LIT

JAMISON

My family wanders down not long after Scarlett leaves my office.

One look at me and Zac pulls me aside right after I've shown everyone where to get coffee and our stash of good snacks.

"You look like a fucking Christmas tree all lit up," Zac says.

I look back to see if anyone's listening. Pappy and Magnus are by the coffee, and Autumn and Ivy are digging into the pastries from Happy Cow.

"I can take you to get something healthier," I call out, but Autumn shakes her head.

"This is perfect. And you know we'll be ready for something else in about an hour and a half anyway." She laughs.

"Hey, spill. You asked her out, didn't you?" Zac smirks.

That would be the normal progression, yes, but…damn.

"Oh, I did a lot more than that," I say under my breath.

He stares at me and laughs, squeezing my shoulder. "Oh shit. You didn't waste any time, did you? I hope that doesn't backfire on you, man."

I sag against him. "Yeah, I had all these good intentions and they all went out the window when she showed up at my office in a—it wouldn't have mattered what she was wearing…I lost my mind."

Autumn turns around and sees us whispering, and her eyes narrow. "What are you guys up to?"

"Not a thing," I say, lying through my teeth and she knows it.

I look at Zac and now he's looking all excited.

"Relax," I tell him. "You look like the fucking Joker right now."

He shakes his head. "You're the one who can't stop smiling."

I growl at him and he just keeps laughing.

"Okay," I say louder, and Autumn and Pappy wander over. "First up, I thought we could take Ivy to LM Kid

Zone and see if she wants to spend any time there. There's no pressure if she'd rather be with us...and I definitely hope she doesn't want to spend *all* her time there."

I grin when she walks over and puts her arms around my waist for a hug. Zac catches her up on what we're talking about.

"Day before yesterday I hired that interpreter I told you about, the girl from Denver," I continue. "Lili. She's excited about the opportunity and when we don't have guests who need an interpreter, she'll teach ASL classes to anyone who wants to learn. Sidenote—she seems great with marketing too, so I think she'll be a huge asset to the resort." I check my watch. "She should be in Kid Zone as we speak if we want to head over there and meet her."

Ivy looks hesitant, and I sign again that she doesn't have to stay in there unless she really wants to.

She decides she wants to check it out before she decides, so everyone but Magnus goes to that area of the lodge. Magnus decides to do a little exploring of his own.

LM Kid Zone is hopping. There are kids coloring at the round tables, two of the staff leading kids in a dance, which gets Ivy's attention, and I point toward the back window, and a few kids are out there building snowmen and one is even working on a snow cave. Lili is out there and when she sees me, she walks over, signing as she speaks.

"Hi, I'm Lili. L-I-L-I," she says as she fingerspells it and then shows us her name sign, laughing. She makes the letter *L* sign with both hands and then uses them for the *talkative* sign. "Yeah, I'm chatty," she adds.

We introduce her to Ivy first and then everyone else,

and Ivy seems to get comfortable quickly, answering Lili's questions and laughing at her reactions.

When Autumn asks Ivy if she'd like to stay for a while, she nods shyly and Lili does the sign for *applause,* making all of us smile. I was really excited when I saw Lili's resume and had a good feeling about her when she interviewed, so seeing Ivy respond to her so quickly just cements that feeling.

Ivy hugs all of us and she and Autumn go with Lili to check in and exchange all the info they need, while Zac, Pappy, and I walk back to the hallway outside Kid Zone. Pappy turns to say something to me and his eyes brighten.

"There's the woman of the hour," he says. "Good morning. Or is it noon yet? My clock is off."

I turn in a hurry when I hear Scarlett's laugh, already smiling before she even looks my way. When she does, her cheeks flush and her eyes dart away shyly.

Oh Scarlett, now that I know we are, if not on the same page, at least in the same manual, there is no limit to the fun we're going to have.

"Good morning," she says sweetly.

"Easy, boy," Zac mutters under his breath. "I've never seen eager on you before. Not about a girl. You look a little deranged."

"Shut up," I say between my teeth.

"Hey, Scarlett. Good to see you," Zac says.

"Is Ivy trying Kid Zone?" she asks.

"Yes, and I think Lili will be such a great fit. Have you met her yet?"

Her brows crease in the center. "Lili? I don't believe I know her…"

"I hired her a couple of days ago. She's an ASL interpreter and also ECE certified. I'm really excited to have her on the team."

An odd expression flits across her face and is gone in the next second. She nods slightly and her hands clasp in front of her.

"We were just getting Ivy checked in and then we're tackling the plans…" I add.

"I-I was wondering if I could sit in on that," she says, still shy.

I want to tuck her next to me and kiss away any inhibitions she has, do away with any lingering reservations she has about being a part of Landmark Mountain's future.

"We would love that," I tell her.

"One hundred percent," Zac says. "We want any input you have."

Autumn walks out, her cheeks flushed. "Sorry to make you wait. They're playing the kids' version of Lizzo," she says, eyes wide. "I can't let that go without dancing."

Zac pulls her close, kissing her. "I hate that I missed that," he says in his disgusting, lovey voice.

"Okay, Ballzac, rein it in. Look," I point at the window where some of the kids have their faces up to the glass watching, "you've got company."

I make a face at the kids like it grosses me out, and some cover their mouths laughing, but I love how Autumn has my brother wrapped around her little finger.

"I better get moving," I tell them. "Steve will be here in a few minutes if he's not already."

We walk back to my office and Magnus and Steve are already talking outside my door like old friends. Steve says hi to Scarlett and I introduce him to Zac and Autumn and turn on the big screen, opening the files Autumn sent.

Steve helped the process along by measuring everything last week.

"These are just the beginning stages," Autumn says, "and now that I'm here, I can already see things I'd change...like this area here by the bookcases," she says, standing up to point at the shelves to the right of the entrance. "And I'd like to see more of the rooms, if they open up while I'm here, but this is a start."

"I love the addition of windows along that side wall," Scarlett says. "And that little rounded edition. Looks like a snow globe..."

"Yes," Autumn says, excitedly. "That's what I was thinking too. And whenever Jamison is ready, if you click on the next, you can see the legacy wall."

"Legacy wall?" Scarlett echoes quietly.

Autumn nods. "I love seeing the history of a place and pictures throughout long spans of time, showing what's stayed the same and what's changed. I was thinking along this wall next to the front desk, we could showcase the history of Landmark Mountain Lodge, spotlights on beautifully framed photographs to make it a showstopper."

I glance at Scarlett as discreetly as I can and her eyes are glassy. She looks down quickly when she sees me watching, and I click to the next 3-D rendering, which is a detailed view of updated decor.

"I thought this married the old and the new," Autumn continues. "Taking this wall out here opens everything up, a light fixture that isn't as heavy but still a statement piece in itself would add a big change with little effort...and the coziest, softest couches and chairs that you sink into and never want to get up."

"I like the sound of that," Pappy says, laughing.

"Add hot tubs here and here, maybe here," she says, pointing at various spots on the next plan. "I don't know what the roof situation is over here, on the southeast corner of the lodge, but an outdoor bar and hot tubs would be amazing there. Or just an outdoor bar and cozy seating. Heat lamps going through the colder months."

"Love that," Zac says.

"And I don't know how you feel about this, but... Magnus and I were talking about this a little bit on the flight over. I thought if we opened up the look of the lobby with more windows, it'll seem even bigger than it is...*even if* we take some of the lobby space and use it for this room." Autumn points to the room that we used for the cocktail hour.

Autumn is really in her element now, and I can't be sure what Scarlett is thinking. I love every idea I've seen so far, but I can see how this would be completely over-whelming.

"Imagine the weddings here if we combined these two rooms and added tons of windows to the back. There's access to the restaurant's kitchen if we tack this room onto the main one...sorry, am I talking too fast? I can just let you look at them too, they're pretty self-explanatory, and y'all know what you're doing when it comes to plans." Autumn makes a face at me, gritting her teeth.

"The Southern comes out in our girl when she's passionate about something," Pappy tells Scarlett proudly. "My wife had a Southern accent too and it's like music to my ears."

Scarlett smiles at Pappy and Autumn groans, her face flushing.

"It comes out when I'm *nervous*," she says. She looks

at Scarlett. "I just really want to get this right. I want to do something that *you'll* love. And I can scrap the whole thing, all of it, and start over. You just tell me what you hate…what you love…if anything…"

She laughs and I've never seen her flustered like this. She's worked with some of the biggest names in Hollywood and practically all the homes of Zac's team, and is looking at Scarlett like she's waiting with bated breath.

Scarlett clears her throat and her voice is slightly shaky when she speaks. "I'm blown away."

She presses her lips together and blinks fast, fanning her face.

"And I'm trying really hard not to cry because this is just…incredible." Her lips wobble and she shakes her head. "The thought to detail, the way you're considering making the most of every space and not just tearing things down…I love everything I've seen."

Autumn sags against the wall, her hand going to her heart as she leans her head back. "Oh, thank goodness," she says.

"You've already given my feelings more consideration in the twenty-four hours we've known each other than my granddad did in the twenty-three years I've been alive." She tries to play it off like she's joking, but I can see the truth behind it, and my heart hurts for her.

She looks around at all of us. "I don't want to hold any of you back. It's clear to me that you've got this…" She stands up and puts her hand on Autumn's arm. "Thank you…it's amazing, *really* amazing."

She looks at me, her eyes shining again, and I want nothing more than to hug her right here in front of everyone. But she's already moving toward the door.

"I have to check on the dogs. I left them alone in my office and that's a fairly new thing I'm trying." She laughs and is out the door before I can stop her.

I look at my brother and Autumn, holding my thumb back toward the door. "I'm just gonna check on her really quick."

Zac nods. "I was hoping you would."

CHAPTER TWENTY-SEVEN

PROUD GORILLA

SCARLETT

I hurry to my office and am turning to shut the door behind me, the dogs rushing to my side, when Jamison reaches out and stops the door.

"You okay?" he asks.

I start to tell him I'm fine like I would everyone else, but he looks at me like he knows I'd be lying.

"I'm a mess," I admit.

"Is it seeing all those plans? Or is it about before? Us...are you wishing we hadn't—"

"No...are you?"

He steps in and closes the door behind him, tugging my waist toward him. "I am reliving every moment of what we did in slow motion," he says, his voice husky. "It's hard for me to think of anything else."

I laugh, my hands landing on his chest. He feels so good, so solid.

"Can I do anything to make this easier for you?" he asks.

And I feel that burning sensation under my eyelids that's been way too present lately.

"Just the fact that all of you care to make it easier for me means...so much." I end on a whisper, my voice breaking.

He pulls me close, hugging me, and a tear drips down my face. I swipe it away and sigh into him.

"Your hugs are really, really nice," I say softly.

"I'm sorry that my dick can't behave in this moment," he says when it's clear that he's hard as a rock.

"Your dick is really, really nice too," I say, still not looking at him.

It jerks against me and he laughs. "Well, flattery is definitely not going to help in this situation."

I lean my head back to face him and he runs his thumb across my lower lip.

"You don't have to worry about me," I tell him. "I'll be okay."

Lucia and Delgado have been sliding their warm bodies against our legs and finally Lucia plops down on our feet.

Jamison laughs. "Guess I'm not going anywhere." He leans in and kisses me and my body melts into his. It's the sweetest kiss, but it still amps up fast, the need for more of him a physical ache.

I break the kiss, both of us breathing hard. "You better get back."

"Yeah, you're right. Hey, they'll be here for a few more days. Be with us as much as you want and are able. We'll be fine-tuning the plans, but I also want to take Ivy skiing and we were serious about taking Grinny to dinner. I'd love for you to be part of any and all of that."

"I don't want to intrude on your family time," I tell him.

He protests and I shake my head.

"No, really. You need a chance to catch up without me. I'll call Grinny though and see if she's free tonight or tomorrow night…"

He studies me, his eyes trying to read between the lines.

"Go," I tell him, laughing.

I move back, which causes Lucia to stand up. She sticks her snout in my hand, wagging her tail excitedly. I pet her and Jamison bends down to pick up Delgado.

"I wish they were staying longer. There's so much I want to do while they're here, but too little time. They need to meet these guys for sure." He sets Delgado back down and pets Lucia. "I'm going, I'm going. Let me know what Grinny says."

I nod, smiling at him, and when he leaves, I collapse into my desk chair. Lucia comes over and lays her head on my knee.

"What am I gonna do, girl?" I ask her. "I think I'm in trouble."

I call Grinny. I talked to her last night but didn't tell her about the dinner just in case it didn't come back up. She's excited and says either night works. After we hang up, I email Jamison, letting him know that and my phone buzzes a few minutes later from an unknown number.

> Should I be offended that Steve had your number and I didn't? This is Jamison, by the way.

I smile at my phone, saving his contact in my phone before texting back.

> You've got my number in a way Steve doesn't.

JAMISON

> Damn. That was totally effective. Not offended anymore at all, but now they're asking why my chest is puffed out like a proud gorilla.

I giggle and Delgado and Lucia look up at me, tails wagging. My alarm goes off, reminding me that I need to let the dogs out and then get over to housekeeping to talk to Deb. I fasten their leashes and grab my phone, hurrying outside. There aren't any other pets in the pet area, so I let them loose.

My phone rings and I frown, another unknown number. I almost answer it, thinking maybe it's Autumn, but then another text from Jamison comes in.

JAMISON

Let's do the Grinny dinner tonight. Would Tiptop be good? I haven't been there yet. Or where would you suggest?

> I love Tiptop and so does Grinny.

JAMISON

Perfect. Is 5 too early?

> Grinny's all about an early dinner.

JAMISON

Pappy too. <Wink-face emoji> 5 it is.

> Grinny and I will meet you up there.

JAMISON

No gondola ride together to the top?

> It only holds six people and with the size of you Ledger men and Magnus, I'd say it'd probably be best to spread out your trips up too.

JAMISON

Again with the puffed gorilla chest.

I'm smiling like an idiot at my phone when it rings again, startling me, but Delgado is done and I need to get to Deb.

"Lucia, come on, girl," I call, and she runs toward me.

The three of us head back inside and I secure them in my office before making the short trek to the housekeeping office.

Deb is there when I walk in and she stands up, walking toward me, her smile wide.

"How about that Ledger family?" she asks, her voice carrying. "They're like the Landmarks, not a bad-looking one in the bunch!"

I laugh and she leans in, her eyes twinkling.

"Heard you might be sweet on the younger one…"

I want to say *well, I should hope so since he's the only single one…and not in his eighties…*but I keep my sarcasm in check. I knew word would already be out. It's like the people of Landmark can smell news.

"They're a wonderful family," I say.

She nods and winks like she knows there's so much more I'm not saying. And she's not lying.

I get behind the desk and motion for her to join me. "Want to show me what's happening when you sign in?"

She shows me and I walk through the steps of restarting and get her back in shape. While we're working, Clara and Becky walk in, and I can tell by the way they come at me all swoony, that the whole resort is talking.

"What have you heard?" I finally ask, unable to take all the side-eyes.

Becky presses her lips together like she's afraid to say anything, but I can tell she's *dying* to spill.

"What do you mean?" Clara asks, but she giggles before she can finish the sentence.

I hold my hand up, waving my fingers like *come on.*

Becky leans in and the rest of us do too. "*Well…*"

I love the woman, but she is the biggest gossip in Landmark and that is saying something. We have lots who qualify. I sigh and refrain from rolling my eyes because she is just now winding up.

"Lisa came in earlier, and she said that Jim said he was talking to Vera outside the offices and they went down the hallway for just a minute and Danny came out, redder than a hornet…"

She looks around for effect and we stare at her.

"Or you know, mad as a horn—what is that saying?" she says.

I wave my hand for her to continue even though my face is on fire too.

"And then they heard something from Jamison's office…*sounds*…" Her eyebrows lift, and everyone else avoids looking at me. "Jim said Vera ushered him out of that hallway so fast, his head was spinning." Everyone cackles. "But he thought he heard your voice in there, and then Danny circled back and waited outside the offices…"

I close my eyes and count to three.

"Poor Danny," Becky sniffs. "Everyone knows he's been hung up on you since you broke his heart."

"I didn't break his heart!" I insist. "We agreed we're better as friends."

Becky presses her lips to the side and gives me a dry look, nodding. "Mm-hmm."

What is with everyone thinking I broke Danny's heart? He didn't even try to convince me to stay with him. What am I missing here?

"Okay, so all of this is speculation that…what? I was in the office with Jamison? Because Jim or Vera or Danny heard a girl in his office?"

"A girl that sounded like you," Becky says. "And you are wearing a healthy glow today, I might add."

The three of them snort and then freeze when I fold my

arms across my chest and stare at them. Becky crumbles first.

"Oh, come on, don't be mad, Scarlett. You know we love you. We would be the first to cheer you on if it *was* you...she's mad," she says, glancing at Deb.

"I'm offended you don't think I'm always wearing a healthy glow," I say, smirking.

Becky nudges my side, exhaling in relief. "Wait, does this mean...was it you?" she says under her breath.

I lift a shoulder. "A lady never tells. Are we all good here, Deb?"

Deb nods and they all look at me, waiting for a sign, any sign...so hopeful.

"Good thing I'm not a lady," I say before I walk out the door, winking over my shoulder.

I can hear them all the way down the hall, hollering and laughing their asses off.

"No, she did not just say that," Becky howls.

I laugh all the way to my office, that little break just what I needed.

CHAPTER TWENTY-EIGHT

A SWEET ESCAPE

JAMISON

We're at Zac's condo, about to leave for dinner, when I get a phone call.

"Mr. Ledger?"

"Yes, this is Jamison."

"This is Blake from Tiptop. I'm so sorry, but I've had to close the restaurant for the night. I was really looking forward to having you and your family here tonight. We're having an issue with our heater, hopefully it will all be up and running by later tonight, but in the meantime, I wouldn't feel right having everyone here with the temp dropping so rapidly."

"Oh, man, I hate to hear that, but we'll be back another time. Maybe tomorrow night if things are looking good again. Can I help in any way? Do you have someone looking at the heater now? One of our friends who was coming with us tonight is great at all that, much better than me, but I could certainly assist him," I add, chuckling when I see Magnus' eyebrow lift.

"Thank you, I appreciate that. I've got a friend coming out in about half an hour though. He's a pro...just can't get here quite soon enough to keep the dinner rush happy."

"Okay, call me back if you see that you need extra help."

"That's awfully kind of you. Goodnight, Jamison."

"Goodnight."

I call Scarlett, hoping I can catch her before she and Grinny leave.

"I was just going to call you," she says.

"You heard about Tiptop?"

"Yeah. There's nothing else quite like Tiptop around here...and I think The Pink Ski is full tonight, judging from their parking lot. The Gnarly Vine seemed pretty full too, when I was by there earlier. I don't know how you'd feel about The Dancing Emu...the karaoke can get pretty excruciating at times."

"Did you say karaoke?" I make a face at Zac and he rolls his eyes, shaking his head while I nod emphatically. "Oh, we are so in."

"Okay." She laughs. "Didn't expect you to sound so excited about karaoke. This should be fun."

"Let the wooing begin," I say.

Pappy snorts out a laugh.

"What did you say?" Scarlett says.

"I said, Whew, I'm in…" And pause to see if that flies.

"Oh…okay. Great." She giggles and I have to close my eyes and think of my dick on ice. Freezing. Shriveled. Not…hard as steel.

The guys barely hold it together before I'm off the phone.

"Someone has finally got Little Squirt's number," Zac laughs, slapping me on the back.

"Nothing little about me," I groan.

The Dancing Emu is hopping when we get there, but the whole town is right now. The lodge is at ninety percent capacity tonight, the highest it's been since I got here, and Heritage Lane is more crowded than I've ever seen it.

I've been so distracted by Scarlett, we've been in the thick of spring break for weeks and it still feels like the crowd snuck up on me.

"We probably should've planned your visit after spring break, not during the rush," I tell Zac as we walk inside.

"This place is so cute," Autumn squeals. "Oh, there she is." She waves and I look over to see Scarlett and Grinny.

Scarlett is wearing a sweater dress and I had no idea until seeing her wear them around the lodge that they're one of my favorite things. Not as much as what she probably has on underneath, but…nothing besides having her laid out bare before me is better than that. This is one I haven't seen her wear yet, and damn. It's a bit lower and shorter than what she usually wears to work and with a bow at the waist that makes me want to unwrap her.

Grinny steps forward, bringing my gutter mind screeching to a halt. She's such a classy lady.

"Grinny, you look beautiful tonight, as always. I'm sorry this isn't quite the night out I had planned for you. I was hoping to wine and dine you." I wink and kiss her on each cheek and when I step back, she's beaming, her hand patting her heart.

"I tell you what, you are a charmer," she says. "And a handsome one to boot," she adds. "Oh, what a beautiful child…"

Ivy's arm wraps around my waist, and Scarlett must have told Grinny that Ivy's deaf because Grinny does the sign for hello.

Ivy's eyes light up. "Hi," she says, signing it back too.

When I fingerspell G-R-I-N-N-Y, Ivy smiles wide and does the sign for *grin* and then *grandma*.

"Exactly," I say.

I keep signing as I introduce Zac and Autumn to Grinny next.

"Such a stunning couple. Wow," Grinny says, turning to smirk at me. "I'm warning you now, if you know what's good for the both of you, don't let my friend Peg see the two of you together. Her heart can't take it."

My laugh is so loud, it makes Scarlett jump and then she cracks up.

Ivy tugs on my sleeve as soon as I'm done signing. "Peg, who?"

"She's my friend and she'll think your daddy and uncle are as handsome as movie stars," Grinny answers.

Ivy laughs when I finish signing what Grinny said. I look around and see Magnus and Pappy walking toward us, Pappy looking like a deer in the headlights. I'm about to ask him what's up when a petite older lady pops up from behind him.

"Speak of the devil," Grinny says. "Oh dear, brace yourselves. Peg is back from a cruise and feeling herself."

Autumn and Scarlett exchange a look as they laugh.

"It's about to get interesting," Scarlett says.

"Pappy, come over here and meet Grinny," I call, trying to save him and also wanting him to meet Scarlett's grandmother.

He looks at me in relief and smiles warmly at Grinny, about to say something when he startles, a little yelp coming out of him. He turns and looks down at Peg, who is all innocence as she bats those eyelashes his way.

"Pardon me," Peg says sweetly. "I wasn't watching where I was going."

"Well, I assure you, my backside's not where the fun's at," he says, eyes wide.

Peg giggles. "Oh, I wouldn't be so sure of that."

Grinny pats my arm. "Looks like you and your brother might be safe from Peg after all. She usually goes for the younger men, but your grandpa seems to ring her bell just fine," she says under her breath.

That sends me and Zac and Autumn into another round of laughter that I have a hard time recovering from.

Scarlett's face is somewhere between horrified and like she's trying not to laugh. "Grinny, I don't think that means what you think it does," she says quietly.

I put my fist over my mouth and try to rein in the laughter, while Grinny frowns slightly, glancing over at Scarlett.

"I'll tell you later," Scarlett mouths.

She presses her lips together and doesn't dare look at me right now.

Pappy pries himself from Peg's grasp and also keeps a lookout behind him as he steps forward, like he's afraid to turn his back on her. This story is going to be told and retold for ages, Pappy getting hit on in a hobbit karaoke bar in Landmark. He lets out a long sigh of relief when he reaches me and Zac, holding out to grip my shoulder.

"Didn't know we were gonna have to keep an eye on you tonight, Pappy," I tease.

"*Please* keep an eye on me," he says under his breath.

He looks apprehensive now as he stands before Grinny.

She holds out her hand, smiling warmly, and he shakes it, his smile somewhat tentative.

"I'm Grinny Landmark," she says. "You've got a fine family indeed."

"Why, thank you," he says, his shoulders relaxing instantly. "And this granddaughter of yours...she is really special."

Scarlett's eyes get a dreamy look when Pappy squeezes her hand and is about to say something when his eyes get wide again.

"Didn't know my girls would be here tonight," Grinny says.

I recognize one of the "girls" and grin at her as she stares back at me. She's the one who dusted me off at the bakery, but she seems like the hardest one to win over in the group.

"This is Helen," Grinny says, taking her hand and bringing her closer.

"Hello," Helen says. No smile, no expression, no *hey, I remember you.*

"Good to see you, Helen."

"And I'm Peg," Peg says, putting her hand on my arm as she smiles up at me. Next thing I know, she's squeezing my bicep. "My goodness, the muscle on you," she coos. "Helen, feel this."

"He's not a wax figure, Peg. He's a human being," Grinny tuts.

"Well, I know. I'm feeling him right now, flesh and bone," Peg practically purrs.

She lowers her lids and sends me a flirty smile. She's a pretty lady, and I can imagine that look has worked its magic plenty.

I hear Scarlett snorting and know I'll lose it if I look at her.

"And look at how tall he is...I'd say around..." Peg leans her head back and taps her upper lip with her finger. "6'3 and a half?"

I nod, impressed. "I think that's about right."

"Oh, for goodness' sake, you act like you've never seen a man before," Helen says.

"I think I just proved that I have." Peg winks at me and pats my arm again. "And he obviously takes after his father." She winks at Pappy.

Helen rolls her eyes. "Oh, for goodness' sake," she repeats under her breath.

"*Grandfather*," Pappy says, mortified.

We're saved when a voice erupts from a microphone.

"Jamison Ledgerrrrr! Come on up!"

I turn toward the stage and a guy I've seen at Happy Cow a few times is waving me up. Scarlett is wiping her eyes when I glance at her.

"Something funny?" I ask straight-faced.

She presses her lips together. "Can't remember when I've laughed so hard…wait…in your office."

I suck in a breath, remembering her naked in my office trying to get her clothes back on and tug my collar, suddenly needing air.

They call my name again into the microphone.

"What did you do?"

She lifts a shoulder. "You sounded awfully excited about karaoke. Didn't think you'd mind."

I put my hand on her waist and her breath catches, making me way too excited for my own good.

"Okay," I say, pretending to be more nervous than I am.

I let out a long whoosh of air and inhale, my nostrils flaring. She giggles again and I point at her.

"You're trouble, aren't ya?"

She smirks and again with the shoulder lift.

The guy calls my name again and I head up to the small stage.

"Show 'em how it's done," Pappy cheers.

I look at the list of songs and pick the first one that catches my eye. When the intro starts, I make the *Ohhh, yeah, yeah* warble just like Natasha Bedingfield, which makes a few people laugh, but then get serious when I get to the first line about a pocketful of sunshine. Scarlett's eyes bulge out and she starts laughing, crossing her arms as she watches me. By the time I hit the chorus at full throttle, she's swaying back and forth with the rest of the place.

When I finish, the place goes crazy and I hop down from the stage, slapping the hands of all the people high-fiving me. I don't stop until I reach her and she does a slow clap.

"What other tricks do you have up your sleeve?" she asks.

I pull her toward me and she gasps, her teeth quickly coming out to tug on her bottom lip.

"Stick around and you'll find out," I tell her, feeling good about the way this night is going so far.

But then Grinny surprises us all by hustling on up there when her name is called. Scarlett watches and for a second I think she might cry.

"I wasn't sure she'd get up there," she says. "She hasn't done this since Granddad…"

We both turn when Grinny says, "I'd like to dedicate this song to my best friend, Peg…"

"Uh-oh," Scarlett says, laughing.

The keyboard intro starts and Grinny does a subtle shake of her shoulders along with the beat, and I lose it all over again when she completely nails "It's Raining Men" as Peg dances her heart out all over The Dancing Emu.

CHAPTER TWENTY-NINE

ENTERPRISE

SCARLETT

Holly and April stop by the office the next morning, making me jump when they stick their heads in the door.

"Sorry," April squeaks. "Didn't mean to scare you."

I hold onto my head and laugh, waving them in. "I'm out of it today. Didn't get much sleep last night…"

They both give me a look, all exaggerated and with plenty of *mm-hmm, we know what you were up to* attitude.

Holly actually says as much and then some. "Mm-hmm. Word on the street is the new man candy of Land-mark is steaking your shake." She leans her hands on my desk and stares me down.

"Oh, that's what they're saying over on Heritage Lane?" I snort. "Well, by all means, what else are they saying? Because I have no idea what that even means."

"They're saying your boy can sing," April says, laugh-ing. "I'm so bummed I missed the Emu...why didn't you tell us that's where all the fun was going down last night?"

"We'd planned on going to Tiptop, but they had to close early..."

"So you chose the next best thing..." Holly laughs and I can't keep a straight face after that.

"He's not my boy, but he *can* sing," I admit. "And Grinny was hysterical...Peg totally put the moves on Jami-son's grandpa and Grinny dedicated "It's Raining Men" to her. Helen was mortified, of course."

They both crack up.

"Classic," Holly says when she stops laughing. And then she leans in, her smile dropping, like she's going for the kill. "But what we want to know is why you didn't get any sleep last night."

"Because I stayed out too late and was wired when I got home?" I barely crack a smile when she slams her hand on the desk. "You're acing the William Shatner over-acting right now," I tell her calmly. "But I thought your *Star Trek* phase was over."

She rushes to the wall, looking back and forth like the meme I send her of Captain Kirk all the time when she's being dramatic. And she keeps going, caught up in the moment and spurred on by our laughter...oblivious to her new audience. I open my mouth to warn her, but I'm too caught up in the entertainment to get it out, and she barrels right into Magnus' chest.

"Oof," she says, bouncing back like a rag doll, winded by the brute force that is Magnus Evensen's chest.

He reaches out and steadies her, and she blows the hair in her eyes out of the way.

"Execute," she says weakly.

Pappy steps around Magnus and claps.

"Live long and prosper," he says, nodding. "Scarlett, I had no idea how endlessly fun Landmark would be…and I haven't even had to play in the snow for it!"

I laugh and stand up, coming around my desk to give Pappy a quick hug. I introduce him to April, and try to introduce Holly too, but she is still locked in a stare with Magnus. The two of them, with their height and all that blond hair going on, are unbelievably striking. I exchange a look with April and she whimpers.

"I don't think I can keep holding out on the tourist fast." She walks toward the door and points at me. "You need to fill us in…I don't want to hear anything else from Lar and Mar that I should be hearing from you."

"Don't believe everything you hear," I tell her.

She taps the doorjamb twice and grins. "Start sharing or I'll have to. 'Kayyy," she says louder and in Holly's direction, "I'm off to find Barney…"

When that doesn't break the spell between Magnus and Holly, she looks at me and points at them, mouthing, *What is happening right now?*

Pappy chuckles. "Spring is around the bend…isn't it? Time for new beginnings and all that. Isn't the snow about to be done?"

"I think we've got one more snowfall to come, maybe two…but it will start melting soon around here." I pause, turning to April, "Wait, Barney's still in town?"

She nods, looking very pleased with herself. "He extended his trip."

"Maybe he's not a tourist any longer?" I laugh when she makes a face and nods excitedly.

"Go get him," I say, shooing her out. "Pappy says it's time for new beginnings!" I yell.

Pappy nods. "You tell 'em, tiger!"

Jamison sticks his head in the door. "Tiger?" he says. "What kind of party am I missing in here, Little Bear?"

I laugh, my heart warming that he remembers my granddad's nickname for me.

"Oh," Jamison says, looking at Magnus and Holly. He lifts his thumb toward them, his eyebrows going up as he looks at me. "What have we here?"

"*Caught up in the rapture of love…*" Pappy sings.

"Oh, I love that song." I put my hand to my chest. "Grinny always had Anita Baker playing around the house. Apparently my parents were big fans."

"Good stuff," he agrees.

"Pappy, we *needed* your representation last night," Jamison says. "Next time, karaoke, you're up."

He smiles at me, and I feel the warmth all the way to my toes.

"You got a minute?" he asks.

"Uh, sure." I glance at Pappy and he reaches out to give Jamison a playful shake.

"Sorry, I forgot my one job," Pappy says. "Jamison was stuck on a phone call and I was sent down here to see if you could stop by his office. He also wanted me to meet the dogs that I keep hearing so much about. I have yet to meet them." He lifts his hands up in the air.

"Shoot. I'll see if you're around when they get back. My nephew is on spring break and I told him he could take them for a while each day. I didn't think he'd really want them every day, but so far, he's been consistent. He's campaigning hard for his own dog."

Pappy takes another look at Magnus and Holly and nods. "I'll walk out with you two…don't want to interrupt this silent conversation they've got going."

We step out of the room, and Pappy waves over his head, whistling. "I'll see what trouble I can get into for a little bit."

"Is he always so great?" I ask as we watch him walk away.

"Always," he says.

He turns to me and takes my hand, threading his fingers through mine. I look down the hall and don't see anyone watching us, but I'm sure someone will be talking about this tomorrow.

"Last night was fun," he says, grinning. "Hated to say goodnight though."

He puts his hands on my waist and leans in for a kiss. Right as his lips touch mine, his phone rings. I step back and he tugs on my hand, trying to hold me in place.

"Do you need to get that?"

He looks at his phone and when it rings again, he sends me an apologetic look and answers it.

"Blake, hi. I'm good. How are *you*—how's it looking over there today?" His thumb traces over my knuckles, and even that slight touch makes my pulse quicken. "I'm glad to hear it—really glad you're up and running again…oh, well, let me see if we can make that work. Can I call you right back? All right. You too. Thanks, Blake."

He hangs up and pulls me close again, leaning his forehead on mine. "I shouldn't have answered that. I just didn't want you to think I ignore the good people of Landmark."

I try to hold back my laugh, but I'm too happy to keep it in.

"Well, I'm glad to know you're taking your job as the owner of Landmark Mountain Lodge so seriously…" My voice is playful as I'm saying it, but there's something about the words being out there that makes it sink in, and I realize that I mean it.

I'm actually glad he's here, glad he's part of this place.

His eyes are hopeful, like he can tell what I'm thinking.

"Yeah?" he asks.

I nod. "You're doing a good job, Jamison. Better than good, really."

His hand brushes across my cheek and dives into my hair, his gaze never leaving mine.

"I had no idea how much I needed to hear you say that," he says.

He kisses me then. A slow, sweet, take-my-breath-away kiss that's over way too soon.

Someone calls his name and he pulls back, dazed.

"Why must I do such a good job again?" he asks, making me laugh.

He turns and Albert sticks his head out of his office.

"There you are," Albert says. "Oh, hi, Scarlett."

I can tell by the way his cheeks turn pink as he smiles

at a point somewhere over my shoulder that Vera told him ALL the dirt.

"Hi, Albert."

"Did Blake get in touch with you?" he asks Jamison.

"Yes." Jamison points at him. "Thank you. I almost forgot." He pivots to me. "Would you and Grinny like to try again with Tiptop…tonight? Your brothers are welcome to come. Blake says the heater issue is taken care of and he's not opening the restaurant until tomorrow, but he'd still love to cook for us tonight while my family is still in town."

"I'm not sure my brothers could all swing it on such short notice, but I'll see who's free."

He steps in closer and my body hums. "And when my family has to go back, I'd like to take you on a date, just you and me."

I get lost in his eyes, only interrupted by the sound of Albert gulping hard and then getting something stuck in his throat, coughing as he tries to sneak away.

"Thanks, Albert," Jamison calls, his eyes laughing as he keeps watching me.

"Uh, sure, sure thing," Albert says.

I bury my face in his chest. "You're not even *trying* to keep this a secret, are you?"

"No, not even a little bit."

CHAPTER THIRTY

NERVES AND SNOWFLAKES

JAMISON

I knock on Scarlett's door, my chest already in that weird topsy-turvy state it gets just at the thought of seeing her.

She opens the door and I stare, speechless. Her head tilts and she grins uncertainly.

"Hi. You okay?" She grabs her coat and starts putting it on, reaching back to grab her purse.

"I-you look…incredible." I lean in and kiss her on the cheek and she flushes.

"Thank you. You look pretty incredible too."

She steps outside and I take her hand, and we start walking toward the gondola station.

Why do I feel nervous all of a sudden? I laugh under my breath.

"Zac says he doesn't even recognize me right now," I confess.

"Why?"

"Because I've never been so…well, whatever this is." I glance at her out of the corner of my eye and then kiss the hand I'm holding. "I'm crazy about you, you know that, right?"

"Uh…I…you are?"

"Yes."

She's quiet, but it's not an uncomfortable silence. I get the impression that I need to let her process all of this, which is understandable. I'm still trying to process it myself.

"Holly and April are mad that they missed the show at The Dancing Emu…and that Lar and Mar were the ones to fill them in about you and me."

I lift an eyebrow. "I bet Lar and Mar have been talking about us since that first morning we showed up there at the same time."

She laughs. "Lots of angsty tension that day."

I shrug. "You were the one putting out the angst, Kitten."

She crinkles her nose and grins at me shyly, which makes my heart dive.

The wind picks up as we're walking, snowflakes falling rapidly around us.

"I knew it was going to snow," she says. "Wyatt and I had a bet going…he owes me five dollars."

I grin. I like that she's so close to all of her brothers. "Is he coming to dinner?"

"Yeah, Wyatt and Theo are the only ones who can make it actually. Sutton and Owen had plans for dinner already and they'll bring the dogs home afterward. And Callum wasn't able to get done with work early enough. Wyatt's bringing Grinny," she adds.

We pass several people we know, locals and some who are guests at the lodge, nodding and saying hello.

"What's it like being so revered?" I ask Scarlett after the last people had just stopped and hugged her and wanted to chat for five minutes despite the snow picking up.

"What do you mean?"

"You're like a celebrity around here," I tell her.

She laughs. "No, I'm not. Everyone knows everyone… I just happen to be a Landmark, but you've had your share of people calling out your name too. Give it another month and you won't be able to go into the grocery store without spending an extra half hour chatting. Sometimes it does sound nice to be anonymous somewhere…"

We reach the gondola station and I'm surprised no one else is waiting to get on with us. "Where is everyone?"

"Well, we are a little bit early," she says, looking at the huge clock on Heritage Lane that we can see all the way from here.

"I was excited to see you," I say, shrugging.

I see the smile she tries to hide and kiss her hand again.

Her skin is cold against my lips and I take both of her hands in mine, trying to warm them up.

"Let's go ahead," I say, and we walk to the entrance, where the operator is waiting.

"Hey, Benny," Scarlett says.

"Hey there," he says. "I thought everyone was either at the Chili Cookoff or the concert at Bethany Christian. You're the first people I've seen in ten minutes. That's gotta be a record during the busy months."

"Well, expect to see some Landmarks and Ledgers before too long," Scarlett says. "Have you met Jamison yet?"

"No, not yet, but I've heard good things about you and your brother." Benny holds out his hand and we shake.

"Nice to meet you, Benny."

"You ready to go up?" he asks.

"Yes, please," Scarlett says, rubbing her arms.

We step inside the spacious gondola and I follow her to the last seat.

"Have a nice ride," Benny says before the doors shut.

We're moving within a couple of minutes, slowly lifting over the lights of the town.

"I wish it was a clearer night," Scarlett says. "Have you been on here before?"

"No."

I can't keep my eyes off of her. Zac's right—I've never been like this about anyone. It should scare me more than it does, given our shaky history and the unknown ahead, but I've never been an overthinker. Don't want to start being one now, and just enjoy this.

She looks behind us. "Landmark is such a gorgeous town," she says.

It's her melancholy tone that has me on alert.

"You say that like you're sad about it."

She faces me and shakes her head. "I'm not sad, just… trying to figure out what's ahead."

Unease shifts through me. I was hoping her uncertainty about staying would be resolved by now. The end of her three-month commitment will be over before we know it and I can't even think about what it will be like when I go back to Boston three months after that. But at least I know I'll be coming back to Landmark often.

It sounds like she still doesn't even know where she'll be. Like maybe she's already saying goodbye.

I can't imagine Landmark without her here.

She *is* Landmark to me.

The rest of our ride is quiet. The visibility gets worse as we go up and I can feel her anxiety building. Neither of us have mentioned getting stuck on the ski lift, but I'm certain it's on her mind as much as it is on mine. She's got a firm grip on my hand and I squeeze back just as tight.

I put my free hand on her cheek and press my forehead against hers. She sighs when my finger dips over her bottom lip, her breath hitching when I bite it. Her lips tilt up at the edges and she tugs my head closer, kissing me long and deep. I moan into her mouth and pull her onto my lap.

"We should've been doing this the minute we got on here," I say against her lips.

"Agreed. I was trying so hard not to have a freakout and this is helping."

"What else can I do to help?" I ask, tugging her hips toward mine.

She arches into me and I reach into her coat and palm

her breast. Her hands wind through my hair as she grins down at me.

"I think we only have seven or eight more minutes," she says.

"Plenty of time," I whisper, tracing my tongue along her neck.

My hands slide up her thighs and up her dress, finding my way to the lace between her legs. I rub my thumb over the wet material and where I know she wants it most and look at her, letting her reaction tell me what to do next. She squirms against my thumb and dick as it jerks to get in on the action. I push the lace aside and dip a finger inside. Her head falls back and I don't let up, keeping a steady rhythm.

"Jamison," she whimpers.

"Tell me something good," I whisper.

Her eyes light up. "You remember."

"I remember everything about you," I tell her.

"You…are good. Your…fingers…are good. Your mouth…" She leans down and kisses me, her tongue battling mine for dominance.

Her eyes are drunk when she pulls back, her thighs shaking as she rides my hand. Her silky channel flutters against my fingers and then her head falls back, and I feel her harder convulses inside, her eyes squeezing shut.

"Best view I've ever seen," I tell her, kissing up her neck.

She lets out a shuddery breath and I pull my fingers slowly out of her, which makes her moan. She arches against my dick again.

"I want to make *you* feel good," she whispers.

"Trust me, you are," I tell her.

She kisses me again and I get lost in her. It takes the sound of the gondola reaching our destination to pull me out of the fog. I make sure everything is put back in place on her and adjust myself before I stand.

She palms me over my pants and leans up on her tiptoes to whisper, "I will make it up to you, I promise."

"I'm fine." I laugh. "This is the state I've been in since I met you. A constant ache."

Her lips twist as she tries not to laugh but fails.

"That was a much better way to go up a mountain," I say, putting my arm around her as we walk toward the exit.

"For me, 20 out of 10."

"So, room for improvement is what I'm hearing."

She laughs and when the doors open, we step off of the gondola and get smacked with a gust of cold wind and snow before stepping inside the station.

"Holy shit, quite a difference up here," I say.

"Yeah, yikes." She turns and looks out the windows. The lights to the restaurant are dim given the lack of visibility.

I curse under my breath. "This isn't looking so good," I say.

"I'm sorry—I felt it coming on that walk to the station, but I ignored it. I thought it was ski lift jitters." She makes a face. "I don't think everyone should come up here tonight.

I pull out my phone. "You don't need to apologize. Benny and I didn't keep it from happening either. I'll text Zac and Pappy to let them know."

She nods. "Okay. I'll let my family know too."

I look down at my phone and see I've missed two calls from Blake. Shit. We're busy on our phones and don't notice the man in front of us until he greets us. Scarlett nearly drops her phone from being so startled.

"I should've said something sooner," he says apologetically. "Blake Gamble. You must be Jamison."

"I am. Nice to meet you." We shake and he keeps apologizing.

"I tried to reach you. We just keep striking out, man," he says, wincing and laughing at the same time. "Uh, now that you're up here, I think you better stay put."

The wind rattles the station and outside the window, snow is whipping around wildly, creating a white-out.

"Stay put?" Scarlett echoes.

"You're welcome to stay with my wife and me at the house...or uh, I don't know how you feel about this, but..." He looks down at our clasped hands and seems to make a decision. "Have you seen those glass domes? Since we work so hard at the restaurant, we thought it would be fun to have a little getaway without really...getting away?" He chuckles and then sobers quickly. "It's hard to explain, but I can show you...after I feed you, of course. I feel terrible that I didn't reach you in time."

"It's okay. I—" My phone buzzes. "Oh, good, my message reached them in time. They're turning back and eating at the lodge."

"I was able to get Wyatt too. They're all staying put."

Blake nods. "Benny has closed the gondola station, so I think everyone is safe for the night. Let's get you guys inside though."

We walk toward the restaurant and the change in weather is unbelievable. I keep my arm around Scarlett, trying to protect her from some of the wind, but it's brutal out here.

Once we stagger inside, the door slamming closed behind us, I take in the restaurant. There are windows on every side, and the decor is elegant. White tablecloths and white oval-back chairs, elaborate crystal votives at every table, and a few chandeliers creating a soft glow.

"This is really beautiful, Blake."

"If you could see what's just outside those windows," he says, shaking his head and chuckling. "I'll get something started for you. Take a seat, any seat."

"Listen, you don't need to go to a lot of trouble for just us. I'm sure with this storm and the heater issue you've had going on, you've got more than enough to do," I tell him. "We'd be happy with raiding your fridge." I glance at Scarlett to make sure she's on the same page and she nods.

"Absolutely," she says.

Blake rubs his hand over his jaw. "It's been a crazy couple of days. I really wanted to do something special for all of you. This girl here and her family have done so much for our community. Some of our favorite people," he says, smiling fondly at Scarlett. "And I wanted to give you a proper Landmark welcome."

"Thank you, Blake. My family and I feel the same about you. Don't worry about this for another second," Scarlett says. "Really. We made it up here safely. Everyone is okay. My dogs are even taken care of for the night. And...I really love grilled cheese...or pancakes if that's easier?" She gives him a wide smile and is so damn adorable, I can't take it. "Or if you trust us near your fridge, lead the way." She laughs.

"What she said," I throw in.

He chuckles. "I do make a mean grilled cheese," he

says. "Can I get you a beer or wine to go with it? A cock-tail, maybe?"

Scarlett's cheeks turn pink and she looks at me with something that looks like a promise in those eyes. "I'd love a lemon drop."

Hot damn.

"A Manhattan sounds great," I say.

"Coming right up."

CHAPTER THIRTY-ONE

SHAKE ME

SCARLETT

"That's the best grilled cheese I've ever had," I tell Blake. "And the peach cobbler, oh my God."

He ducks his head, pleased.

"I can't believe your grilled cheese isn't even on the menu," Jamison says.

"Maybe I'll have to add it." His laugh rumbles through the empty restaurant.

We ended up sitting at the table closest to the bar so we could talk to him. He still hasn't stopped apologizing.

"Can I get you another lemon drop? Manhattan?"

"Two's my limit or I get loopy," I say, holding my hand up. As it is, I don't feel loopy, but I have a nice happy buzz.

"I'm good too, thank you," Jamison says. "This has been so nice."

"Well, you're welcome to stay in here as long as you want, or I can show you the dome. My wife calls it the bubble. If that doesn't suit you, she's got a room…or two ready at the house."

I glance at Jamison and a bolt of heat steamrolls through me. My body is loose from the orgasm and alcohol, but I only want more of him. The desire in his eyes makes me glad I'm still sitting down.

"I'm fascinated about the bubble," he says. "I think we have to see it, don't we?"

I nod, my eyes locked on his.

Blake rubs his hands together. "I'm pretty excited to show you. It's been a really fun project. Come on, let's get out there. It's probably best if we get settled wherever we're going to be before too long. It doesn't seem like it's slowing down at all out there."

We stand and follow Blake through the restaurant, into the kitchen, and out the back door. Blake leads the way with a big lantern and it's a good thing—I don't think our cell phone lights would have cut it.

It's already snowed at least six inches and I'm glad I went with my over-the-knee boots instead of the heels I almost wore. We trudge down a path away from the restaurant and house and when he stops, he tries to shine the light on the dome as best he can.

"It's all clean and should be plenty warm." His keys are jangling as he shuffles to the right one and unlocks the door made of glass. When he turns the light on, I gasp.

"Blake. This is a dream," I say, turning in a circle, completely enchanted.

It really is a large glass bubble and has the prettiest bed piled high in snowy white linens. A small wooden tray sits at the end of the bed with a decanter of rum or bourbon maybe, and two crystal glasses. At the foot of the bed, there's a plush alpaca rug.

"It's truly magical when you can see the view," he says, shaking his head. "Stars like you can't believe."

"Heaven," I whisper.

"I'm blown away," Jamison says. "I've never seen anything like this."

Blake beams. "Thank you. We've really enjoyed it. Taken up star-gazing. If you like it out here, you can come back and stay on a clear night." He motions behind him. "The bathroom's not much, but I didn't want to ever make Camilla trudge outside. And I should tell you, no one can see in from the outside." He chuckles.

There are no doors, but there is a curtain where the toilet is, the wood flooring shifting to tile just for the space around the shower. My body heats at the thought of staying in this intimate space with Jamison.

I used the restroom at the restaurant, but I doubt I can go all night without using this one. It might be ridiculous that I'm shy about that when I've had sex with him, but...I don't imagine getting over that any time soon.

"Well, I wanted you to at least see it," Blake says,

clasping his hands together. "More than happy to take you to the house now, if you'd prefer that."

Jamison looks at me and reads my face right because he nods and turns to Blake. "We'd love to stay right here, if you're okay with that."

"Absolutely. You've got my number. Let me know if you need anything. I have a jet ski parked near the hot tub...it's such a shame it's not a clearer night. But if you change your mind and want to come to the house or need anything, here are the keys."

"Thank you, Blake. Are you okay getting back to the house with it like this?"

"Oh, yeah. I'll be fine. But I'll shoot you a text to let you know when I'm inside, just to be on the safe side." He grins and turns toward the door. "You guys make a cute couple, by the way," he says.

He taps on the door and leaves, the quick burst of frigid air sweeping through the room.

Jamison turns to look at me. "You okay with him knowing we're a couple?" he teases.

"Are we?" I ask.

He levels me with a look. "Hell yeah, we are." He growls and tilts my chin up to look at him. "I'll make sure you don't have any doubts come morning."

The fire in his eyes makes me shiver and he doesn't miss it, his lips quirking up in a grin.

He shakes his head. "I can't believe this place. And is he the nicest guy or what?"

"I know. I had the biggest crush on him, growing up. He's close to my brothers, especially Sutton."

He lifts his eyebrows. "Did anything ever..."

"No," I laugh. "Blake never saw me as anything other than the kid sister."

I take a deep breath, happy to have a second to catch my breath. Everything feels bigger, weightier with Jamison, and while I'm loving every second of it, my brain hasn't fully caught up with it all yet.

"I always really liked Camilla too," my words rush out. "She's just as great. I had no idea they'd done this. I'm just…in awe. And I can't believe the news of *this* hasn't made it around the rumor circuit yet."

"He's probably wanting to keep it on the down-low… his little love nest with Camilla." He chuckles, his hands tugging me against him.

I already know that I love it when he does that.

"I should probably feel guilty about how happy I am with the way this night turned out," he says against my lips. "But I'm not at all…"

I smile against his mouth, my senses on overload from the walk in the cold and now in this warm bubble with his hands on me, fresh snow and pine mixed with the scent that is all Jamison. When he kisses me, the lingering taste of whiskey and the cherry he popped into his mouth before we left. My hands roam underneath his coat and over his broad chest and arms, a solid shield that comes alive at my touch.

When we kiss, I don't know how he does it, but somehow he makes it feel even better than the last time… every single time we kiss. There's that same current, that spark that has been there since the first night we met, but it's intensified with every look exchanged across the room, every sparring session we've had, every heated touch.

He kisses me senseless, until my knees are so weak, I'm relying on him to hold me up.

"Are you warm yet?" he asks as he kisses down my neck.

"After that kiss, yes," I whisper.

He smiles, pushing my coat off my shoulders and tossing it over a chair. I shove his off and we stand there looking at each other for a moment before both moving toward the bed. His mouth finds mine again and we kiss between stripping the clothes off of each other.

He pauses when he sees what I'm wearing underneath.

"Fuck," he says, his voice hoarse. "You're the best present to unwrap."

His hand traces reverently down my neck and over my barely there lingerie. This one has more skin than anything else, with a few iridescent embroidered flowers strategically placed over thinly stretched tulle.

"This one is…absolutely my new favorite."

"You say that every time."

"And I mean it every time."

His thumb rolls over my nipple and he pinches it just hard enough to make me gasp.

I pull down his boxer briefs, his erection slapping against his stomach, hard and velvety and fevered when I take him in my hand and wrap my fist around him. He hisses out a curse and our mouths crash into each other. His hands are everywhere and then on my backside, squeezing my cheeks so hard I hope it leaves a mark.

Nothing feels close enough, the need in me growing, building. He lifts me up and wraps my legs around his waist and I feel him right where I want him and move against him, chasing that feeling. He urges me on, his hands lifting me up and down with my tempo, making me get there faster than I thought possible.

But just as I'm about to come, he tosses me back on the mountain of covers and stands over me.

He palms his cock and grins. I lean up on my elbows, breathing hard.

"You're looking good, Wingtip." My voice is breathless, but the nerves from a moment ago are gone.

His nose scrunches as his body hovers over me. My eyes are conflicted over where to look because it's just all *so amazing*.

"Not sure how I feel about that name when I'm naked."

"I don't know…" My eyes trail down to where he's more than ready for me. "When I look at you like this, Wingtip has a superhero vibe to it."

"Yeah? Like I'm about to make you fly?" His smirk is cocky and sweet sin all at once.

I lean up and pull him down on top of me. "I have *no doubt*," I tell him.

"You're so beautiful. The things I want to do to you…"

I want him to sink into me right then, but he makes me wait for it, kissing down my body and landing between my legs. His tongue flicks over the material, slowly at first and then faster and harder, making me crazy with want. It feels so good, the friction and his teasing flicks, but I want his mouth on my skin.

I slide the satin straps off my arms and down my stomach and he continues to torture me in the best ways. I whimper and arch into his mouth and he laughs and hums against me, continuing his onslaught. When he finally, *finally*, pulls the material down my legs, tossing it over his shoulder, I breathe a sigh of relief, only to feel a cold rush of air over my wetness when he leans up.

He reaches over to grab a condom, but I lean up and take him in my mouth, surprising him. He's teased me long enough.

"*Oh*," he breathes out. "Scarlett…"

He's long and thick and warm, and it surprises me how much I love having him in my mouth. I swirl my tongue around his tip, looking up at him. He stares at me, mouth parted and hand in my hair, as his eyes glaze over. I take him in as far as he'll go, still not able to take him all the way, and work my hands around him, wishing I could swallow him whole. I lean my forehead against his stomach to get a better angle and feel his muscles clench.

"Oh, Scarlett. Fuck. You're too good at this." He thrusts into my mouth once and then pulls back, my mouth falling off of him with a pop.

His thumb slides over my bottom lip and I swirl my tongue around it as he puts the condom on. He gives my chest a little shove and I fall back against the pillows.

"Are you still craving me, or should I warm you back up with my tongue?" he asks.

"I'm ready," I tell him, lifting my arm over my head in a stretch.

"I'm not so sure," he says, leaning back down to take another taste. "I need you so ready that you shatter when I fill you up. Do you remember? That's what you did on our first night together."

I moan as he swipes his tongue down my slit and then goes back up to suck my clit.

"Jamison, please," I whimper. "Don't make me wait…"

He ignores me and keeps going until my thighs are trembling, every part of me crying out for more of him, all of him, and then he leans up, his hands on either side of my face, and he thrusts in as deep as he can go.

I go to another place, a feral release that tumbles through me and doesn't stop. I clench around him and he just keeps going deeper and deeper, making my orgasm feel endless. Our breaths are ragged, bodies frantic as we stare at each other and connect, body and soul.

Around us, the snow swirls against the glass, as we shake and shudder inside the globe, making each other fall apart.

CHAPTER THIRTY-TWO

ALTERING

JAMISON

She's on top of me now, looking like an angel with her hair covering each breast.

I keep pushing it back so I can see her tits bounce as she rocks my world, but I love her hair, love her skin, love every curve and crevice of her.

We haven't slept. We've talked, we've taken time to

watch the snow in this incredible glass dome we're in, and we've fucked while doing all of the above.

"What do you think would've happened if we'd met for the first time at the lodge?" I ask now.

She swivels her hips, her breath catching when she hits her clit, and I reach out and rub it with my thumb, loving the way she flutters against my dick.

This is a lazy, leisurely fuck, like we're worn out, but it still feels too good to stop. We've had it frantic, crazed, gentle, and soul-deep, and each time is more earth-shattering than the last. This time feels playful and like I want it to last forever.

"I think it would've taken longer for us to get here," she says.

"But you think we eventually would've?" I ask.

She nods and closes her eyes, her head falling back when I arch into her. I sit up and put my hands in her hair, watching her expression change as she trembles around me. She moans when I thrust into her again.

"I do too. We were made for this. Look at me," I whisper.

Her eyes open and I just barely pull her hips down to get deeper inside before she detonates. I flip her onto her back and fill her to the hilt.

"Jamison," she cries out.

My name falling off her lips in ecstasy never fails to do something to my ego and my cock.

It's not a lazy fuck anymore. I pound into her, and she meets me with every thrust. How is it possible that I still haven't had enough of her? We go on overdrive, like there is no tomorrow, like we haven't already fucked all night long.

My body is yours, my heart too.

Her eyes fly open and I realize I said that out loud. We come together, our worlds and bodies colliding into the perfect explosion.

She has a grip on my ass, her legs wrapped around my waist, and we both press into each other as deep as we can possibly go. I feel every quiver, every shake, and she feels every jerk, every swell, our bodies responding to each other even now. I wish I could stay buried inside her forever.

"It's like little hugs from you when you're coming," I say, smiling against her neck as I kiss her pulse. "It's the best feeling, your pussy holding on for dear life."

She puts her hands on my cheeks. "Is sex always like this for you? I've never…experienced anything like this."

I lean my forehead against her. "No, it's never been like this for me and it wouldn't be with anyone but you."

"I'm falling in love with you, Jamison," she whispers.

And then her mouth drops like she can't believe she said it out loud, and I swoop in and kiss her like the greedy bastard I am. I want her to know I feel the same about her, but I'm unable to resist her lips.

She has my heart in her hands.

As the sun begins to rise, we catch the beginning stages of the beauty before giving in to sleep. When we wake up a few hours later, the snow has stopped and the view is unlike anything I've ever seen. Snow-capped mountain peaks surrounding us, and every branch on the trees near us outlined with snow, the bottom third of the dome is buried with white fluff.

"I can't get over this view," Scarlett says.

She's on her stomach, looking at the view behind our bed.

"I've been up here so many times, but I've never seen it quite like this." She glances at me out of the corner of her eye and her cheeks get pink. "And I'll never look at it the same way again."

"Think Blake would let us make a tradition out of this?" I ask, my hand trailing down her back and landing on her round, perfect ass. I knead her cheeks and her head falls forward, her hair curtaining my view of her eyes and chest.

"Does that mean you'll be back to Landmark after the six months are over?" she asks, her voice tentative.

I push back her hair and when she doesn't look at me, I tilt her chin toward me. "Of course I'll be back. Will you be here?"

She swallows hard. "I'm sure I will be at least some of the time."

"Where are you gonna go?"

Her eyes flutter down. "That's just it. I don't know. But now, it's hard to imagine being here when you're not, and the past few months have already been so confusing…"

My phone starts ringing and I glance around in surprise. "I thought I turned my sound off. That must be my dad." I look around and see my phone on the floor by my clothes. I get up and grab it.

"Dad?"

"Son…" My dad's voice breaks and my heart takes a nosedive. "I'm really sorry to tell you this over the phone.

I'm at the hospital with your mom. They're doing an emergency bypass…she wasn't feeling well, so I brought her in and she had a heart attack in the ER."

"Oh God." I feel winded and startle when Scarlett places her hand on my back, but then it steadies me. "I'll be right there. We had a snowstorm here last night, but I'll get there as soon as I can."

"Can you let everyone else know? I hated to call Zac so early when he's on vacation. I hoped you were up already."

"Dad, you never have to worry about that. We'll get there. Tell Mom we're coming. She…has to be okay."

"I know," he says, his voice cracking again. "I don't know what I'll do if—"

Tears prick my eyes and I press my fingers into them. "She'll be okay. She will. I'm gonna hang up so I can get to you faster, but I'll check in soon, okay?"

"Okay. Love you, Jamison."

"I love you, Dad."

He hangs up and I stand there in a stupor, trying to wrap my mind around my mom having a heart attack.

"My mom is so healthy," I say. "She's having an emergency bypass right now. What the fuck?"

Scarlett leans her head against my back and hugs me close. "What can I do to help?"

I turn and pull her against me, taking a deep breath as I hold her for a second before pulling away. "I need to get everyone home. As soon as possible."

She nods, already walking to the pile of clothes near the bed. She hands mine to me and moves toward the tiny bathroom, while I stand there numb.

"I'll let Blake know and then make a few phone calls,

see who can get all of you out of here the fastest," she says.

She jumps into action and it stirs me out of my fog. I get in touch with Zac and then Pappy, hearing the shower turn on and off in that time, and when Scarlett comes back out, she's dressed.

"Blake says it's safe to head down whenever we're ready, and there's a flight leaving at noon from Denver, which is cutting it close with the drive. But George is willing to take you in his personal plane, if you're comfortable with that. He insists it's in prime condition and ready to go. He can leave within the hour."

The relief is overwhelming. "Thank you. I can't believe how fast you did that."

I text Zac and Pappy about George and then take a quick shower.

We're out of our glass bubble within half an hour, my life changed in more ways than one.

CHAPTER THIRTY-THREE

PLAN

SCARLETT

I let Lucia and Delgado into my condo before I step inside.

My energy is depleted after having *another* most incredible night of my life with Jamison and then seeing him climb onto that plane with his family, waving until they were out of sight and uncertain when I'll see him again.

I collapse on top of my bed and am too wired to sleep at first.

The dogs are glad we're together and I think my nephew wore them out because they hop up on the bed, and as soon as I turn to my side, they curl up next to me. Delgado curls into a ball at the back curve of my legs and Lucia turns and turns until she finds the perfect spot to plop down, eventually stretching out against the front of me like we're spooning. I put my arm around her and she falls right to sleep while I stare blankly at TikToks.

I wake up to Delgado licking my ankle and sit up in a panic, searching for my phone. It's tucked under one of my pillows and there are no messages. I slept for almost three hours.

I stumble into the bathroom and then take the dogs out on autopilot. Grabbing a Coke from my fridge, I change out of the dress I still had on from last night and into my coziest sweater and leggings and fuzzy socks.

My planner sits on my desk, mocking me. I'm so far from a plan right now, I don't recognize myself. I promised Jamison that everything would be taken care of here, so I sit down and start a list.

- *Meet with Albert to discuss the week and figure out what backup I can provide.*
- *Check Jamison's calendar.*
- *Dinner with the Golden Girls, 5 pm at The Gnarly Vine.*
- *Get on the pill.*

My eyes lose focus and I drift off, seeing Jamison hovering over me, his body in tune with mine...and then the anguish when he heard about his mom, the lost look in his eyes when we said goodbye.

He said he'd let me know what's happening there, and I believe him, but he had no idea what to expect when he got home. The surety I felt through the night, the peace about being with him and maybe not trying to figure out my exact plan just yet…is on a precarious highwire that could topple over at any second.

I'm not used to floundering and I don't like it, so I do what I do best—I go to work. But before I leave my condo, I look longingly at my sewing machine and the pretty lace that came in a few days ago. I've been so busy having fun with Jamison and his family, I haven't had time to make anything with it.

The dogs are ready to be outside, so they don't give me time to linger, and after a quick walk, we go to my office and dive in.

My meeting ends up being with Albert and Magnus, who stayed to keep working on the plans with Steve. We don't talk for long, not because we don't have plenty to discuss, but because the lodge is a hub of spring break activity. In the past we've hired extra staff to cover this stretch, but with me being stubborn about being hands off and not doing what I could've to prepare Jamison for what this time of year is really like, it's coming back to bite me now.

I end up working at the front desk with Elsie for a few hours and clean a few of the suites when Clara goes home sick. As I'm leaving, we get a call about the dishwasher in one of the condos, and I text Albert to see if he can look into it. He says Magnus is willing to check it out and I let

Albert know I'll come back in tonight after my dinner with Grinny.

Lucia and Delgado are stopped every few minutes on our walk, people asking if they can pet them.

"My two little celebrities," I tell them as we're walking in my door.

They follow me around while I freshen up and look forlorn when I tell them they're staying.

"I'm sorry. I'll be back before you know it."

All the way to The Gnarly Vine, I wish I'd gotten out of dinner. I love being with Grinny and her girlfriends more than just about anything, but I'm still exhausted from last night and feel like I'm needed at the lodge.

The Golden Girls are always early, so they're already at a table and have two bottles of wine and my favorite charcuterie board—the one with the fig jam, crostini, prosciutto, the best cheeses I've ever had, and a variety of chocolates.

They're so happy to see me, I feel bad for ever wanting out of it.

Except they have a clear agenda for tonight's dinner.

And surprisingly, it's Helen who starts it off.

"Jo says the numbers are highly in your favor over at Sunny Side." Her tone is no-nonsense, her white curls tighter, like maybe she visited Rosie's today and got a perm.

A few days ago, Grinny had said Peg was going to broach that subject with Helen—that maybe Helen should give up perms. I don't blame Peg for backing out...or maybe Helen just ignored her.

Highly possible.

"Numbers?" I ask, still making my rounds with the

hugs. I reach her last and she tilts her cheek up for me to kiss. As I lean in, I catch the scent of her powdery floral perfume and yep, perm.

"For the girl to win Jamison's heart," Peg says, leaning in, her eyes shining.

Grinny glances at me apologetically. "Let the girl sit down before you start talking about that nonsense. How was your day, ang—"

"Nonsense!" Peg pipes up. "The way to a man's heart is never nonsense. And from what I've heard, you're ninety-nine point nine percent there!" she squeals. "Tell us everything, Scarlett. Is that man as huge as he looks?"

"Peg!" Grinny huffs, reaching out to pat my hand. "She didn't mean that how it sounded."

I laugh, knowing exactly what Peg meant.

"I most certainly did. His hands can probably fit around your waist and overlap," Peg says dreamily.

It's true, his hands do fit around my waist and overlap, and it's not because I'm the tiniest person. His hands are big, just like everything else about him.

"And I don't have to tell you what they say about big hands and you know what," Peg keeps going.

Grinny's head falls into her hands. "Oh, hogwash," she says, cocking her head toward Peg. "You don't really believe in all that, do you?" She turns and winks at me. "I didn't even notice his hands because of those eyes and broad shoulders." Her shoulders shake as she laughs.

I put my hand over my mouth, trying not to choke on any of the food I'm chewing as I laugh. A sip of wine helps.

"About those numbers," Helen says, completely unamused by Grinny and Peg. "We've been talking about a weekend trip to Denver, and I'd like to have a little extra spending money." She looks at me pointedly. "Anything you'd like to confirm or deny?"

"I'm telling you, it's totally true. Think about the men you've dated and their fingers." Peg taps her lips with her finger, little miss one-track mind. "On the other hand…I once dated a man who had smaller feet than me, but he wasn't struggling in the other department, if you know what I mean." She giggles and nudges my side.

Grinny lifts her eyes to the ceiling like she's praying for heaven's patience. "I can't take you guys anywhere."

"It's not about the feet," Peg says, excitedly. She leans in and holds up both index fingers. "It's all about these right here."

I look at her, waiting for the punchline.

"Disco fingers?" Grinny says when Peg continues to point toward the ceiling.

We all laugh and Peg does too, but she falls back in her seat and shakes her head, waving her hand dismissively. "No, silly. Studies show that the size of a man's index finger is connected with how much testosterone he got in the womb and voila, there you have it."

Jamison's long, wide fingers come to mind and my body floods with heat.

Grinny's eyebrows squish together. "I don't really want to think about the womb and the size of—"

"Jo tells me Nellie Thompson is in the running," Helen cuts in, pressing her lips together. "She's at Sunny Side every time Jamison is and they usually talk. And there's a new girl that works at the lodge that made the list…" She looks at Grinny, motioning with her hand. "Starts with an L—Grin, do you remember what her name was?"

Grinny sighs heavily, like she's given up on this night altogether.

I frown, wondering if Jamison *is* interested in Nellie at all. Or the new girl, Lili, I'm assuming…she does know sign language, which gives them another level of communication that I don't have with him. Yet.

My body is yours, my heart too, he said last night. It was a powerful night, ground-shaking. I would understand if he said that in the heat of the moment…but then I told him I'm falling in love with him. My body thrums with excitement even now, and the way it has ever since I said it, thinking of that moment.

Does he love me too?

Or did I scare him by saying it?

I turn my phone face up and there's still no word from him.

"He had to go back to Boston," I say to the table, interrupting their chatter. I've been lost in my thoughts and they've still been going on about fingers and dicks and the list.

They turn to me and start talking at once.

Grinny's hand falls on my wrist. "When will he be back?"

"I don't know," I say, shaking my head. "His mom had to have an emergency bypass and I haven't heard anything. He's really close to his family…he'll want to be there while she recovers."

If she recovers.

The thought makes me sick to my stomach.

I look at Grinny. "I'm really worried about her." A lump starts forming in my throat. "And he'd never planned to be here full-time beyond six months anyway—did you know that?" I ask Grinny. "Did I tell you that?"

She looks at me intently, her hand squeezing mine. "You did mention that, but...well, I hoped we'd all give him a reason to stay." She forces a smile and bumps her shoulder with mine. "We should send something to the family to let them know we're thinking about them...and to let Jamison know he's made a significant impression around here in a short amount of time."

Her eyes are reading me the way they have since I was a little girl. She could always see right through me, any sadness I tried to hide, any attempts at lying were futile around her.

The subject changes to what's acceptable to send to someone who's in the hospital since flowers aren't always allowed, and I try not to check my phone every five seconds.

CHAPTER THIRTY-FOUR

UPHEAVAL

JAMISON

By the time we get to the hospital, it seems impossible that it was only this morning that I woke up with Scarlett by my side.

I've thought about her nonstop, the night we had the only relief in the also nonstop worrying I'm doing about my mom.

The plane ride was quiet and somber, and the gravity

of everything hits even harder when we step inside the waiting room and see Dad. His tall frame is stooped when he moves to hug us, the circles under his eyes deeper than I've ever seen them. Zac, Pappy, and I surround him, and he cries, something I've only seen him do occasionally since Gran died, and pretty soon all of us are wiping our eyes too.

"Any word yet, son?" Pappy asks.

"No, and it's been longer than they said," Dad says. "Where are Ivy and Autumn?"

"They went to Jamison's condo to wait until we send word since it's so close. I wasn't sure how many of us could be back here with the new restrictions, but they let the three of us in," Zac says.

"Oh, I didn't think of that," Dad says. "And it's better that Ivy doesn't have to be confined in here anyway."

"Can we get you anything? Have you eaten?" I ask.

"I don't think I can eat just yet. I keep expecting the surgeon to walk through that door at any minute." His eyes fill again. "I've spent more of my life with your mother than without, and I can't imagine—"

I squeeze his shoulder, my head against his. "She'll be okay, she has to be."

I glance at Zac and he looks how I feel, absolutely wrecked.

"There's so much more we want to do," Dad says. "So much more life to live…"

None of us know what to say because we can hope and pray for the best outcome all we want, but sometimes the worst still happens.

Dad and Pappy move to the chairs and I stand nearby,

wishing I could go run or work out to get rid of some of this nervous energy.

I pull my phone out of my pocket and text Scarlett.

> Made it to Boston and at the hospital now. My mom is still in surgery. Thanks again for stepping into action this morning. If it had been up to me, I'd probably still be in Colorado, pacing the airport.

She texts back within minutes.

SCARLETT

> Glad to help. Thinking about all of you... you especially. <Heart emoji>

I smile, bolstered just to hear from her.

> I haven't stopped thinking about you for a second. Last night was...

The surgeon comes in and says, "Mr. Ledger?" and we all rush toward him.

"My sons and my dad," Dad tells him, stumbling over his words to get to the news.

Dr. Freeman nods at each of us, his focus returning to my dad.

"Everything went well. She's stable now, vitals are good. She had eighty percent blockage in one artery. We put a stent in, and she's responding well. Once she's back in her room, you'll be able to see her." He pauses, glancing at each of us again. "Any questions?"

"How do we keep this from happening again?" my dad asks.

"Healthy diet—we'll go through all of that—exercise…stay on top of cholesterol and high blood pressure… and don't ignore the signs with chest pain or not feeling quite right. Sometimes in women, it can present more with shortness of breath and nausea."

"She didn't say anything about that," my dad says, his voice cracking.

"And sometimes there are no signs." The doctor crosses his arms, his demeanor brisk but not uncaring. "But you got her here just in time."

That gets all of us, the weight of those words. My dad breaks down again and it guts me to see him this way, to know we almost lost my mom. She's too young for this, seems too vibrant, too healthy.

"Thank you, Dr. Freeman," Pappy says.

He nods and shifts on his feet. I notice his bright orange sneakers for the first time. Hard to miss them.

"A nurse will let you know when you can come back," he says.

We thank him again and when he leaves, we huddle around my dad.

"I guess that means no more S'mores pie," I say.

"And I'll be swinging by to pick her up on the way to my workouts," Zac adds.

"Count me in," Dad says.

We all laugh softly, grabbing onto any lightness when we should probably just bawl our eyes out. We break from the huddle and Pappy squeezes Dad's shoulder.

"She's okay, son. She's gonna be okay." Pappy's eyes are glassy and before long, tears are spilling down his cheeks.

He pulls a handkerchief out of his pocket, never without one, and dries his face with it.

"I want to tell you something," he says to my dad. "You've been given a second chance here. You and-and our Daisy. I want you to live this next phase of your life exactly how you want. You and Daisy want to travel? You travel. You want to putter around together, hitting those antique shops she's into, you do it. I tell you what you *don't* do…you don't worry about me. You guys have gone above and beyond what most kids would do for me, moving in after Gran died, looking after me. I'm doing all right. You need to focus on you, focus on *her*, don't let this old coot hold you back for a second." He smiles a shaky smile at Dad and squeezes his shoulder again. "You hear me?"

Dad nods. "I hear you. It hasn't been a hardship to look after you, just so you know…" He grabs a tissue from a box nearby and winces as he blows.

"Oh, I know I'm easy as all get-out," Pappy says, winking. "We all know I've been a sad sap for a long time without Gran. But I'm still here, so I figure I've got some living to do yet, best make the most of it. And so do you. This is *your* time. Don't let anything or anyone keep you from living it up."

Dad nods and we shuffle back to sit. Zac calls Autumn to let her know about Mom and I look at my phone, looking at the text I left hanging with Scarlett.

Thinking about the words Pappy said…I don't want to look back on my life when I'm my dad's age and Pappy's age and have regrets. Both have been workaholics at different times in their lives and I've been following that track for a while now too. Zac and I have talked about it some—the adjustments he's made having Ivy and then marrying Autumn—it takes a conscious effort to prioritize what's important. I didn't think I'd be ready to take this look at my own life so soon.

I send the text before I can overthink it.

> I don't have any idea yet of how we do all this, but I want to figure it out with you.

And then I add…

> My mom's out of surgery and it went well. We haven't seen her yet, but hopefully soon.

It's quiet for a while before I get a text back.

SCARLETT

> I'm so glad it went well! Keep me posted.
> <Heart emoji>

And then I second-guess whether we're on the same page at all.

CHAPTER THIRTY-FIVE

CLUES

SCARLETT

The past week has been madness.

We get a rush of families coming in, the lodge is at max capacity. I barely have time to sit down, helping at the front desk when it's busiest and making sure everything is operating seamlessly behind the scenes. It's what I used to do all day, every day, but it feels completely different.

In such a short time, Jamison has infiltrated every part

of the Landmark Mountain Lodge and Ski Resort. Where I thought I'd always miss Granddad's presence, I miss him more when I'm with Grinny or at their house.

The void at the lodge is Jamison. He brought a new energy to the place, an excitement and fresh approach that I'd been trying to carry on my own. With him here, it had just started to feel like I could relax a little bit. I stayed busy at the lodge, but it wasn't all-encompassing.

I haven't made any lingerie in almost a week. And I miss it.

I haven't had time to hang out with Grinny or Holly and April, and I miss them.

I haven't talked to Jamison much, and I *really* miss him. More than I ever thought possible.

We've done staff Zoom meetings with him, so I've seen him that way, but between his time at the hospital, and me taking care of everything here, there's been little time to talk to him one-on-one.

He texts every morning and every night, but there's been no discussion of when he's coming back, or much conversation beyond me asking about his mom and him asking about the lodge and the puppies.

When he first got there and texted that he wanted to figure out how we do all this, I wasn't sure how to respond to that. I didn't want to assume anything, and he hasn't brought it up again. So, I've just stuck to what I do know…the easy topics.

And really, I've had little time to think about any of it with being so busy, except that it still manages to permeate my thoughts no matter what else I *should* be doing.

Holly pokes her head in the door. "Come on, I promised April I'd get you out of here tonight. It's nine o'clock on a Friday night, you should be taking a break. Aren't you exhausted?"

"It's already nine? Yes, I'm exhausted, but I still have a million things to do."

"Nothing too pressing though, right? You can leave it for Albert, Vera, and Doug until the morning, can't you?"

I made a face. "I'm not so sure. You know how it's been around here lately, and with Jamison gone…"

"Have you even eaten?" When she sees my face, she moves forward to pull me up. "You need to eat."

"Why don't you see if Magnus is around? I bet he needs to eat too," I tease.

Her cheeks turn bright pink, her ears a deep red, and I stare at her in shock. I've never seen her this way over anyone. Ever.

"You are really into this guy," I say, smiling.

"NO. No, it's not, I'm not…I don't think he—" she stutters and gives up when I smile blankly up at her.

"My bestie has finally found a man who makes her speechless and makes her flush. I didn't think you were capable of either." I laugh and hug her.

She rolls her eyes but hugs me back. "Yesterday we were walking toward Happy Cow at the same time and when I saw him, I turned and walked in the opposite direction." She looks horrified when I gasp. "I know."

Her forehead lands repeatedly on my shoulder as she groans.

"Did he see you?"

"Yes," she whimpers.

"Holly! That's so rude." I laugh and she does too, although hers is tinged with hysteria.

"I didn't have time to get caught in another freeze-frame with him—I had to get to work!"

"Funny, he doesn't have any problem talking to me and anyone else around here." I hold her cheeks steady so she doesn't start banging her head on my shoulder again. "Seems like you're both equally smitten. We just need to figure out how to get you talking to each other."

"Uh. Have you *seen* him? I've never even been attracted to a blond guy before…didn't know I was into long hair either, but I want to wrap my fists in it and hold on for dear life. And his eyes and those full lips…" She holds her hand up in front of her lips as if recalling his back to memory. "I thought I was going to throw up if I talked."

"Geez, that's a strong reaction." I frown. "Maybe we shouldn't get the two of you talking…"

"No, I want to. Maybe I just need a little liquid courage." She clasps my hands. "Do you think he's out tonight? Let's see if we can find him."

I look back at the pile of paper on my desk and check my phone. There's a text from Theo. He has the dogs at his place to run with his dog, Fred.

THEO

I think I wore the dogs out. Dropped them back at your place at 8. See you tomorrow at Grinny's.

Thank you! You're saving me. XO

Nothing from Jamison.

I go back and forth between understanding that he's

busy with his family and obsessively wishing I'd hear from him more often.

I *hate* being this girl.

"Okay, I'll go look for Magnus with you...but I can't stay out late."

"Yay, I'll text April and see if she's still free or if she gave up on us."

Within the next twenty minutes, we've looked in the windows of The Pink Ski and done a thorough inside sweep of The Gnarly Vine, when we hear back from April.

"She's at The Dancing Emu," I tell Holly. "I hope Magnus is there because I could go for some food now."

"Sorry," she says, putting her arm around my shoulder. "I get you out to feed you and end up taking you on a hunt for Viking man meat."

I wrinkle my nose, unsure if that sounds hot or disgusting. He is a good-looking guy, but I can't seem to see past Jamison Ledger. I check my phone one more time to see if he's texted.

"Any word on when Jamison will be back?" Holly asks.

"Nope. No word."

"Sorry, Scar. That sucks."

The Dancing Emu is packed, an awful singer belting "I Will Always Love You" and people slow dancing to the right of the stage. There's not really a dance floor there, but sometimes Pierre clears a few tables out if the crowd wants to move.

April sees us and waves, hurrying toward us.

Holly reaches out and clamps her hand around my arm. "He's here."

I look for Magnus and sure enough, he's at the bar, and his eyes are locked on Holly's.

"Holy hot staredown," April says, looking between Holly and Magnus.

"You should have seen them after you left my office," I tell her. "They did this for at LEAST another half hour. Maybe an hour. I had to leave and they still hadn't spoken to each other."

April shoots wide eyes my way.

"I know." I shrug.

"Let's go talk to him," April says, grabbing both of our wrists.

I feel a hand on my upper back and turn, seeing Danny there. "Hey, Danny, how are you?" I have to yell it because the singing is so loud.

"I heard Ledger's gone back to Boston," he says.

He doesn't seem as angry as he did when he quit, but he doesn't look happy either.

"Yeah, he had a family emergency and had to go back."

Holly and April watch and wait while Danny and I are awkward with each other. Bo stumbles up to us, slurping a beer and maybe on number three or four, judging from the way he's hyped up. He pops up between me and Holly, so I'm sandwiched between him and Danny, and he does a screenshot from his phone of all of us.

"Wooo, we're out on the town tonight," Bo yells. "We don't do this often enough. This beats getting stuck on a ski lift, doesn't it, Scarlett?" He cracks up and I join in just as he goes snap happy with his phone.

"Can I talk to you for a few minutes?" Danny asks.

I glance at Holly and April, and Holly points toward

the bar. "I'll go get drinks for us before we do anything else."

"Okay. One lemon drop. One." I hold up my finger so they know I mean it. I need to get up early tomorrow and have a clear head.

When I turn to look at Danny, he tilts his head toward the door. "So we don't have to listen to that godawful singing at the same time?" he says.

"Sure." I walk outside, wrapping my coat tighter around me. "What's up?" I ask once the doors close behind us. The music still bleeds through the windows, but it's not nearly as grating as inside.

"I just wanted to check on you. I…felt weird about the way I quit, and then with Ledger gone this week…I guess I wanted to see if you're okay."

"Oh. Yeah, I'm okay. It's been really busy without Jamison here, but I've been handling it."

"Like you always do," he says, smiling.

"Like I always do," I repeat. "Are you considering staying? I had no idea you wanted to quit…"

"I didn't want to quit," he says. "I thought I'd be working at Landmark Mountain for the rest of my life… hopefully one day running the resort more than I am now, but…" He lifts a shoulder and leans against the glass of The Dancing Emu. "I want to talk to you about something…"

He turns to face me, his head still leaning against the window, but he takes my hand and it's like he pulls away the blinders from my eyes and his because I suddenly see what Holly and Jamison…and Granddad always said about Danny.

I take a step back. "Oh," I whisper. "Danny…"

"I want you back, Scarlett. You know I've never stopped loving you," he says earnestly.

"I did think you stopped…in that way," I say, panic jumping to my throat. "We decided…it was best."

"I never wanted that. I thought you'd come back to me once you saw how right we are together."

"We're friends. We've always been friends…"

"I've always felt more," he insists.

"Danny, I really—I have feelings for Jamison. Strong feelings," I say, unsure of how much to say.

"That guy's not cut out for Landmark Mountain," he says, his forehead creasing with his frustration. "You really think he'll stick around? He's already out of here, and during our busy season too. What makes you think he'll stay?"

"I like that he's with his family when it's important. That's where he should be right now. And I don't know if he will stick around or not," I admit. "I just know my feelings."

He scoffs. "You barely know each other. And I heard you've hated each other for most of the time he's been here. You don't know what you feel. You can't possibly, not yet…"

That makes me see red a little bit, but I try to hold onto what little patience I possess.

"I broke up with you before I ever met Jamison because I knew I didn't feel the way I should," I tell him. "We weren't in love with each other, Danny. And my feelings for Jamison…they're…different…*stronger*."

I don't add the rest—*than what I felt for you*—but judging from the way he stands straight and the coldness that creeps into his eyes, I think he knows exactly what I'm saying.

"I've never wanted to hurt you," I whisper. "I thought we were on the same page this whole time."

"I've been in love with you for as long as I can remember. I was just waiting for you to come to your senses," he says, putting his hands on his head and then letting them fall on his hips. "I've been so stupid."

"Don't say that. You're not stupid. You've never been stupid. I'm so sorry, Danny."

The ragged look he gives me makes me feel like the worst person alive. I should've listened to what everyone said about him.

"Well, don't make the same mistake I have. If he's the one you want, you better lay it out for him and hope that he's straight with you in return." He takes a deep breath and adds, "You're not that great at seeing what's right in front of you."

CHAPTER THIRTY-SIX

HEART TO HEART

JAMISON

I crawl into bed at midnight, ready to crash so hard.

It's been a long week of very little sleep and hours that blur together at the hospital.

We've been staying at my condo while Mom's in the hospital, just long enough to shower and sleep a few hours before heading back, but we got her home this afternoon.

She's doing so much better, says she feels like a new person.

Turns out she's been struggling with shortness of breath longer than any of us knew and just thought she needed to lose those extra fifteen pounds she'd accumulated this winter. We've all agreed to do regular physicals after this. Zac stays up on all that and we make sure Pappy does too, but my parents and I have slacked.

I'm staying at my parents' house, at least for the weekend. They live near Gillette Stadium and I live in downtown Boston, so the drive isn't too bad, but it's far enough that I didn't want to be traipsing back and forth and missing anything going on here.

I pick up my phone, checking to see if there's anything from Scarlett. I texted her earlier and usually I would have heard something by now. I'll try to call her tomorrow now that I'm finally not surrounded by either my dad, brother, or grandpa. They're nosy as all shit.

My eyes close, but my mind keeps racing. After five minutes, I give up and grab my phone again. Still nothing from Scarlett. It's amazing how quickly I've become such an infatuated tool. Never thought I'd see the day. I scroll through Instagram, checking the lodge's feed first. There are some great shots from guests tagging Landmark Mountain and a post about the Easter egg hunt tomorrow. And then mindless scrolling…

I pause and scroll back when I get to one Bo posted. What catches my eye is that Scarlett is sandwiched between him and Danny, looking happy as can be. She's laughing and looks stunning—the stunning part is no surprise. How happy she is next to Danny—the hell? I stare at it, my heartbeat galloping too fast. What's that bastard Danny doing by her side?

I look at when it was posted—not that long ago since I have a couple of hours on them—and I go to Bo's stories to see if I can find anything else out.

And *score*.

Bo's feeling pretty happy tonight. Story after story of shaky video. There's nothing like the picture he posted, but there's brutally pitchy singing in the background as he does a sweep over the crowd at The Dancing Emu, and I search for Scarlett, certain I'll see her cracking up at the singing. Bo pauses on a girl he thinks is hot, which he yells over and over again—someone needs to give that guy some lessons on *game*.

Hold up.

I play the story again and behind Bo's hot girl, standing outside, is Scarlett. And holy shit, Danny's out there with her. He's looking at her longingly and getting closer and closer. And then it's over. I go back and watch it a few times, wanting to throw my fucking phone across the room the more I watch it, but instead, I call her.

When she doesn't pick up the first time, I wait five minutes and call her again. This time she answers, her voice breathless.

"Hey," she says, sounding surprised.

"Hey." My tone is flat and angrier than I intended.

"What's—is everything okay? Your mom, is she—"

"Everything's fine. Mom's good. She got to come home late this afternoon. We're—I'm staying with them."

"Oh, that's such good news. I'm so glad, Jamison," she breathes out.

There's scuffling in the background.

"Settle, *settle down*. Hi, loves," she says in a playful voice. "Oh yeah, I missed you too. Sorry…I just got home and the dogs are losing their minds."

"Oh, so you weren't talking to me." I try for lighter, but I still sound like a grumpy brute.

She giggles and yep, that sound still shoots straight to my dick despite the long distance.

"Guess it depends—do you need to settle down?" she says, laughing again.

"I think I do because I want to know what the fuck you were doing looking all cozy with Danny tonight?" Damn. That wasn't subtle at all.

"*What?*" There's no playful sweetness now. "How did you—"

"I'm not even gone a full week and you've already moved on, looking all doe-eyed up at the guy who was too good for Landmark Mountain—"

"I'm gonna give you a pass because you're clearly deranged from the hard week you've had, and I don't want to discredit the pain you've been in because I know it's been difficult worrying about your mom, but what the hell, Jamison?"

I feel like an idiot but keep going, proving that it's more than just a feeling… "*Exactly*, what the hell?"

"I've been working my ass off, covering for you and glad to do it so you could have time with your family. I've barely heard from you all week…which I've understood. But this is the first time you've even called me, and it's to go all caveman on me? No, I don't think so. I'm exhausted and I don't have time for this. Goodnight, Wingtip."

Dammit. Back to being Wingtip and not the sexy 2.0 superhero version either.

She hangs up on me and I run my hand over my face, mostly mad at myself now. I almost call her right back, but I don't because she said she's exhausted, and I am too. And the part of me that's still mad at her might say the wrong thing while I'm—what did she call me?—going all caveman on her. I'd love to be going all caveman on her body right about fucking now, but I don't think she meant what I do by that phrase. And she fucking hung up on me, dammit.

I put the phone on the nightstand and shove the pillow over my head, grumbling as I turn over. It's possible I overreacted, but I guess I won't know until tomorrow.

I sleep in, shocked when I glance at the clock and see that it's nine. I can't remember the last time I slept until nine, even with a short night as an excuse.

It helped. I feel a lot better.

The first thing I do is check my phone, hoping for something from Scarlett.

Nope.

I can't blame her, since I did kind of go barbaric ogre on her last night. This long-distance thing isn't going to work for me. I know this week isn't a good one to base anything off of with the state of mind I've been in, but I think I'd feel the same no matter what: I hate every second of being away from Scarlett. Especially since we were just getting on what I thought was solid ground.

In the light of day, all the things she said about her and Danny being friends come back to me.

Shit, I totally overreacted.

My text is to the point.

> I'm sorry. Please call me when you feel like talking to this caveman.

When my phone doesn't immediately buzz with a response from her, I get up and shower and wander downstairs in search of caffeine. Pappy and Dad are at the table, still in their pajamas.

"What's doin'?" Pappy asks.

I shake my head. "Don't know yet—too short of a night. How 'bout the two of you?" I ask them. "Mom okay?"

"I slept like a dream, but this one didn't get much," Pappy says, pointing at my dad.

"Mom slept well, only woke up once and told me to stop staring at her," Dad says, laughing. "She was awake for a while earlier and just fell back to sleep. I'm already driving her crazy, hovering. But it's hard not to. I thought she was fine before…can't believe I missed the signs." He sighs and takes another sip of coffee, looking dead on his feet.

"Ma is the best at staying positive, so even if she felt awful, she'd try to rally without worrying ya. Can't be blamin' yourself."

"That's what worries me. She can't be keepin' that kind of thing from me. I gotta know the truth," he says. "This can't happen again."

"You should rest while she is, Dad. You've hardly slept

at all this week. We can't have you getting sick too," I tell him.

I reach for the biggest mug and pour what's left of the coffee, looking around for the half-and-half.

Pappy holds it up. "This what you're lookin' for?"

I nod and rub my eyes as I fill the rest of my mug with the creamer.

"Havin' a little coffee with your cream still, I see, Little Squirt." Pappy laughs. "You need to take your own advice. Go back to bed and get your rest. Daisy's better than she's been in who knows how long, and I think she's learned her lesson—she'll let us know if she's not feeling right."

I slump into the chair between them and Pappy leans forward and squeezes my shoulder and then Dad's.

"And come Monday morning, I want the two of you to have your physicals scheduled for just as soon as they can get your sorry patooties in there, you hear me?" He gives us both the eagle eye and Dad rolls his eyes like a sullen kid with peach fuzz on his upper lip.

I chuckle and Pappy's grip tightens.

"I mean it. The way you chuckleheads have stayed after me, making me go to the doctor if I even glance at you sideways, while you've been avoidin' your own health…I oughta bust both your asses, I tell ya." He huffs and while I know he'd never bust either one of our asses, this is about the most aggravated Pappy ever gets.

"I hear ya, Pap," I tell him. "I hear ya."

Pappy loosens his grip on my shoulder and turns his focus on my dad.

"I hear ya," Dad grumbles.

"What are you hearin' from out West? Son, you oughta

see our boy with this Landmark girl…Scarlett." Pappy smirks. He points at me and shakes his head, his smile getting wider and wider. "She's something special and I've never seen this one so smitten."

"You're kidding. Why am I just hearing about this?" Dad frowns, but he's having a hard time holding it, too happy about this news.

"We've been a little preoccupied with more important things." I take a long gulp of coffee. "And why don't we talk about Pappy and the way he was turning the ladies' eyes in Landmark?"

Pappy lets out a loud snort and his ears turn red. "Don't know what this kid is talking about. Tell him about Scarlett!"

"Pappy's right—she's remarkable. Gorgeous, smart… capable of singlehandedly running Landmark Mountain on her own."

I see her on top of me in that bubble, the way her body felt moving over mine, one of many memories of that night that I can't stop reliving.

I exhale a long, ragged breath. "And I might've blown it with her already. We…had words last night. I was just getting on her good side again too."

"I can't imagine you blowing it—not with the way I saw her looking at you. Fill your dad in on the backstory while I'm in the hoppah," Pappy says, standing. "All that time at the hospital and I'm about to have a medical condition of my own. Been backed up for days, say a prayer that I come out of this alive." He walks toward the door and calls over his shoulder, "Take your time and save what I haven't heard yet until I'm back. I'll check and see if the queen is up while I'm gone."

Never thought having a one-night stand would be something I'd discuss with my dad and grandpa, and it's not like any details are given, but it's part of our story. I couldn't have known that one night with Scarlett would change my life…

And now I need all the help I can get to make sure I don't lose her.

CHAPTER THIRTY-SEVEN

CONFESSIONS

SCARLETT

I wake up foul.

Too little sleep.

Angry at Jamison.

The whole thing with Danny…

I'm feeling foolish about all of it.

My to-do list is pages long. It's been a while since I've
had this much to do. It used to fire me up and today I just

feel daunted by it, but the good news is it helps get my mind off of last night.

Barely.

After walking the dogs while it's still dark out, I get to the lodge before the crew starts arriving to set up for the annual Easter egg hunt. We used to do it on Easter Sunday, but in the past few years, we've done it on Saturdays, so Bethany Christian and St. Mary's won't get offended when all of Landmark skips their egg hunts for ours.

It's a big to-do. Pictures with the Easter bunny—Albert dressed in a bunny suit. Or live bunnies for those who prefer that. Callum brings over a few of his nicer goats for the kids to pet, and Lar and Mar close up the shop with a sign on their door that says, *Find your Happy Cow pastries at the Landmark Mountain egg hunt!*

There's still snow on the ground around here, but that's never stopped us. What could be better than a *ski down the hill and find the eggs* kind of day? The inside of the eggs are filled with small packaged candy, tokens for the games inside the Landmark Mountain game room, and coupons for the local restaurants and activities. Everyone who enters the hunt is given a number and at the end of the event, the big prize is a massive basket full of the best goodies Landmark has to offer. Every shop on Heritage Lane contributes to the basket, and even some off of the main street.

Right before the festivities begin, I get a text from Jamison and I read it but don't text anything back. Not because I don't want to, but because in the next moment, I get caught in the crosshairs of a snowball fight and end up taking on the teenage boys with a few snowballs of my own. And then we think we're running low on baskets, but

I find the stash tucked in the side room of the banquet hall, no idea how they got there.

But Jamison…I can't seem to get away from thoughts of him. An apology is promising. I'm just not sure what the hell he was thinking, but if he can apologize about things…

Vera calls me saying I'm needed in the lodge—the family in 303 hasn't checked out yet and they've already been asked twice. I'm on my way inside to give her backup, deep in thoughts of Jamison, when I feel surrounded and it's my brothers walking alongside me without saying anything until I notice them.

"What?" I say, jumping when I realize it's them. "And all of you? All of you at one time—what did I do to deserve this?"

Wyatt puts his arm around me. "This is always a busy day for you and we heard the Hawaiian shirt lover is out of town…what can we do?"

"Lover?" I say, eyes wide. Who told them?

"He loves Hawaiian shirts, doesn't he?" Wyatt says, shrugging.

I take a deep breath, relaxing a little. My sex life is not a topic my brothers and I ever go near. They don't want to see me cry, but the amount they want to know about my sex life is in the negative numbers.

"And we wanted to see if you're still mad at us," Theo says.

I sigh, sagging into Wyatt. "No, I'm not mad. I've seen you since that conversation about the lodge—have I acted mad?"

"You've been quieter than usual," Sutton says.

"I've been thinking about what you said and

wondering why I've had such a hard time admitting what I want." I watch the families lining up to get their pictures taken with Albert. "But today's not the day to figure it out."

Wyatt chuckles and his arm tightens around me. "Just know we're here when you're ready to."

Callum mutters something in agreement on the other side of me.

"Thanks, guys. Where's Owen?" I look around Sutton, who's walking behind us with Theo.

My nephew is nowhere in sight and he's usually the first one to hug me.

Sutton points at Owen running around with a couple of his buddies, their baskets piled high with plastic eggs.

"We didn't see you when we first got here, so he went ahead and got started. Hopefully this will get his mind off of getting a dog for more than two seconds. He won't stop…thanks a lot." He makes a gritted-teeth face, and I lift my hands up, laughing.

"You're welcome. Get the boy a dog." I bump Wyatt with my hip. "You need one too…and Grinny. Everyone needs a pet or two in their life."

"When I get home from work, I don't want to take care of anyone or anything else," Wyatt says.

"Fair enough. I suppose you're off the hook since you do have one of the most selfless jobs on the planet."

"I don't know, some say being a judge requires being selfless," Sutton says.

"Who says that exactly?" Theo asks, lifting an eyebrow.

"Yeah, no one," Wyatt says. "No one has ever said that."

We all laugh and Sutton grumbles about us all being in on the puppy treaty with Owen.

We reach the door of the lodge and Callum opens the door, holding out his arm for me to go first. "Thanks, Cal."

He grins and then follows me inside, cutting off the rest of my brothers.

"Rude," Theo pipes up. "Callum doesn't have a pet or the most selfless job on the planet—why aren't you hounding him?"

"Callum has dozens of pets." I turn back and wait for them to all get inside.

"Doesn't count if they don't live in the house," Theo says, folding his arms over his chest like he really cares about this.

"Totally counts," Callum says. "Maybe more so since I have to go out in the freezing elements just to feed them."

I hold out my hand toward Callum and nod at Theo like *see?*

"And Delphine has started sneaking in the house when she can," Callum adds. "She's got Irene trying it now too, but Irene's not as smart about it."

"Oh shit," Wyatt says, chuckling. "That can't be good."

Most people never know when Callum is joking or not and usually assume he's angry based on his expression, but when it comes to his cows and goats, he's the biggest softie.

"Irene doesn't know she's not Delphine's size," he says softly.

I giggle, imagining Irene the cow trying to follow Delphine the goat in the house.

Vera sees me coming and a sheepish look flits across

her face. "I'm so sorry I didn't catch you in time," she says. "They just checked out and then I got distracted with something else." Her face lights up when she notices who's with me. "Well, this is a treat."

"Isn't it? No worries. It gave me a chance to hang out with these guys on the walk over." I lean against Theo when he moves next to me and they all take turns hugging Vera.

"You should stay a while," Vera tells them. "Maybe we can finally get you bachelors a wife if you stick around long enough. You don't want your sister getting married before you do, do you?" She winks at me and my mouth drops open.

They turn as one toward me, closing in as they loom over me, all talking at once.

"What's she talking about?"

"So that's what Jo meant the other day..."

"You got something you want to tell us, Scarlett?"

"It was the Hawaiian shirt, wasn't it."

"I knew I didn't trust that guy."

I hold up my hand and give Vera a scorching look that has her hustling off to do something very important...as far as she can get from my wrath.

"Yeah, you better run," I call after her.

When I look at my brothers, they all have various degrees of scowls on their faces. I put my hand on my hips, mostly to brace myself, but it's also the way I've been dealing with them since I was little.

"Wipe the scowls off your faces. No one's getting married, so you can just calm down."

"You like the guy though," Theo says. "I knew it."

"He deserve you?" Callum growls, chest all bowed up. "Where is he right now?"

"His mom just had a heart attack and bypass surgery," I say, enjoying the deflate in his stance. "And it remains to be seen if he deserves me or not." I think of his apology this morning and my heart thaws almost all the way. "He's pretty incredible."

I try not to go full-swoon since they wouldn't be able to handle it.

"You up for long distance?" Sutton's brow is crinkled and I reach out and smooth it with my thumbs.

"Stop it. You're too old to frown like this, it'll start sticking," I tell him.

He curses under his breath. "I knew I should've looked into him more thoroughly."

"Oh, for crying out loud," I groan. "Grinny adores him."

"She know you're marrying him?" Wyatt snaps.

"No one's marrying anyone. But I get the impression that Grinny wouldn't mind if I did." I smirk, and that just makes them scoff, their expressions like sullen five-year-old boys. "I'm twenty-three and you haven't liked anyone I've ever dated, but you like him, I know you do."

"So you *are* dating him…" Wyatt says.

His arms fold across his chest as he studies me like I'm his next patient.

"We're…seeing where this goes," I say.

Callum grumbles *where is he* again from under his breath and I shoot him a look that would normally have him caving, but he doesn't back down. "He wants you? Once his mom is taken care of, he figures out a way to close up shop in Boston"—he attempts Jamison's accent when he says Boston—"and he gets his ass by your side."

"Oh, so now you're wanting him by my side? Make up your mind, brother." I laugh and reach out to poke his side. He jerks and scowls and I go put my arm around him. He's stiff for a second but then relaxes against me and I lean back to look at him. "You're not gonna start taking tips from them and get all barky with me now, are you?"

"Sorry," he mumbles. "I just...you..." He pulls me back in and pats my shoulder awkwardly.

"No one's barky," Theo says, sounding medium barky. "Just looking out for you. Holly said Danny was giving you shit the other night at The Emu and Regg was the biggest bastard on the planet—"

I look around, making sure no one is hearing this. "Keep it down."

"It's the truth, and if we know it, the rest of the town already knew it weeks ago," Theo says. "You haven't had the best track record with relationships, and you've been through a lot this year. We just want to be sure that you're not rushing into anything and that he's worthy of you... and I'm hurt you didn't tell me... didn't tell us," he adds.

His phone buzzes and he glances at it as I lean my head against his shoulder.

"Shit," he whispers.

"What is it?" I ask, frowning up at him. He's pale. "Theo?"

"It's...Sofie. She's-I guess one of her horses needs help."

"I'd heard she was back. Watch your heart, brother," Wyatt says.

Theo shoots a dark look toward Wyatt and runs his

hand through his hair. "I better go. Are you okay?" he asks me.

"I'll be fine. Will you?"

His jaw clenches and he stalks away without answering me.

"So help me if she wrecks him again," Wyatt mutters.

Growing up, I always adored Sofie, but when I heard she'd moved back after her father died, I didn't know how to feel about it. Still don't. She must be avoiding us since, as far as I know, none of us have seen her yet. An almost impossible feat to pull off in Landmark.

Discussing her is off-limits with Theo, so we're all a little shaken as we look at each other.

"I'll check on him in a while," Callum says.

"I will too. And about Jamison—I'm still trying to figure it out myself. I know you guys care and I love you for it."

I pull the three of them in for a hug.

"You really are the best brothers, despite being a little oblivious at times," I tell them, laughing at their sheepish reactions. "I did try to get us all together while his family was here—when he comes back, we'll have to make sure that happens. If this does end up being a thing, I need all of you to be on board. And I don't mind if you give him the third degree…" I bite the inside of my cheek as my smile grows way too big. "But I think he can take it."

CHAPTER THIRTY-EIGHT

DICKENS

JAMISON

By the time I say goodnight to my parents and Pappy that night, I've given up on Scarlett calling me.

Despite checking my phone more times than I'm comfortable admitting to myself, it was a good day.

Mom said it's the best she's felt since her surgery, and it was obvious. Her cheeks had more color and she had more energy.

I'm tired from not sleeping much but too wired to sleep, and tonight I refuse to go down the social media rabbit hole. I check email, sending out an email to everyone who participated in the Easter egg hunt, thanking them for all their hard work and stating again how much I wish I could've been there. And I opt to just go for it, clicking on Scarlett's number. I can't wait another second to know if she's still mad at me.

She answers right before I expect it to go to her voice mail, sounding out of breath.

"Hey. Did I catch you at a bad time?" I ask.

"No. I just got home," she says.

"You sound exhausted."

"It was an exhausting day. Best crowd we've ever had at the Easter egg hunt and with the fewest mishaps."

"That's excellent. I followed the updates throughout the day and it looked like an amazing day. Weather looked perfect."

"It was. Couldn't have been any better. And I got to see my family for a lot of the day, and we hung out at Grinny's tonight…it's been a while since I've had that much time with them. Took the dogs with me and they are nice and tired."

"I'm glad," I say quietly. Glad about her day, *really* glad she's talking to me.

"How's your mom?"

"Today she seemed the most like herself. My mom is normally full of energy, so it's been strange to see her so subdued, but she was chatty today and ate a little more, looks better too."

"That's great news."

It's hard to tell if she's just being polite when she really wants to hang me up by the balls or if my apology did the trick. So I double down.

"I'm sorry I was a prick last night."

"You *were* a prick," she agrees. "Thanks for apologizing."

"Do you forgive me?"

"I do," she says.

I blow out a long gust of air, relief knocking me sideways.

"I'm so gone over you, Scarlett," I say, leaning my head against the headboard. "And I'm gonna blow it a lot probably. For example…I don't think I've called a girl in a decade."

"You're more of a texter?"

"I guess so, yeah. More of a plan things in person and then do the follow-up with texts kind of guy. I haven't ever done a long-distance thing, haven't had the agony of waiting all day for someone to call…" I pause when she laughs. "Honestly, I usually regret giving my number to anyone, not this…wishing you'd call."

"You could've called me at any time," she sings.

I hit FaceTime on my phone, and she accepts, grinning wide.

"Oh, could you FaceTime me again and I'll answer from my laptop? I want to see you better," she says.

We hang up and I grab my laptop, calling her from there. When she pops up on my bigger screen, my stomach and chest flutter erratically.

"Well, this is a helluva lot better. Why haven't we been doing *this* all week?"

She's on her bed, positioned about like I am, only she has Lucia and Delgado nestled in next to her. Delgado's body is snug against her thigh and his little head is propped up on her leg.

"God, I miss you. I want to be where Delgado is right now."

Her cheeks flush and she looks down, her teeth sliding over her lip. "I miss you." She sounds hoarse and I frown.

"Are you getting sick?"

"I think I just yelled too much. We do this relay toward the end of the event, where everyone has to leap with all their legs attached to a partner and see how many of their eggs they can keep in their basket. It's hilarious. The winners were these twin little girls who are staying at the lodge this week. Owen was certain they'd cheated. I wish Ivy had been here—she would've had so much fun."

"I wish she could've been too. Her week hasn't been even half as much fun as all that—lots of hospital time and worrying about Daisy. She's been really anxious about my mom and it's hard to see that little girl sad about anything."

"She's so happy, it breaks my heart to think about her going through all that heaviness," she says. She shakes her head. "Why can't everyone live forever?"

"I know. I don't like the dark places my head has gone this week," I admit. "Anyway, we're on the other side of it...and I hope we won't have to deal with any of this again for a very long time. Never works for me. What else is happening over there?"

"Vera let my brothers know—about the two of us."

Her pink lips press together, her dark eyes pulling me in. She seems shy still, unsure of how to be with me and I want to reach through the phone and reassure her.

"Yeah?" I grin, and she makes a face. "What? You didn't want them to know? How did they react?"

"They'd be happiest if I'd join a convent, maybe start one right here in Landmark so I'm never far..." She laughs, and yep, clockwork.

Hi, dick. I shift my screen up so my bulge doesn't take over our chat.

"I reminded my brothers that they all liked you before they thought we were...whatever we're doing..."

I think about Pappy telling me it was time to woo her and how I've failed spectacularly in that department, but hopefully it's not too late.

"We've gone about this whole relationship a little backwards, but I'm not complaining," I tell her. She grins and my heart thumps against my ribcage. "What we're doing is...we're getting to know each other...and enjoying the ride. As I think I've confessed a few times now, this is new for me. But I've never been one to hold back once I'm sure of something."

She fans her face with her hand, and I laugh. I don't mind seeing her flustered this way, not when she's looking at me like she wants me as much as I want her.

"Do you always sleep in a sweatshirt?" she asks. "What is that on there?"

I roll my eyes. "I should've thought this through before I called in this." I stretch out my obnoxious yellow sweatshirt so she can see the grapefruit with *Squirt* slanting across it in bright red letters.

She laughs. "Did Zac give you that?"

"How'd you guess?" I laugh. "I left it here so the only people to see me in it would be family—to keep the nickname from growing outside these walls."

"It looks good on you," she says. "It'd look a lot better off." She lifts a shoulder and my poor dick weeps and bucks against my sweats. Dramatic bastard.

I yank my sweatshirt over my head with one hand.

She grins. "This *is* fun."

"What do you sleep in when you're home alone?" I ask, wishing this screen could be life-size.

She stands up and places her laptop on her nightstand and undoes her jeans, giving me a much better view.

"Oh, I love where this is going," I say.

She laughs. "Don't get too excited. You haven't seen what I end up in yet."

She shimmies her jeans off and there are too many good places to look at once. Today's lace is navy with subtle purple and pink swirls through it.

"Turn around," I say, my voice husky.

She turns and with her sweater on, all I see are the bottom curves of her bare cheeks.

"Perfect," I tell her.

She looks at me over her shoulder and pulls her sweater off, and her back is bare except for the crisscross straps that lead to the lace on her hips that is only there to highlight her full, round ass.

My mouth waters. "I want to take a bite so bad," I groan.

She gives me a flirty smile and then turns around to face me, and I groan again. There's a deep plunge with a small crisscross ribbon straining between her tits.

"You would be wearing the best one when I'm two thousand miles away."

"You think all of them are the best." She laughs and starts to move away.

"No, don't go," I tell her, gripping my dick with my fist to stave off an eruption.

She leans toward the camera, looking like the only fantasy I'll ever need to die a happy man, her pouty lips parted.

"But I don't sleep in this," she says.

"Okay." I nod, reaching out to trace her lips on the screen. "Let me see. Do you sleep in the nude?" I ask hopefully.

She did the two nights we spent together but also curled around me like a little koala. I wish I could warm her body up right now.

She doesn't answer, lowering the straps so slowly and then leaning back before doing the unthinkable and stepping out of the frame.

"Nooo. Come back."

She giggles and I hear her opening a drawer and then it's quiet for a moment.

"Okay…next time definitely take the laptop with you. The curiosity is killing me."

She steps into the frame, hands clasped primly in front of her, and I stare at her for a moment before I burst out laughing. Covered head to toe in vertical purple and white stripes, little details in the white, and lace trim around the very high neck and sleeves that go all the way to her wrists.

"What's that in the white stripes?"

"Hearts and flowers," she says, trying not to laugh. "Grinny gives me a new gown every Christmas. I have one in red and blue and green and all white and this—" She does a sweeping motion over her.

"Is that flannel?"

"Sure is."

"I am so fucking turned on right now."

She cracks up then, her eyes bright. "Mm-hmm, I bet." She picks up the laptop and gets back on the bed. "At first I'd just tuck these gowns away in my drawer, feeling bad that I hadn't donated them somewhere or something, but then one night I came in from a long day, chilled to the bone, and the gowns beckoned me…"

"Like a siren's call?" I fill in.

"Exactly." She grins. "Slipped one over my head and damn, life-changing. It's like wearing a flannel sheet."

My laugh is loud in this little room, and I cover my mouth with my fist, the other still firmly gripping my dick.

"So you're sexy little lacy vixen during the day, and come nightfall, you're sexy little ghost of Christmas past."

Her eyes close when she laughs, and I'm smiling so hard my face hurts.

It's not the only thing that hurts.

"And what's underneath that flannel goodness now?" I ask.

Her eyes open and she smirks, her shoulder lifting. "Not a thing." Her grin widens with my tormented look. She tilts her head up. "Let me see what you're wearing. Your face is nice, but I want to see all of you. Tell me you've got some raggedy plaid pajama pants going on or something…"

I let go of my dick, figuring she may as well see that I wasn't lying about being turned on, and hold the laptop out so she can see my grey sweats. I adjust myself, making sure I'm tucked in, but I'm so hard, it's a fight.

She gasps and I give her a smug look.

"Told you."

She licks her lips and my dick jerks to life, trying to sneak back out the top.

"Hey, Little Squirt," she sings.

"Don't you dare."

She giggles. "Since there's nothing little about you, I'd think it'd be okay." Her raspy voice and the hunger in her gaze as she stares at me have me cursing under my breath.

"I was trying to keep this situation under wraps and have a conversation with you, but you're making it really hard…" My laugh rumbles in my chest. "Not what I meant, but also perfectly accurate…"

My hand winds through my hair, tugging, adrenaline surging the longer I look at her.

"It's the granny gown, isn't it. That does it for you?" she teases.

"Lie back and slide those hands up that granny gown, let's see if I'm the orgasm whisperer from over here."

Her face flushes. "I've never sexted before," she whispers.

"Neither have I, but I like the way it's going so far."

"Me too." She pulls something toward her and sets the laptop down. It's at the perfect angle to see her now. "Huh, who knew my portable desk would be so handy?" She lies back and I sit up more, still leaning against the headboard, my laptop placed in front of me so I can see her front and center.

She looks shy all of a sudden, her brown eyes huge as she looks up at me.

"Let me see if I can tell from here how wet you are," I say softly.

As hilarious as this gown is, when she lifts it up her leg, showing more and more skin, I get the allure. Cover up those goods and then reveal the package bit by bit. I can get behind that.

I can also get behind her stripping it off, but I don't want her to be chilly. When she gets to the apex between her legs, I stop breathing for a second, leaning in to see her closer.

"I wish I could zoom," I whisper.

She giggles.

"Spread your lips for me, let me see." She doesn't hesitate and I groan, seeing her practically dripping for me already. "I wish I could have a taste," I tell her. "Dip inside with your middle finger, nice and slow, and back out. Swirl around some of that wetness. And this time, make sure you glide over your clit on the way back in, can't leave her out."

She does as I ask and her breath hitches, her teeth clenching down on her lower lip.

"I want to see you," she says, her fingers repeating the motion, her eyes glassy as her hips start to arch to meet her hand.

I pull my dick out, fisting up the length of it with a tight hold, and she whimpers.

"I've never seen anything so hot in my life," she says.

She lifts up and yanks the gown over her head, her tits bouncing as she lies back and resumes her strokes. Her nipples are dark red pebbles, just asking to be sucked.

"Pretty sure my view is the hottest," I tell her. "I don't think I'm gonna last long. I've been hard as a rock since we started talking."

"I'm close," she says.

"Go faster," I tell her.

She picks up her speed, her middle and ring finger flat

as they glide over her clit and inside and out, faster and faster and faster. Her breathing gets shallow, her mouth parting as she watches me in rapt attention. I follow her tempo, imagining my hand is her tight channel clenched around me.

"That's it. I love being inside your hot, wet heat. You look so fucking beautiful. I love watching you…come," I choke out.

Her head tilts back into her pillow and her eyes squeeze shut as she chants my name and bucks against her hand. It's more than I can take. It's hard to keep from shouting as I come so hard, streams shooting onto my stomach and chest.

I wipe myself off with the sweatshirt and she smirks. I shake my head, laughing.

"I think you can only be *Big* Squirt," she says.

"It's better than Wingtip, I guess."

CHAPTER THIRTY-NINE

CRUSHES

SCARLETT

I'm dragging more and more as each week passes.

The following Friday I feel like I could sleep for twenty hours straight, and the week after that, even more so.

By the week after that, I'm catching catnaps at my desk when I have an extra ten minutes. Jamison and I text when we can during the day, and then at night we Face-Time for hours.

The range of topics we cover every single night is vast. We've talked about everything from our childhoods and funny stories with our brothers to what's going on at the lodge and with his mom.

Usually we're covering the trivial and the deep all within the same few minutes.

"Grinny makes good meatloaf."

"Mmm, I will do my best to pretend I like it, but it'll be difficult. I dipped everything in ketchup until I was fifteen and then never wanted it again…"

"What does that have to do with meatloaf?"

He laughs. "Sometimes people put a ketchup-y thing on the top." He shudders. "It feels wrong."

"Hmm. Seems kind of like ketchup on a burger which feels pretty right to me. Who was your first kiss?"

"A girl I met at a week-long YMCA camp. We both had braces. It wasn't great."

I laugh.

"Who was yours?"

"A tourist named Kyle." I grin at the scowl on his face.

"He sounds like a twit."

I shake my head. "Not at all. He tasted like strawberry-watermelon Hubba Bubba."

He scoffs at that. "Everyone knows Hubba Bubba loses its flavor."

"Who did you lose your virginity to?" I ask.

He doesn't hesitate. "Charity Farling. She's the daughter of some of my parents' friends."

"Oh, do you still see her?"

"I do, yeah. She lives in Boston…with her husband and three children," he adds, grinning.

"Do you ever regret not being the one she married?"

He makes a face. "That has never once crossed my mind. No."

That makes me unreasonably ecstatic.

He's already heard the details about Regg and Danny and didn't gloat when I told him he was right about Danny. He knows how Danny has avoided me since he admitted his feelings, and that I'd heard he was leaving Landmark. He's not threatened that I'm sad about Danny, which I appreciate. I'd worried when he'd gone caveman on me that he'd be the jealous type and I didn't think I could handle that. He's apologized more than once about reacting that way.

I personally think he was just freaked out about his mom, exhausted, and we were still in such a tentative place with each other that it was the perfect storm.

I think he might know more about me than I've even admitted to myself, many of our conversations going much deeper than I'm used to.

The hurt I've always held inside about Granddad not treating me like my brothers, despite his love.

The shame I've felt for how much I miss my parents when I don't even really remember them when Grinny and Granddad have done everything in their power to give us the best life.

How I've felt attached to the lodge as a way to show them how grateful I am for the way they've raised us, the way Grinny gave up so many years of her life when she should've been a doting grandma who could hand us back to our parents after a little visit and instead was a full-time parent to five kids.

The last few nights I've fallen asleep while talking to him and wake up in the morning to see him looking like hot sin with his rumpled hair as he sleeps, or to his sweet eyes on me, heating me up from the inside out every time.

And the man is still an orgasm whisperer from two thousand miles away. Holy hell. The things he says, the things he tells me to do to my body, the power that comes from watching him fall apart over *me*—I don't think I'll ever get used to it.

His insatiable hunger to know me in every way, body and soul...the way he's the perfect combination of sexy and playful. I was close to certain that I was in love with him, but after the past few weeks of getting to know him in a way that we might not have if we'd been together in person, there's no doubt in my mind now that I am completely and madly in love with him.

What I've also learned that has been almost as surprising as falling in love, is that I don't want to run the lodge by myself anymore. I was figuring that out even before he left, but doing it without him—it's just not the same.

Last night he wanted to watch me sew one of my lacy things—his words—and I had him pick the color. He thought that was too hard and ended up going with a sheer black leopard print with black lace. I tried something a little different and I'm really happy with the end result. There's a ribbon waistband like a lot of them, but the rest is unique to me. Sexy lace cutouts attach to the ribbon, a cheeky thong in the back that's mostly bare, the little strip of leopard material coming to a swooping V right before the tiny lace scallops.

I tried it on afterward and he was speechless. It's the fastest he's ever come and then he stroked himself leisurely while he told me to get on my stomach on the bed and rub against the mattress until I came so he could watch.

I've always felt a little weird about touching myself— which we've also discussed—and especially at the thought of doing it in front of anyone—it was more of an *in the dark when I'm too pent-up to ignore it* occasional occurrence or sometimes in the tub. But he's woken up my body —it's stirred up and constantly craving him.

He texts while I'm helping Lorena get the floral arrangements inside and I try not to smile at my phone, sticking it in my pocket before I read it to put the last arrangement on her cart.

"You've been so happy," Lorena says, smiling wide. "When I first met you, you were not so happy. Want to share your secret?"

My cheeks flush and she smiles bigger.

"It's hard to put into words," I tell her as we start rolling the cart toward the lodge. "I've always been such a planner, needing to have my life all plotted out, and panicking when it didn't go to plan. And now that I'm living the life that I thought I wanted, it's not what's making me happy. Not that it's making me sad either, it's just…it's a guy," I finally say.

Her eyes light up, but then she frowns, sticking her lip out in a sad pout. "But it's not Mr. Jamison? Is he never coming back?"

The bet at Sunny Side has paused since he's been gone

and I've had more than one local asking when he's coming back for that reason alone. We've never fully confirmed or denied all the rumors and I'd rather not when he's across the country. The bet is just a small part of why I've kept my mouth shut about how things have progressed with Jamison and me, but the truth is, I like having this all to ourselves for a little bit longer.

And I still have no clue what the future holds for me, for us…but I love what is happening right now.

It's a whole new concept for me to think this way. A complete mind shift. I don't even put the little things on the to-do lists just to check them off anymore, only what I have to get done for the day.

"It seemed like there might be something there with the two of you," Lorena says, her eyes narrowing.

Bill and Andy open the doors for us and we roll inside the lobby.

I lift an eyebrow at Lorena. "How much money have you placed on it?" I ask.

Her cheeks turn rosy and she glances around us before leaning in to whisper, "More than I should've."

"I think he'll be back," I say over my shoulder.

Her eyes widen and she starts to say something, but Vera and Albert step in to help unload and I'm glad she doesn't push for more in front of them.

It's an hour or so before I pull my phone back out to check his text.

Dammit.

JAMISON

Do you have a minute to talk?

I wish I hadn't waited to check it, the worry niggling in

the back of my mind still about his mom. I call him, walking back to my office. It's not like I could have talked to him an hour ago anyway, but I could've texted to let him know what was going on.

It goes straight to his voice mail, so I text him back.

> Sorry I missed you. Lorena was here with the arrangements and we were low on help when she first got here! I'm around for the next hour if you're free, and then I'll see you in the meeting with Magnus and Steve and the team they've put together. XO

He doesn't text back then and when I'm done with the meeting a couple of hours later that he never Zoomed in on, he still hasn't.

I send another text.

> Meeting went great! I hope everything is okay with you over there. Renovations are starting next week, May 1st as planned. They're doing it in the order you suggested: Condos first, then upper floors before the main level and lobby, pool and hot tubs last. <Dancing girl emoji>

I start to text more and then pause. We might have come a long way and I feel more and more secure sharing how I'm feeling, but I don't think I'll ever be someone who texts a bunch when no one is responding. Okay, two texts aren't a bunch, but for me, it is. I included a lot of sentences in those two texts.

I get a call half an hour later and am disappointed when it's not him. It's from a number I don't recognize, but I always answer anyway since it could be related to the lodge.

"Hello, is this Scarlett Landmark?" a woman asks.

"Yes, it is."

"My name is Annette Tremblay." She has a slight accent and pauses frequently between her words. "I got your number from Jamison Ledger…" She leaves me hanging there, and my stomach dives to the floor while also feeling like it might have jumped into my throat.

"Is Jamison okay?" I ask, my voice rushed and higher than normal.

"Oh, yes," she laughs, "at least as far as I know. I'm sorry if I worried you. Jamison wanted me to reach out—he said he'd let you know I was calling, but it sounds…uh, maybe it was a surprise? Jamison found me through Summer and Liam…I met them at a dinner party here in LA…and uh, Jamison and I…we had a Zoom meeting… about you."

I have to sit down. Jamison contacted Summer and Liam—Autumn's famous director sister and movie star brother-in-law—about *me*?

Annette is still talking and I try to focus. "—friends," she's saying.

Shit, what did I miss?

"I am the owner of Belle Lace Textile, a wholesale lace and fine fabric company, and Jamison says you are a very talented seamstress."

Belle Lace Textile—I've only lusted after the lace on their website for the past two years. I fan my face with the new brochures we just got of our alpine slides and coaster.

"Again, I'm sorry for catching you…unaware. I will have…words with Jamison." Her laugh catches me off guard but not as much as her next words. "He is just too…*delicious* to stay mad at."

My eyebrows lift and a little zip of possessiveness rushes through me.

It's like she can read my thoughts. "Never fear, I have been happily married to my wife for ten years, and Jamison seems…uh, he is quite taken with *you*, but between you and me, if I, uh—how do you say it—if I *swung* that way, and I *don't*, he would catch my eye." She laughs and I join in this time. "*Charmant.*" She sighs.

I quickly Google *charmant* in various spellings to be sure what it means and grin when it's what I thought —charming.

When it feels like she's waiting for me to say something, I throw in, "He *is*…pretty charming and delicious."

My face flames—I don't really use delicious, or charming for that matter, to describe how hot a man is, but with Jamison, both do apply. But then I realize she was probably waiting for me to say something about her company, not Jamison.

"Mm-hmm," she says.

No, I think she'd be happy just talking about Jamison.

Fan, fan, fan. The thin layer of sweat forming on my forehead chills as I fan my face.

"If you would like to see my swatches, I will send our latest collection. Or even better, come visit my showroom. Recently I have been more exclusive to luxury bridal designers and a few costume designers, but just give me a few days' notice and I will have everything ready for your visit."

"This is—thank you so much," I say, still shocked that Jamison did this for me. "I've wished I could order from

Belle Lace for a long time. But you should know that I don't have a shop or anything yet."

"Jamison told me you are just starting out...we all have to start somewhere, do we not? Let's just say he was *very*... compelling." She laughs again, and I so wish I knew what Jamison told her about me.

"I'd love to see your swatches," I say. "As much as I wish I could, I'm not able to get to LA right now, but I'm so excited to see what you have...to *touch* all of it."

"You are going to fall in love," she says. "Well, something tells me you already are in love with our Jamison!" Her voice lilts up at the end with what sounds like excitement and I have to pinch myself. "I am a hopeless romantic, you see. But you will fall in love with these laces and fabrics too."

"Oh, I'm sure I will. I can't wait."

"Tell me your information and your shipment will be sent today...most likely a Tuesday delivery."

I give her my address and thank her again and before she hangs up, she says, "Tell Jamison hello for me, and between you and me, that man needs an *énorme* thank you —" She bursts into a long sentence in French. "I wish I knew how to fully express it in English. Big, big adoration for his thoughtfulness. This is not something I have ever done. He was—what is that expression? He was *that* convincing."

She giggles and again, I'm fanning as we hang up.

I wish I could show him my *énorme* thanks. I jump up from my desk and shake my booty before I check my phone again to see if he's texted.

Still nothing.

CHAPTER FORTY

CROWD PLEASER

JAMISON

It's been the longest fucking day and hasn't gone even close to how I thought it would, but I'm here.

I made it.

Damn, I'm glad to be back.

I breathe in the mountain air and take note of how most of the snow has melted since I've been gone. I wish I'd gotten in another ski day before the lifts closed in mid-April.

It's almost nine o'clock, so after my first errand in town, I go to Scarlett's condo, wanting to surprise her before anyone tells her I'm here. I knock and the dogs bark, so I wait for her to answer, but she doesn't, so I knock once more and then head to the lodge, going in the office entrance.

Her office is empty and it's quiet as I walk down the hall. I check my phone and she hasn't sent another text since this afternoon. I should've called her when I landed, but I didn't want to give anything away.

When I walk into the lobby, the low hum of laughter and chatter feels good. Inviting.

And then I see her.

Scarlett is over by the couches near the bookshelves, clinking champagne glasses with Holly and April. I can't stop the smile that spreads across my face.

Will there ever be a day that she doesn't take my breath away? I don't think so.

Holly's facing me, so she sees me first, pausing mid-clink.

Scarlett turns to see what got her attention and I hear her say something about Magnus being in the room. Her mouth drops when she sees me and Holly takes her glass as she rushes toward me, wrapping her arms around my neck and hugging me hard.

My arms close around her waist and back and I sigh into her hair.

"It is so good to see you," I say.

"I was trying so hard not to worry," she says.

She pulls back and looks at me, swatting my chest and then placing her hands on my cheeks.

"I want to be mad at you for making me worry about you, but I'm too happy to see you." She laughs, but her eyes are shy.

I lean my forehead against hers. "I'm sorry—I was supposed to be here hours ago and the flight kept getting—"

"Does this mean the two of you are official?" A lady I've never seen pops up next to us.

"Rosie," Scarlett hisses.

"I'm sorry, but the pot is up to three thousand now and my salon could really use a few updates." Rosie shrugs, not looking sorry at all.

I look at Scarlett and tilt her chin up.

"As far as I'm concerned, we're official," I whisper.

Her lips tilt up and the heat in her eyes is unmistakable.

"I sure hope so, Wingtip," she whispers.

I grin and lean in to kiss her the way I've wanted to for so long. Her arms tighten around my neck, her hands tugging my hair, and we get lost in each other, barely coming out of our fog when applause erupts around us.

We part reluctantly and turn to see a small crowd cheering for us as they clap. Whistles fill the lobby and I see Rosie running out the front door. She's not the only one hightailing it out of here.

"Sunny Side is about to get a mad rush right around closing time," Scarlett says. "Serves Jo right."

"Should we head over there and set the record straight ourselves?"

She grins. "Absolutely."

We walk hand in hand to her car and she tosses me the

keys. I open the passenger side for her, taking the opportunity to kiss the back of her neck and her cheek before she gets in. She lifts her lips to mine and then pulls away when it heats up.

"We're on a mission," she reminds me.

"Almost forgot."

I drive as fast as I can and there's only one parking spot in the Sunny Side lot. Scarlett laughs when she sees the crowd inside.

"Grinny will be sad she missed this."

The patrons of Sunny Side are so focused on arguing about who got there first that they don't notice us.

"Scarlett!" Grinny says in surprise. Her eyes widen when she sees me and she winks. "Speak of the devil."

"Don't tell me you're part of this bet too," Scarlett says, laughing.

"No, but…Helen dragged me here when she caught wind of…happenings." Grinny smirks and lifts an eyebrow at me. "She wanted me to manage the crowd to make sure she got to the front, but she managed that all by herself."

She points and we turn to see Helen, pounding her tiny fist on Jo's counter. Lar and Mar are behind her scowling, I guess because they know they don't stand a chance behind Helen.

"How did all of these people get here before Rosie?" Scarlett turns to me, her eyes wide.

I clear my throat and put my fingers between my lips, the whistle piercing through the noise. Everyone turns to look at me and when they see me with Scarlett, there's a whole new buzz of excitement that carries throughout the restaurant.

"We thought we'd come and settle this wager once and for all," I say, taking Scarlett's hand in mine.

A few cheers erupt and I lift my other hand, grinning as I silence them.

"I didn't know my heart was up for grabs," I start, pausing when a few people chuckle, "but when I met Scarlett, everything changed."

"Awww," rumbles through the room.

I lift her hand to my lips and kiss her knuckles. "I have tunnel vision for this woman right here, so all bets are off. Scarlett Landmark has my heart."

"What about you, Scarlett?" Jo shouts from the back. "Does Jamison have your heart too?"

Scarlett's cheeks tinge with pink and she squeezes my hand before nodding.

"Completely," she says.

I put my hands on either side of her face and kiss her as the restaurant celebrates. It's hard to pull away from her, but I want to say something else while I have everyone's attention.

I squeeze Scarlett's hand, our fingers threading together, and I look at her as I say the next part. I want to see her face.

"And you're looking at the newest official resident of Landmark…"

Her mouth drops and she puts her hand over her mouth. I put my arm around her and she leans into me.

"Really?" she asks. "I can't believe it."

"I didn't want to be away from you for another minute." I lean in and whisper the rest in her ear, "Let's get out of here. We have a lot to talk about."

She nods, her eyes shining. We kiss Grinny's cheeks

just as Helen is declared the winner. The restaurant is still flying high when we make our escape.

"I can't believe you're moving here," she says on the way to the car. "I'd tried to not even hope..." She looks embarrassed to admit that much and I put my hands on her waist before she gets in the car.

"Hope for everything you want, Scarlett Landmark. The sky is the limit for you. And I'm not going anywhere."

CHAPTER FORTY-ONE

MEANT TO BE

SCARLETT

By the time we get to my condo, talking nonstop the whole way, any earlier inhibition I felt at seeing Jamison again is gone and I'm amazed at how easy all of this feels, how much we've progressed since he was here.

All those hours we've spent getting to know each other online have made this transition more seamless than I could've imagined.

Delgado and Lucia flip when they see him. Delgado's entire back half swishes back and forth like he's wagging his entire rear end, not just his tail. Lucia goes between Jamison's legs and stays there, standing tall like she's his pony, and the joy the two of them bring him is infectious.

"I feel terrible for hogging them all this time," I say, as they vie for his attention. "You're clearly meant to be with them."

"I'm meant to be with all three of you," he says, his smile making my heart skip over itself.

I move toward him and ignore the wet puppy noses and wrap my arms around his neck, looking up at him. "I'm really glad you're back and that you're staying..."

His hands on my waist feel so good, having him in my space feels so good.

"Do you think you might decide to stick around in Landmark too?" His voice is light, but I can tell that he's nervous about my answer.

I bite the inside of my mouth, my heartbeat picking up. "I've realized some things since you've been gone."

"Tell me everything."

I smile and I feel his body relax into me. "I like working with you. A lot. It got challenging with Granddad because I was doing most of the work for such a long time, but that's what I was used to. I didn't think I'd like having someone else in here, mixing it up, challenging me. At all."

He grins and stays quiet, waiting for what I have to say.

"But when you were gone, I missed you, not just because of my feelings for you, but because I think we're a good team. And I know I said it at dinner that night, but I believe it more than ever now: I trust that you're taking this place beyond what I could've ever done on my own." I take a deep breath.

"We are an *excellent* team," he says, grinning. "That's my favorite part of what you said."

I laugh and he leans his forehead against mine for a second before leaning back to look at me again.

"I'm excited to have more time to work on fun projects. When I tell you how shocked I was to hear from Annette today—well, there's no putting it into words. That you would do that for me—it means so much."

I put my hands on his cheeks and lean up to kiss him.

"Thank you," I whisper. "Your belief in me has been—well, I haven't even known how to wrap my head around it. I think that's why I was so resistant to working with you in the first place. I'm not used to being so validated. And with the lingerie, I don't know what will come of all of it, but I'd like to try to do *something* with it."

"A shop in the lodge?" he asks hopefully.

"I was loving that idea and it's amazing of you to offer the space…but I thought maybe…I'll just start with a website at first, see how that goes…see if I can keep up with the workload…" I pause, unsure if I have to spell it out for him.

He tilts his head.

"You want to keep working at Landmark Mountain?" he asks, eyes lighting up.

I nod, my smile giddy. "Yes, I do. With you."

He lets out a loud, "*Yeah,*" which gets the dogs all worked up, and when he twirls me around and dips me back, kissing me hard, they're right there in the big fat middle of us.

"Nosy little fuckers, aren't they," he says, wiping Lucia's slobber off of his cheek. I wipe my face too, laughing as I try to push Lucia back.

I pull him to the couch and we sit down, our legs tangled together, touching everywhere we can.

"Well, this is a monumental day," he says, pushing my hair back. "Everything feels right in the world now that we're in the same room. I've missed you so much."

"That's the other thing I'm not used to—this missing," I admit. "It consumed me, wanting to talk to you more than work or anything else."

I flush with how honest I'm being—it was hard to do that with him for a while when I wasn't sure of his motives, but I've always been a straight shooter, and it feels safer than ever to say what I mean with him.

"I also...*wentonthepill*." My last four words come out so fast, he tilts his head.

"What?"

"I went on the pill," I say quietly. "Do with that what you will, but...throwing it out there."

One of our conversations while he was in Boston was the admission that neither of us have ever had sex without condoms. And on our first night together, despite using condoms, we'd already covered that our last tests were negative.

His eyes burn with intensity. "I haven't been with anyone but you since the night we met, and you're the only one I want. I love you, Scarlett."

I straddle him and he's already hard, his hands tugging me tighter against him.

"You're the only one I want," I whisper against his mouth. "I love you."

He lifts me up, my legs going around his waist, and he carries me into my bedroom, laying me on the bed as he leans over me.

"Say it again," he says.

"I love you."

I keep whispering it in his ear and against his skin, as we undress each other. When he sinks into me, bare, we both gasp and shudder with the sensation.

"Sitting next to you in that bar was the best decision I've ever made," he says, his face straining as he pulls out and works his way in deeper with the next thrust. "I haven't told you this, but...I watched you before I ever sat down."

My breath catches as I look up at him, loving how full he makes me feel.

"I thought you were the most beautiful girl I'd ever seen, way out of my league."

He drags in and out, so slowly that I clutch his backside and tug him in deeper.

"I thought you were out of my league too," I say, breathless.

He buries himself as deep as he can go and groans, his eyes shutting tight for a moment as he stills.

"We're perfect for each other," he whispers. "You're still out of my league, but I'm going to spend the rest of my life up for the challenge."

I flutter around him and he swells, making me moan. I clench around him and he grins.

"I love watching you come more than anything," he says.

"You might have to fight for bed space with the dogs," I whimper when I can breathe again.

He lifts an eyebrow like I'm daring him and starts a faster assault on my body.

"I love that you're fucking planning to have me in your bed."

I can't even be embarrassed because I want him here too much. "Yeah, you're not going anywhere…"

I lean up and he flips over, pulling me on top of him.

"I'm yours," he says, grinning up at me.

He's not grinning a few minutes later, as I rock against him. Our skin is damp, our faces flush as we move as one. He sits up to face me, taking him impossibly deeper.

"Tell me something good," he says. "I can start. Being so deep inside you, I don't know where I end and you begin…"

"Having you in my bed, living in Landmark, and doing this whenever we want," I say.

"Loving you, you loving me…starting a new life together."

He presses his fingers between us and I cry out, another orgasm taking me by surprise. He comes with a roar, and I love how everything feels so much more intense this way.

I hang on for dear life as he wrenches everything out of me and then some, making me see stars and beyond.

"I have something to tell you," he says, when we fall back on the pillows, chests heaving up and down.

He says something and I'm still delirious, so I think I'm hearing things.

I turn my head to look at him, my body still winded. "What did you just say?"

"I said, 'Landmark Mountain is yours.' Well, technically, it's *ours*. Your name is next to mine and Zac's now. I went to show Grinny the papers before I came to see you, and she approves. It's how Helen knew about us before everyone else...she showed up as I was leaving and Grinny said, 'Go get our girl!' which told Helen all she needed to know."

He grins and leans over to kiss me. He pulls back when I'm still staring at him.

"Are you okay? It doesn't mean you have to do anything more or different than what you're already doing, but the resort is now in your name. Zac and I agree that it should be yours."

My eyes fill with tears. "I-I can't believe you," I say, my voice cracking. "Jamison!"

He laughs, his hands winding through my hair, as he kisses me hard.

"You are my something good," I whisper.

EPILOGUE

JAMISON

A year later…

I have the best view on the whole mountain as I hike behind Scarlett in her white yoga pants, both dogs on either side of her, Lucia continuously turning around to make sure I'm still coming.

Delgado finally stops and Scarlett does too, laughing when he stretches across her feet.

"I guess he's done," she says, bending down to pick him up. "We're so close to the top. You sure you want to give up now?" she asks him, kissing his little head.

He nuzzles up to her, his eyes smug as he looks back at me like *yeah, I give up, now kiss me again*.

Lucia winds herself around our legs and I lean down and kiss Scarlett, unable to help myself.

"Guess what today is?" I ask.

"What?" Scarlett asks.

I love how free her smiles are with me now. It's become my mission to keep her smiling as much as humanly possible.

"Happiest day of our lives," I tell her.

She giggles. "Yeah?"

I nod. "I'm happier than I ever imagined I could be, Scarlett."

She sighs, leaning her forehead against my chest before she looks up at me. "I am too."

I put my hands on her waist and make a point of frowning as I look past her. "What is all that?" I ask.

She turns and gasps when she sees a picnic basket sitting on a blanket. "When were you up here?"

I shrug. "There might be a reason Delgado is so wiped out. He's already been up the mountain today."

She laughs and Delgado's sleepy eyes open as he stares fuzzily at us. We walk the rest of the way and stretch out on the blanket.

I open the basket and there's a combination of treats from Happy Cow and The Gnarly Vine. She digs into it excitedly and I watch her, feeling a wave of nerves hit me.

"Is this to celebrate the spread in *Boutique Resorts*?" she asks, taking the glass of champagne I offer her.

"Yes. And the fact that all the renovations are finally done. We can breathe a little bit now."

"I'm so in love with how everything turned out," she says. "I never dreamed it could be so magical. You made that happen." She clinks my glass and leans in to kiss me.

"*You* made that happen," I tell her.

"We did," she says, laughing.

I put my hand on her face, tracing her jawline with my fingers, her big brown eyes luminous in the sunshine.

"Don't underestimate what you're capable of," I say. "I've been in complete awe of all you've accomplished with your lingerie business and your vision for the resort that has come to life too."

Her cheeks flush. Her lingerie is in a dozen boutiques nationwide, and more are calling every day. Since the renovations, the lodge has been booked solid.

I pull out a black velvet box and her mouth drops before I even open it.

"Jamison," she whispers.

"Will you marry me?"

I hold up the ring and she's nodding, her eyes never leaving mine, tears spilling over.

"Yes," she says, wrapping her arms around me and then pulling back to hold out her finger. "Oops, I forgot about the ring."

Her fingers are shaky when I put it on, or maybe mine are, but once it's on there, the huge stone radiant, we both start laughing and kissing, and the dogs dance around us, knowing things are about to get even better.

———

She tries to distract me as we're getting ready, and normally I'm all about the distraction, but I have a plan tonight and don't want to be late.

I kiss her and pull her arms off of my neck, kissing her palms. "I'll make it up to you later, I promise you. But for now, get that lacy goodness out of my face and get some clothes on."

I slap her ass and she yelps, laughing before she pretends to pout. I leave the bathroom before she can convince me to change my mind.

We drive to Grinny's house and Scarlett looks at me in surprise when she sees all the other cars. We can hear the party around the back as we step outside and walk hand in hand toward the festivities.

There's a loud cheer when everyone sees us, and Scarlett laughs over at me when she realizes they're all here to celebrate us. Scarlett's brothers and Grinny are here, along with my family.

"Very sneaky," she says, leaning up to kiss my cheek.

Everyone comes over to hug us and to see Scarlett's ring. When her brothers come over to hug her, they slam my back, offering me veiled threats along with their congratulations, all said with a smile.

"He officially won us over when he asked for our blessing," Wyatt tells Scarlett.

She looks at me, her eyes shining and her smile so bright.

"He didn't tell us until after the fact that he already had Grinny's," Theo says, rolling his eyes. "So, I guess it's a good thing we didn't have any objections."

My parents and Pappy are beside themselves, and Ivy can hardly stand still, she's so excited to be a flower girl.

We eat and talk and dance, and at the end of the night when we've had a lot of wine and so much laughter, Grinny taps her glass.

"I'd like to make a toast to the most beautiful couple and to share a couple of secrets with you all," she says.

That gets our attention and we all turn to look at her.

"First of all, I would like to announce that the Alpine House is yours if you want it, Scarlett and Jamison."

"Grinny!" Scarlett gasps.

Grinny waves her hand like it's nothing. "It's too much house for me. I'd prefer to have your condo, if that's an option," she says, laughing.

"Whatever you want, Grinny," Scarlett says. "Thank you."

"And there's something I never told anyone about when I met your grandmother, Jamison," she says, her smile so sweet when she looks at us. "Something that I'd thought about over the years but couldn't see how it would ever happen."

She presses her lips together, her eyes filling with tears.

"You see, the two of us made a plan that day. She knew she didn't have long...and she cared about what happened to her grandsons." She looks at Zac. "She said she hadn't spotted anyone around here for you, but it looks like she worked that one out from heaven."

Everyone laughs and Zac pulls Autumn closer to him, looking so damn happy.

"But when your grandmother saw my Scarlett, she said she just had a feeling about her. And that if there ever came a time when it seemed like Scarlett might need a kind, hilarious, and…I believe her words were *a little too handsome for his own good kind of guy*…to keep her grandson Jamison in mind. And so I did."

Scarlett gasps, turning to look at me. I stare back at her, just as shocked, not knowing where this is going.

"The funny thing about it is, I didn't see how this could ever come to be. I was so angry that Granddad hadn't given you the lodge, angel, I could hardly see straight. I believe he knew better than anyone that you could handle running the lodge, but it was his silly notions about what he wanted for your life that got in the way. You know how he wanted you to just get married and settle down…give us a bunch of grandbabies."

Everyone laughs and Scarlett nods, rolling her eyes but smiling.

"But then I saw who the buyers were, and well, I knew it was meant to be." Grinny laughs, shaking her head. "Since your grandmother and I had exchanged names and talked specifically about you, Jamison, I laughed out loud when I saw your name on the title. I figured since your Gran had done her part from up above, getting you here, I'd better do the rest."

She points at Scarlett and makes a face. "So it's really *me* you should've been angry with all along…I'm the one who made the sale contingent on Jamison coming here for the first six months." She lifts her hands up. "I knew once the two of you spent any time together, the rest would work itself out."

Scarlett still looks stunned, but she starts laughing and can't stop. I'm laughing too and feel winded. She leans into me and I wrap my arm around her shoulder.

"Did you know about this?" she asks, barely able to get it out.

"No…I had no idea." We start laughing again.

"Thankfully, it all worked out!" Grinny says, holding up her glass. "To meddling grandmothers and the most incredible love stories!"

Our families cackle and everyone clinks their glasses together.

I tilt Scarlett's chin up and kiss her plush red lips senseless.

When we pull apart, she's dazed, and I lean into her ear to say, "I don't think our grandmothers could've predicted us falling into bed with each other within an hour of meeting, do you?"

Her head falls back as she laughs and I kiss her neck and hair. She puts her hands on either side of my face, her forehead on mine.

"I'm glad we did it our way," she says softly.

She gives me a quick kiss, a promise of more to come, and lifts her glass to say, "Thanks for the help, Gran and Grinny! We'll take it from here!"

We kiss again and I feel all of my dreams aligning because of this woman by my side.

I plan to give her an unforgettable future.

THE END

Thank you for reading *Unforgettable*!

. . .

Would you like more of Jamison and Scarlett? Click HERE: https://bit.ly/UnforgettableBonusScene

Do you want to know what happens between Theo and Sofie? Preorder *Someday,* a Second-Chance Romance HERE: https://geni.us/Someday

To read how Zac and Autumn fell in love, click HERE: https://geni.us/AutumnNights

FIND OUT WHAT'S NEXT

Linktree @willowaster
Newsletter http://www.willowaster.com/newsletter

ACKNOWLEDGMENTS

There are so many people to thank in my life, for so many things, but for here, I'll try to mostly stick to the ones who helped during the writing of *Unforgettable*.

Nate, Greyley & Kira, and Indigo, thank you for all the love. Time with you will always be my favorite. Kira, I'm obsessed with the map. You made Landmark Mountain come to life. Thanks to both my girls—Kess Fennell, you're part of this too!—for the swag artwork. I'm in awe of your gifts. Greyley, Happy Cow is perfection. And Kess, thank you for bringing Lucia & Delgado to life. I love all of it so much.

Laura, thank you for convincing me to keep going with the Willow books, for all the sprints, for your unwavering belief in me, the love, and all the laughs every day.

Catherine, thank you for always being willing to get to the heart of the matter, for cheering me on as I go small town, and for your consistent care and friendship.

Christine, thank you for keeping my head on straight for the past decade in one way or another, and for your eye for detail.

Nina, your guidance and friendship have been such a gift. And to the entire VPR team, I am so grateful for all of you.

Erin, Maren, Kat, and the Slack sisters, thank you for the sprints, encouragement, and laughs.

Emily, you and your covers are magic.

Lynette, thanks so much for your ASL expertise!

For those who encourage me in my daily life with so much love and support: Christine Maree, Tosha, Courtney, Claire, Tarryn, Terrijo, Kalie, and so many more.

My family and friends, I love you so much.

And to all of you who have read my books, reviewed, shared, sent me messages, and had me on your IG lives or podcasts—I'm so grateful!

ALSO BY WILLOW ASTER

Standalones

True Love Story

Fade to Red

In the Fields

Maybe Maby (also available on all retailer sites)

Lilith (also available on all retailer sites)

Miles Apart (also available on all retailer sites)

Falling in Eden

Standalones with Interconnected Characters

Summertime

Autumn Nights

Landmark Mountain Series

Unforgettable

Someday

Irresistible

Falling

Stay

Kingdoms of Sin Series

Downfall

Exposed

Ruin

Pride

The End of Men Series with Tarryn Fisher

Folsom

Jackal

The G.D. Taylors Series with Laura Pavlov

Wanted Wed or Alive

The Bold and the Bullheaded

Another Motherfaker

Don't Cry Over Spilled MILF

Friends with Benefactors

FOLLOW ME

Website willowaster.com
Facebook @willowasterauthor
Instagram @willowaster
Amazon @willowaster
Bookbub @willow-aster
Tiktok @willowaster1
Goodreads @Willow_Aster
Asters group @Astersgroup
Pinterest @WillowAster